She Speaks

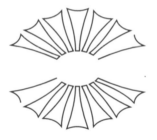

SHORT STORIES BY
INDIAN WOMEN AROUND THE WORLD

First published in 2019 by

Becomeshakespeare.com

Wordit Content Design & Editing Services Pvt Ltd
Unit - 26, Building A-1, Nr Wadala RTO, Wadala (East),
Mumbai 400037, India
T:+91 8080226699

Wordit Art Fund helps deserving authors publish
their work by providing monetary support.
To apply for funding, please visit us at
www.BecomeShakespeare.com

©
ISBN - 978-93-88930-09-3

Contents

Europe

Introduction

This anthology project was discussed by a small group of Indian women living in Switzerland in March 2018. The idea was to form a group of writers, consisting of Indian women living in Switzerland, India and abroad based on our personal contacts; and to ask each writer to contribute one story each. The writers whom we would choose for this project did not have to be professional writers, but they had to be women who would be willing to raise their voices and write about what women feel and encounter in modern times, through their short stories. We spread out this idea all over the world and received several abstracts and 20 full stories by the end of September, 2018, from Australia, India, Indonesia, New Zealand, Switzerland, UK and USA.

Most of the writers, who joined this anthology project, came from diverse backgrounds like finance, marketing, science, engineering, management, arts and literature. We requested each writer to come up with a unique voice, through a female protagonist. Since, most of us were penning a story (for a book) for the first time, there were occasional hiccups, but with a strongly motivated writers' team in place—ready to help each other, with friends—old and new, all coming together under one creative umbrella, we were able to finish this project well within a year's time.

In this book, we followed a contextual editing style, so that the author's voice and choice of words remained intact, with minimal intervention. Each writer, in her own genuine voice attempted to address an issue. Our writers didn't exchange their storylines with each other and yet when all stories came in, we found a 'common thread' - dealing with a woman's constant need to accept good and bad, adapt to change, and move on. We believe this theme will also resonate with our readers.

For this book, first and foremost, I would like to thank all the writers who believed in this idea and contributed with their beautiful stories—despite their hectic professional and personal engagements. This is your book, our combined project! Also my personal thanks to all friends who helped us get connected. Amongst the writers, Nayana, spent countless hours on this book from start to finish and sent her developmental editing remarks to all writers during the review-revision-re-review stage—reading and re-reading the stories at every stage, Munmun helped us find a Publisher and helped in promotion along with other fellow writers. Poppy planned distribution through book fairs in Indonesia, Sumona compiled all writers profiles and photos over a very tight schedule and with her prompt market surveys and polls she helped the project progress faster, Jyoti helped with her photoshoots for promotion, Kamalika helped with her suggestions overall, Parvathi edited two stories (thanks again), Sameer, Pooja and the entire Publishing team was very professional and supportive throughout and a big thank you to all—who came forward to motivate us and helped us in this project.

The entire writers' team voted and decided about every step that we took for this book, from the cover page selection to the title. This book is truly a team effort and we sincerely hope that more and more women will come forward and take this idea ahead and publish more often. Writing is a dream, which can come true, only if we take a step forward. Stay inspired and I hope you will enjoy reading this collection of short stories written by 20 Indian women around the world.

Thank you.

Brindarica Bose.

Foreword

To make time for writing when one is caught up in the act of living life itself is no mean feat. Beyond the fact that we - the women who bring you this collection - are all women of Indian origin, we also have one more thing in common. We have all been writing stories in our heads or scribbling ideas into our notebooks which we have left on our bedside table 'just in case' the muse invites herself into the backs of our minds at midnight. But, even as our stories have grown in length, in breadth and in scope, we have all been guilty of finding ourselves push our writing to the back of our minds as we have been caught up in the currents of life and swept away in its ceaseless tide. So, yes, while we have conceived of characters during the daily commute, we have also been juggling our day jobs, families, marriages, deadlines and dentist appointments... Indeed we have all been spinning and in fact, continue to spin so many plates that adding another plate to the circus act in the form of writing constructively had not even had the opportunity to cross our minds. Until, of course, this project came along and we all inspired each other to come forward and write.

Conceptualised by Brindarica Bose, a published author and celebrated artist of Indian origin living in

Switzerland, our 'writing project' and our tribute to 'the female voice' (which, incidentally is the name of our WhatsApp group!) gave us the platform and the incentive that we needed to write. It was and is and will remain a perfect example of a group of women coming together across the world (because we truly are from everywhere as you can see from our contents page) to support each other, empower each other and hold each other up. I believe that to a certain degree, the authentic voices of women 'like us' don't often make into print. 'Women like us' are caught up in the throes of multiple responsibilities and commitments, we often do not take up the pen and hence we are often written about rather than writing. Indeed, at times, we are written out altogether and this is also something that we wanted to change. We wanted to take back our voices and put our collectively creative feet forward.

As you read your way through our offering, you will see for yourself that the stories all treat certain themes and that they aligned themselves to some fundamental issues while simultaneously exploring critical fault lines in society. There are some universal themes at work such as anger, joy and sadness and how that is manifested forms the crux of each tale.

One of the overarching themes throughout is the theme of how female voices and bodies negotiate domestic and urban (along with gendered) spaces. For example, in *Padma* by Kamalika Ray, we witness the protagonist fight to take back control over her domestic space as she tries to rise up and break the shackles of her disenfranchisement. In Ashwathy Menon's *The Inner Voice*, the protagonist is compelled by the quirks of life itself to overcome child abuse and also break through social prejudice about mental health. Once again, she has to fight to take back her space and assert her right to overcome trauma.

In both Shweta Dasgupta's *The Survivor* as well as in my story *The Goddess is Missing'*, the issue of female foeticide is treated albeit from very different angles and very different spaces. The differences not with standing, both stories talk about social hypocrisy as well as indifference. They also offer contrasting outcomes and appraise the striking difference that caring support can mean.

In *Shades of Amara*, Sindhuja Manohar's protagonist tries to find a balance between her private and public self, social acceptance and social exclusion but, ultimately, to what cost? This is also the question that Brindarica Bose asks of her character in *Sita's Vacation* once again, the two authors treat this universal question in strikingly different ways which recalls one of the fundamental truths of storytelling which is that while there may just be a handful of Ur-narratives, there's an infinite number of ways to tell them.

Indeed, *Khushi* by Tania Basu tells a tale of joy when the protagonist finds herself being welcomed and respected in a new and different space as does *Paksh/Vipaksh* by Munmun Gupta. Again, told in very different ways, both stories talk about accepting joy and courage into our hearts in order to seek out joy and acceptance in spaces which could have been otherwise forbidding. Rejina Ramchandran Sadhu's *The Forgotten* also tells the tale of what happens when love is deferred, not to be found in expected quarters. Here too, joy is found in surprising quarters.

Jyoti Kapoor's *Ageless* and Pallabi Roy Chakraborty's *Durga's New Dawn* both take us into new planes and dimensions altogether. The former transports us into the future with a world built around space-age technology while at the same time concentrating on issues of mental health and burn out, the latter takes us into heavenly realms and works with the ancient and enduring idea that the gods are not all that different to us after all and that they too tug and tussle over domestic and professional spaces, responsibilities and duties. Richa Chauhan's *Radha and Govind* also has a spiritual theme and is inspired by the mythology that played a big role in many of our childhoods. The story takes into the protagonist's interior space and explores the concept of love, falling in love and memory.

Love, of course, is one of those universal themes which finds mention in virtually all of our stories. While Agomoni Ganguli Mitra's *The Remains of Goodbye* tells of the end of love and how that enigmatic sense of loss tinged with a strain of freedom and yet coupled with longing haunts a space once shared, Abhilasha Kumar's *Five Half Lives* discusses the issue of sustaining it in a marriage filled as it is with domestic duties while also exploring the manner in which one might seek to escape the domestic and marital space by falling in love outside the marriage. But, what happens when reality comes calling? Well, dear reader, you must read the stories themselves to find out!

Journeys,memories, the minutiae of life, the very texture of a life well lived also form the meat and bone of some of our stories. In some cases, as in Sujatha Ramanathan's *Solitude*, the mind of the protagonist dwells upon the people of places left behind; where one has to achieve a sense of closure in order to move on with life. Other stories speak of the journey through the eyes of the trailing spouse and here too, the stories which are so similar in theme are so unique and different in scope. Sumona Ghosh Das writes movingly in *A Journey To Remember* of how the protagonist, a trailing spouse must learn anew while negotiating a new space both as a wife, a daughter and a mother. In the process of living her life and conflating two cultures together the protagonist is also able to discover herself as an individual and as a woman. On the other hand, in *Sour Apples and Hot Peppers,* Suparna Basu strikes an almost Proust-like note as she shows how the protagonist is moved to deal with the present in a different country with its different class system and social mores by seeking out lessons from her past as she begins a quest to strike a balance between all the different and disparate areas of her life. Poppy Choudhury's *Gari* brings together the concept of a journey, tying it to the tale of the trailing spouse while also dwelling on the themes of love, longing; in this story we also see how one domestic space haunts another. Indeed, time appears to be a palimpsest, each lived moment mingles a love and appreciation of the present while never losing sight of the love that the protagonist feels for the childhood home that she has been forced to leave behind.

Furthermore, in Ekta Sharma's *Languages,* she posits that learning languages can be a great boon. She also weighs up the pros and cons of such a commitment and questions the impact that this has on one's internal monologue. Finally, in Ipsita Barua's *A Half Ticket,* acclimatization and acceptance of the new space and of the new space is brought about through the act of forging ownership by moving around, the very act of making oneself familiar in the host country and building relationships.

We have endeavored to remain true to our own voices and inspirations throughout this project and we hope that you will enjoy reading our words and the voices that we have found as much as we enjoyed writing them. I would like to take this opportunity to thank each and every member of our team. It has been a privilege to be able to read your stories and to learn from them.

By Nayana Chakrabarti

India

Padma

By Kamalika Ray

I have been waiting on the steps of the *ghat* for nearly an hour. He arrived, a few minutes ago.

Even with my back to him, I can see his tense face in my mind's eye. He sits perched on the very edge of the first step. His taut, wiry body is hunched forward. This is in an attempt to be ready, to catch the first look of my face, *if* I happen to turn around. His left hand, however, holds on tightly to the adjoining railing. Just in case.

His posture gives away his uncertainties, much more than his eyes do. I have looked into them, far more openly than he has ever looked into mine. I straighten my drooping shoulders, pull the edge of my sari around my body firmly, get up, and decidedly, turn around.

He is still in his work clothes today. He looks flustered when our eyes meet for a brief second before I casually look away. I start climbing up the stairs, faking hurry after making sure that he has stood up too. From the corner of my lowered eyes, I see that he is heading towards the *ghat's* exit, while keeping an eye on me. I continue my fast pace and surpass him, it is me who enters the crowded main road first. We have just ten minutes, if he wants to catch his six-thirty train.

****

I am Mrs. Choudhury. Although there is also a 'Padma' in between, nobody has ever cared to know that. I am Mrs. Choudhury, the daughter-in-law of the Choudhury household of Rashbehari Avenue, Kolkata. This identity is enough for me to get ushered into every place of interest with a distinct reverence.

My in-laws have been residing in this locality for more than sixty years now. A prominent sycophant of the British Raj, my grandfather-in-law, saluted his way through a remarkable career and amassed huge wealth.

My father-in-law, the only son, witnessed this ascent and observed it closely. Naturally, he was appropriately stimulated by the increasing stacks of cash at home. Upon reaching adulthood, presumably confident of becoming an even greater success than his father, he started off with a business, that of supplying labourers. Poor ignorant villagers' lives changed overnight. With a single press of their 'misguided' thumbs, they went from being hungry farmers to becoming bonded labourers on commercial ships, voyaging abroad. However, after a while, the daily sight of scrawny farmers and hollowed-out eyes left my father-in-law bored. The business failed, miserably. It was said that some of the villagers who went, were never sent back. Their lives were the currency that my father-in-law paid to set right some unfinished dealings.

Soon enough, to make him 'responsible' enough for a job, the family married him off to a 'good girl' of a 'matching status'. The new lady who entered, however, did a far better job. My mother-in-law turned her husband, into the managing director of a big multinational.

In a society where respect-shown is directly proportionate to the amount-of-money-earned, the Choudhury family grew used to being treated almost like royalty.

Before I became a part of the lineage, the Choudhurys were also known for their sacrificial ceremonies. In the family temple, every Durga Puja, on the evening of Navami, surrounded by murderous onlookers, three hapless goats were butchered off, in order to appease the Devi. The frantic screams of the goats were drowned in a din of incessant bell-ringing and the lusty cheering of a bloodthirsty crowd.

Interestingly, one year, a little boy in the crowd fainted on seeing the gory sacrifice. My anglicized mother-in-law who herself never liked the idea of eating the 'prasad' - the mutton-curry cooked afterwards - seized the opportunity to cook up a storm. And it was her power at last, not the Devi's, which saved the ill-fated goats. The sacrifices turned vegetarian from the very next year (nowadays, three ash-gourds are slaughtered by a sober priest).

Meanwhile, something 'non-vegetarian' enough soon started brewing inside the Choudhury household. My elder brother-in-law, Mrinal, the scholar, returned from London with an English wife.

After the initial shock subsided, pretty and submissive Emily quickly adapted to the customs and struggled hard till the family grudgingly accepted her. Eventually, they started to flaunt her at social gatherings, she was, after all, the 'Mem Bouma'.

However, four months to the day after arriving in Kolkata and living with Mrinal, Emily declared in a quivering voice that her 'Indian Holiday' was over, and she now wanted to return home. On pressing her further, it was revealed that, it was Mrinal who had 'broken up' with her. And then, the final bomb exploded, when, in between her hiccupping sobs, Emily blurted out their well-kept secret. They were still not married.

The saffron flags of Indian culture and traditions inflamed Emily's sky, and in no time the 'Mem Bouma' was 'rebranded'. She became the 'unchaste whore' who had maneuvered her way into their 'innocent boy's' heart in order to further her ulterior, selfish motives (nobody was any the wiser as to what these were but the accusation remained nonetheless). After four days of mortifying curses and taunts, the 'innocent boy' packed her off in a flight back to London.

Nobody ever mentioned Emily again. Not in public hearing at least.

Mrinal, the foreign-returned, scholarly-son of the wealthy Choudhury household was married within a month, to the nineteen-year-old only child of the illustrious Dutta family of Bardhaman.

The family portrait started looking perfect. Until, I entered it. Two years later.

****

Boro-Mami told me that Moloy was handsome. But when I first saw his picture, I didn't find him to be handsome at all. The artificial surroundings of the studio were as flat and unimaginative as his own facial expression. His round eyes were almost bulging out, as if shocked by the fact that he too, was getting married. The corners of his mouth drooped, giving him a gloomy look, like that of a child who had just been scolded. It was as if melancholy had crawled into the entirety of his thin body, which reclined loosely on an old wooden chair. As if he already knew, that it was all futile. That I would never like him.

At that moment, an as yet unrecognisable surge of maternal affection had gushed into my heart and tugged hard at my insides. I knew what it was, to be rejected, didn't I? In my twenty years of life, I too had been rejected. Twice. First, by a father who committed suicide when I was just three-months-old. Second, by his family, who hurriedly packed off my 'dangerously' young, widowed mother, and returned her to her own reluctant family, with me in tow.

So that day, standing on the terrace of a house in which I had myself grown up as an unwanted burden, I looked through Moloy's plainness and saw only another child, looking up for acceptance. I said 'yes' to Boro-Mami, and added an aptly grateful smile.

****

Three years ago, a young bride was decked up in a red Benarasi sari and the huge garland weighing down upon her neck was made of a thousand red roses. Her dry, painted face felt like a mask and her bejeweled body looked entirely alien. Gold, rubies and diamonds, her new family had not left out a single inch of her body to display the 'wealthy love' they had readily showered the new bride with.

But nobody cared to notice that underneath those wet red roses, the new bride was shivering. That it had been hours since her body had started burning with fever. The fever of fear. Of that gnawing feeling of things gone wrong. That foreboding sensation of something worse still waiting around the corner.

But the bride had decided to be brave and strong.

And thus she put on her best smile yet.

Three years ago, blinking away those anxious tears, in

the midst of a pretentious crowd of well-wishers, that young bride was me.

****

Moloy, my husband, had first shown symptoms of mental disbalance when he was in his teens. He kept slashing his limbs to simply gaze upon the oozing gouts of blood. Otherwise, he was gentle. Keeping to himself, sometimes talking and cackling like a child. With imported medicines, regular doctor visits and the help of amenable school principals, he finished matriculation at the age of twenty-five. But, attending a college was definitely out of the question. He needed supervision, round the clock. Someone was needed, all the time, to keep an eye on him.

It was my mother-in-law who finally thought of taking her own sweet revenge, and decided to get hold of another girl to put through an experiment which, years ago, she herself had participated in; a test subject who was put to task immediately, to rear and manage another wayward son.

Moloy accepted me as his new nurse quite quickly. I assume he had been told exactly that, earlier, by his family. I was acknowledged as 'Sister' by him for nearly a month after our marriage. When slowly, with time I told him that we were married, and he was my husband, my name changed from 'Sister', to a simple 'Bou'. At night, he preferred sleeping on the bed alone. Once, he almost kicked me out of the room when I forcibly lay beside him.

By the end of the first six months, I was contemplating committing suicide. I had no other way out it seemed. My mother's sobs became louder whenever I suggested that I return to her. My only childhood friend, Banani had gone off to Mumbai where her husband had been transferred. I yearned to share my frustration. The servants at the house, though sympathetic, kept a safe distance from me, knowing very well the volcanic condition I was in.

My in-laws left no stone unturned to drill down to me the very fact that my life was now irreversible. They went on reminding me about the luxurious life that I was getting to lead, which would have been unattainable had I married into any other family. Gifts, apropos of nothing became almost a weekly affair.

Until the night of my first wedding anniversary.

Most of my in-laws' friends, relatives and neighbors had been invited. Particularly those who had advised against their decision to marry off a lunatic. It was a party to celebrate their success in retaining my bejeweled presence beside that very insane son of theirs, even after one whole year.

So what if from the morning, all I had done that day was to clean imaginary pools of vomit on the floor of our room? Puddles which only Moloy was able to see. He had kept me on my toes all day, and by late afternoon when I was too tired to even lift an arm, Moloy had, for the very first time, hit me with his chappal. His first act of violence.

Something snapped inside me the very moment his hands came down on me. And I just knew that this could not continue. I had sprung back up on my feet and stopped the third blow, holding on tightly to his wrists as they twitched in mid-air. We struggled for a whole minute, while his bulbous eyes threatened to burst. Then, as fast as it had come my fury suddenly disappeared. My wrath spent, I stood there with his chappal in my slack hand, looking blankly at his silly face. We had never looked at each other this way before. His mouth twitched and he lowered his eyes. He glanced up again, this time with a sadness so evident that I had to look away. Hot tears of indignation welled up in my eyes and for a change, I let them flow. The world was a big black hole, sucking me in with all its might. I had never felt this weak before. After the lifetime of another minute, Moloy snatched his chappal back from my hands, and ran out of our room, barefoot. As usual he tripped near the flowerpot kept by the corridor. But he didn't look back at me and giggle this time, as he always did. He just picked himself up, unsure on his feet, and hobbled ahead, till he disappeared around the corner.

I never saw him again.

It was quite late that evening, when everybody started to look for Moloy in earnest. Till then, there were just casual enquiries. I had been in my mother-in-law's room till the guests started arriving. And when I came out, I was too ornamented to role-play as a nurse. With all those diamonds glittering on me, I had tried to keep myself near their owner, my mother-in-law.

Three hours later it was she, who grabbed my shoulders in front of the whole throng, and planted a resounding slap on my tear-stained face. Moloy's disappearance, by now established by the men of the house, was apparently completely my failure. They were so adamant that, for a second, I began to believe it myself. My mother, standing amongst the murmuring guests had then done almost a 'heroic' act. If only it would have been really for my benefit as she termed it later. She had thrown herself at my grandfather-in-law's feet, begging for mercy. And later, it was she, who instilled the idea of my penance, into the criminal minds of my in-laws.

I don't know, what really made the Choudhury family decide to keep me with them, months after Moloy's disappearance.

Was it hope? A belief in his inevitable return? Or was it only to tackle the weekly police visits, updating us on their search for Moloy? The absence of whom now hardly irking anyone anymore. Or was it something else, which I couldn't yet fathom?

I now lived like a maidservant, but with a small room to myself. What was it, which made them this humane? I got the answer; the day Inspector Pratap finally told me to stop waiting, apologetically, over a year after Moloy's disappearance.

That night, I saw a new twinkle in Mrinal's eyes when

he came into my room to ask about Moloy. And at that precise moment, the universe handed me my answer. It was my youth.

Ever since Mrinal's pregnant wife returned to her paternal home and began to wait out the birth of his child, he had developed an eye for me. Every evening, after returning from office, he invented new requirements, chores, that were to be completed only by me. In my presence, he became fidgety and kept clearing his throat until I, growing frustrated, was compelled to ask him what had happened. Then he became overly talkative, pausing only to stare at my breasts.

It was then that I started to plan my escape.

With the help, of my new friend, Pratap.

I confess. Inspector Pratap became a friend, if only because of my desperate need to talk.

It began during his numerous visits to this house, which happened in the presence of an anxious family at first and then boiled down to just him and me sitting under a whirring ceiling fan, discussing absurd possibilities. He watched my 'devaluation' from close enough. From my silks to the coarse cottons I now wore, he worried now, I could see, for my safety. At times, he gave me information, thrown in casually, apropos of nothing, in-between professional updates. About NGOs and self-help groups. I carefully noted all that he told, in my mind. Later, I was the one to initiate our secret meets, on my visits to the temple by the ghat. His agreement had nervousness. But, it was his unease, which put me to rest.

****

Today, it is our seventh meeting.

He is a bit annoyed, when he spots me at the bus-stand. "Too public", his eyes say. Pratap's uniform is already attracting second glances. He makes sure I am watching, before dropping an envelope near the dustbin and then scurries past me, towards the station. I pick it up, by dropping my purse nearby.

"Wait for two whistles", his letter says, "Tonight at eleven, outside the gate", and "Come prepared".

I press the precious message tightly to my bosom and hurry towards a standing cycle-rickshaw. And on my way back, I tenderly take out the main thing I had come for today. The ticket.

I contacted Banani through him, last week. And though I have not yet heard from her, I am willing to take the risk. Pratap has bought my ticket to Mumbai, for tomorrow. He has his friends there too, he has assured. For once, I have willed myself to believe.

No, there is no romance brewing here. Not yet, at least.

It is still humanity at work. For the very first time in my life, I am experiencing humaneness.

And I want to enjoy it, I have told myself, I wish to cherish it with a grateful heart.

This evening, without displaying even the slightest speck of haste I finish all my duties, for the last time. Then, I calmly go up to my room, stuff my modest life into a handbag, and finally, with a pounding heart, start to wait.

But when the clock strikes twelve with still no sign of Pratap, my bravado starts to crumble. After about ten minutes, I hear a soft knock at the door. With soft, careful strides I reach the door, just in time to hear the muffled sound of a familiar throat-clearing.

A sickening chill runs down my spine, making me swoon and I clutch the doorknob with all my might.

I crouch near the door and wait.

Seconds plod by, separated by eternities in between.

The next knock, is louder, and it kills the surrounding stillness.

Something within my depths rises and hits me hard this time. Mrinal's audacity cuts me open. Huge reservoirs of pent up fury unleash and start clawing up my insides. Blood oozes out of my scabbed, scarred heart.

I lift myself up and slowly pick up the brass vase near the door that still stands by the edge of the room.

I take a long deep breath and step forward.

And just when I slowly begin to turn the sweaty doorknob,

I hear the sound,

of

two

guarded

whistles.

Glossary:

Ghat: Embankment
Prasad: Food offered to God
Boro-Mami: Wife of mother's brother
Mem: A foreigner lady
Benarasi Sari: A special silk sari woven in India
Bou, Bouma: Wife

The Inner Voice

By Ashwathy Menon

66 I t's a girl! Congratulations!" a faint voice said. The effect of the anesthesia was wearing off. Ayesha felt drunk, heavy headed. She wanted to respond but couldn't. The nurse was patting her cheek, trying to wake her up. A plethora of emotions tumbled through Ayesha's mind. She mumbled something and the doctor responded, but nothing of what she said registered in her mind. She drifted back to sleep or at least that's what she thought...

Ayesha had always wished for a girl and despite her mother-in-law prophesying to the whole world that Ayesha was going to have a boy; she had secretly hoped that the baby would be a girl. Now that her wish had come true, she was feeling anxious! *Why*? She thought. Why are happiness and joy eluding me? I have always cherished the idea of being a mother to a girl and when the moment has finally arrived, why am I not feeling ecstatic? Am I being hypocritical? A tumult of mixed emotions flowed through her. She was trying to be happy but something was holding her back. Maybe this was just the effect of postpartum hormones!

Raised in an industrial town in Northern India, young Ayesha was a happy-go-lucky girl; talented, boisterous and full of enthusiasm. She had always been responsible. She helped her parents with their household chores and took care of her younger brother Ajay. Her parents both worked, in fact, her father travelled quite frequently. This led to Ayesha donning the mantle of household responsibilities.

When Ajay started pre-school and it became clear that he needed some guidance with his writing, their mother made arrangements with Neeta Ma'am, who also happened to live in the same neighbourhood. Neeta Ma'am was meant to help bring Ajay up to speed since both Ayesha and her mother were busy with their various responsibilities. Ayesha was given the responsibility of dropping and fetching Ajay from tuitions. She felt proud and excited about this 'new' role as a big sister. After all, she was ten years old. Neeta ma'am stayed four buildings away on the second floor. A short flight of stairs led to their flat. *Good exercise*, Ayesha thought to herself.

Neeta Ma'am's husband, Dhiren, was a friendly man. He would come home for lunch and he would play with the tutees present in his home at that time. A tickle here and a tickle there….

High fives and jokes all around...

Strangely enough, none of the children responded very enthusiastically. At most, his jokes would only earn him a forced smile and nothing else. *Maybe he disturbs them while studying*, thought Ayesha. If only, she would later come to wish, her intuitions had been stronger.

Initially, for the first two days, all went well. Until, on the third day, while she was climbing the steps, Dhiren stopped her and asked Ajay to proceed to class. Ayesha was surprised but she nodded anyway. Just when she was about to leave, Dhiren held her hand, smiled and kissed her on her lips.

"Bye darling," he said before pulling away and dashed off to his flat.

Ayesha felt uncomfortable but didn't know what to make of it. She pushed the niggling feeling that what had happened was not right, aside. She tried to think better of him and give him the benefit of doubt, maybe he was just being affectionate, she reasoned. She continued to feel uneasy but did not mention the incident to anyone. Then, when he kissed her again the next day and the day after that, she realised that it definitely could not be that. This was not avuncular affection. He was making her very uncomfortable and she definitely did not like it! The fourth time that it happened, she tried to resist. She begged him, pleading, *"Please leave me"* but her muffled words didn't reach his ears. He held her all the more strongly and carried on kissing her aggressively. He then put his hand under her skirt. By now, Ayesha was pushing Dhiren away with all her might.

It was Neeta ma'am's call for her husband that saved

her from further harassment and abuse that day. Dhiren straightened up and sternly told Ayesha not to mention what had happened to anyone. He warned her that if she did, she would face consequences.

Ayesha was shaken.

Tears rolled down her cheeks.

She didn't know what to do or whom to tell. She was shivering.

Somehow, she gathered her senses and ran back home. For the next hour, Ayesha kept crying! She was scared, she felt dirty and she felt peculiar, as if her body was not her own anymore.   The time was fast approaching for her to pick up Ajay. She was dreading it. She prayed that Dhiren wouldn't be around. What if there was a confrontation? What if there was screaming? What if there was an ugly scene? She wasn't sure if she could handle this all alone.

For the next few days, Ayesha made excuses about the pickup and drop-offs and kept missing Ajay's classes.

Thankfully, her mother did not pester her much. Maybe I am expecting too much from a ten-year-old. Ajay is just in pre-school and doesn't need regular tuitions, for now, pondered her mother.

Much to Ayesha's relief, the classes were stopped.

Ayesha was careful to avoid Dhiren whenever she left the house. She even stopped going out to play for a long time. When prodded about it, she would attribute it to a 'lot of homework' and 'assignments'. Her busy parents failed to notice anything was amiss. Then one day, as an answer to her prayers, her father was transferred and they left town for good. She was thankful, happy and very much relieved to leave that colony.

However, the harrowing experience continued to play havoc on Ayesha's mind for many years to come. Any bit of eve teasing or harassment she faced, made her cringe with disgust. Ayesha started distrusting people. She was wary of strangers and also of people she knew. She looked at every man who cajoled or caressed a child with suspicion. Eventually, on the professional front as well she encountered a number of sly womanisers. Some, she was able to handle deftly but a few of them were just too much for her to take. She felt disgusted but she told herself that crying was not an option. She wanted to be strong and face this grim reality with courage. *I must deal with it,* she kept telling herself.

Over time, the bubbly and boisterous Ayesha became very reserved. She herself remained completely unaware of this transformation. Lack of trust led to her having very few friends. So few, that she didn't even need to count them. She was unable to open up even to the few friends that she did have.

But life is such. For every 'bad' there is a 'good'. For 'hate' there is 'love'.

Even Ayesha couldn't escape Cupid's arrow. She met Prem at work. Her marriage to Prem was entirely without complications. Neither family objected. She was very happy and felt blessed to have him in her life. Their days of courtship were lovely, filled with affectionate moments as Prem was very caring. Their marriage was a dream come true for both of them but Ayesha was very scared of consummating her marriage. She wanted to run away from physical intimacy. The thought of it filled her with anxiety. She knew that physical intimacy was part and parcel of being a newlywed and she found her own aversion to it confusing. It was incomprehensible to her.

Prem attributed her 'avoidance' to anxiety arising from all the adjustments that she had to make as a new bride, from a new household to a new family. He gave Ayesha time to settle. But as time went by, and Ayesha still did not seem very favourable with intimacy, he grew sad and concerned. Eventually, going against his personality, he confronted Ayesha about it. Initially, she was just quiet; even after all these years, she was unable to express herself. But later, somehow, she mustered up the courage to narrate the nightmarish incident of the sexual abuse she had faced as a young child.

"It isn't easy for me Prem. I love you and want you to know that my avoidance has got nothing to do with you. I am trying but I will need your help."

She wiped her tears and hugged him.

As time went by, she surrendered herself to love - of Prem and for Prem!

A month of missed periods led her to take a pregnancy test and when it turned out to be positive, she was elated! Her in-laws doted on her and took care of her well. Ayesha never missed home and thanked God that she had been married into such a lovely family. All in all, it was a good life, or so she thought…. Until the 'D day' arrived!!

"Look at our beautiful daughter sleeping blissfully," whispered Prem softly into Ayesha's ear. Ayesha groggily opened her eyes and looked at her baby in the cot. From that position, she found it difficult to catch a glimpse as her stitches ached yet she smiled, nodded and said, "I can't see much of her for now but I'm glad she is a healthy baby."

Before Prem could respond, she had lost consciousness again.

When the effect of the anesthesia had worn off, Ayesha found herself and her baby surrounded by relatives, neighbours, her parents and in-laws. They were hovering around the baby. Sharma Uncle was holding the baby and smiling at her. There was chatter all around the room. A gush of anger surged in her. *Where is Prem? Why is Sharmaji holding my baby?* She was restless and struggled to sit. Her movements caught her mother's attention. Ayesha signalled her mom to hand over the baby to her. She felt relieved when she finally held her little angel in *her* hands. She kept admiring her daughter as she saw her, up and close for the first time. Just then, Prem walked in. Before she had time to check herself, she reacted angrily and asked him in a hushed whisper, "Why are so many of them inside the room?"

"It's visiting hours... How can I say anything?" replied a surprised Prem. He tried to change the topic. "How are you doing?"

"Much better, and glad that I finally get to hold our angel," said Ayesha, even though she felt calm, she could not hold the sarcasm back from her voice.

Ayesha kept looking at her daughter, checking on her and dreading the visiting hours for the next three days at the hospital. She felt uncomfortable when any man held her child; an unexplained feeling of fear and restlessness would engulf her. She would feel her temper rising each time. A great deal of restraint had to be exercised. Everyone who knew her grew confused with this *new* Ayesha. They all brushed it aside thinking that it must be some manifestation of postpartum depression.

"Everyone goes through it. She will be fine!" Her mother-in-law insisted to a thoughtful Prem.

The homecoming of the baby was a simple affair with just the immediate family around. Ayesha was very hands-on with her angel and wanted to do everything for her with as little help as possible.

'*You are being a little obsessive,*' said the right side of the brain.

'*Rubbish! Being the mother, I am responsible for her care. What's wrong if I fuss about it?*' said the left side.

Ayesha knew she was battling inside but she refused to acknowledge it.

The following week saw a barrage of visitors coming in to see the baby. Since when did Prem have so many relatives? thought Ayesha, cursing beneath her breath. Why can't they just let the newborn and the mother settle? She was fuming.

They had yet another visitor. Prem's cousin Nitin, who insisted on holding the baby. Her mother-in-law handed over the little bundle of joy to him without batting an eyelid. *Ma didn't even feel like checking with me?* When Nitin bent to plant a kiss on the baby, Ayesha could feel her blood boil with rage. Nitin gently patted the baby. Ayesha's heart was palpitating! She wanted to somehow take her daughter to the safety of her room. She made an excuse of wanting to nurse the baby and dashed off to the bedroom.

"I am tired of so many visitors Prem. Can't you talk to Ma and ask her to tell all those wanting to visit to come later? I can't bear this stress."

Prem was in a fix. He tried talking to his parents but 'customs' and 'rituals' preceded all logic!

The day of the naming ceremony rolled around. Ayesha dressed up her daughter. *Guests galore*, she thought while looking around, feeling irritated at the sight of the crowded hall. She wasn't happy. She had wanted a private affair but her in-laws had remained adamant! She had felt forced into giving in. It was

Ayesha who had chosen the name. Prem whispered it now into their daughter's ear.

'Aparajita'

~*The one who cannot be defeated.*

After the ceremony, every guest present wanted to hold the baby and cuddle her. Seeing Aparajita passed around and exchanged like that was making Ayesha cry with anger. She felt like screaming out loud. Just then, Aparajita cried. It was like an answer to her prayers. Ayesha rushed to pick her up from Mrs. Batra and then ran inside to the adjoining room, to nurse her infant.

That night, Aparajita was tired and cranky. Ayesha couldn't bear to see her daughter in distress. "That big crowd, all that changing of hands has affected the baby," cribbed Ayesha to Prem.

Her inner voice niggled, *'Or, is it my anxiety that is affecting her....'* She had once heard that the thoughts of a mother could have an effect on the child.

A tired and stressed Ayesha sat down on the bed, thinking. Aparajita meant the whole world to her. She could not let her daughter face defeat because of her fears. She had to battle this or hell was sure to break loose. Not only Aparajita but everyone around her was getting affected. She herself could hardly bear the stress any longer!

Ayesha lay on the bed staring at the ceiling. What will happen when Aparajita starts schooling? Will I be able to let her go? She is going to be all alone amongst the teachers, the staff, the security ... What then? There will be umpteen elevators and stairways in her life. Ayesha shuddered at the thought of Aparajita on a stairway. It was then she realised that the incident of her molestation had left a *deeper* scar on her than she had ever imagined. She knew she would protect her daughter fiercely from prying eyes and would be vigilant throughout but she could not afford to raise Aparajita in fear and anxiety.

I cannot put her in a birdcage forever and let her lead a restricted life. I will 'need' to work on this monster in my head! Sleep took over her thoughts.....

Motherhood engulfed Ayesha completely. Her world revolved around Aparajita. Their shared cup of tea in the morning was the only time Prem and Ayesha had to themselves. It was during one such moment that Ayesha broached a topic that had been sitting heavily on her mind.

"Why don't we go to a therapist? Maybe it will help." Ayesha's tone contradicted her determination to try.

It was then that Prem noticed, Ayesha looked incredibly stressed. Her face was riddled with lines of tension now. It was evident that there was a lot going in her mind.

"Therapist? Why Ayesha? I do not see anything wrong with you. We are all there for you," said Prem. He sought to be reassuring. Ayesha sighed.

"I know you are there for me and will stand by me. Yet, it will not be long before things start to go wrong with your parents and even more so with Aparajita. I need to do something about my fears, or else it will get in the way of parenting. I do not wish to affect our daughter negatively in anyway."

Epilogue

It was raining heavily. The taxi pulled close to the gate of a formidable building. Ayesha opened her umbrella, adjusted her saree and walked towards the entrance. She checked for the name and it said second floor. Hesitating, Ayesha took the first step. *Steps* still made her feel uneasy. Yet, she surged ahead.

Reaching the reception, she spoke softly, "Would you let Dr. Dey know that Ayesha is here? I have an appointment with her, for 2 pm."

The Survivor

By Shweta Ghosh Dasgupta

The lantern swayed, casting eerie shadows on the ground, as Kamla emerged, almost ghost-like, from the cluster of trees, with a plastic mug in her hand. She was on her way back from her morning ablutions. She looked up. It was still dark. She increased her pace. As she reached the fringes of the sleepy village, she became aware of a soft wail. Her curiosity brought her to the heap of garbage which appeared to be the source of the sound.

Every time she tried to move away from the heap of garbage, the wail pierced at her heart. It was unmistakably the faint wail of an infant.

Kamla's heart was breaking into a thousand pieces. It seemed as if she had been standing there forever….. but in reality only a few minutes had passed. For the umpteenth time, Kamla stood there contemplating whether or not to pick up the little bundle, but courage failed her.

Who could have been so cruel?

An infant girl child on a heap of garbage!

This didn't come as a complete surprise. In this remote village of North Bihar, Madhopur, such incidents were more or less a common occurrence. As a senior worker for the *'Ladki Bachao Ladki Padhao'* mission, by the Central Government, Kamla knew about previous track records. Little did she know that she too would face one such situation in her own life.

Gently she picked up the 'living' bundle. The wailing immediately stopped.

Maybe she was hungry?

Maybe she was sick?

Worse, maybe she was injured and already dying?

Bloodstains!

The girl was not even cleaned properly before being 'disposed' of!

Red ants were crawling all over her flimsy cover. There were mosquito bites on her tiny legs and face, abrasions too! Houseflies were stuck fast on her eyelids….

Kamla tenderly wiped them off with her *anchal*.

The baby dozed off….hungry, tired, and cold.

Kamla looked around cautiously and brought the infant closer to her bosom. It was the infamous girl child, alright...unwanted, uncared for, and left to die. The east skyline had lit up. The new dawn ushered in a new story.

Few cyclists passed by, looking curiously at Kamla with a baby wrapped in her arms. She was a well-known figure in Madhopur, pretty much disliked by the menfolk, for her unorthodox and challenging outlook. She was a threat to their dogmas and chauvinism. Her actions intimated them. As for the women of Madhopur, it was envy mixed with awe. Her courage, her honesty, and her no-nonsense attitude worked against her.

For, who cares about the *baloom* and its usage when you get the pleasure for nothing? Who wants to get involved in a police case for having two wives… or a dowry death? Never mind a child every nine months, ligation was like going against God. The more children, the more *marad* one was! When the spouse did not object to another hungry mouth, who was *SHE* to give 'sermons' to all ? Incidents of abortions, by the local midwives, killing or selling of the girl child… such events were rampant, but that was the wish of the men-folk. Who was she to meddle in their private lives?

Kamla cared and protested and as a result, often had to bear the brunt of their anger.

"Ladki ko school kyun nahin bhejte Kaka?" Kamla was frequently known to ask the senior men of the village why they didn't send their girls to school.

"humhar ladkin ke tohar jaisan nahin banawe ke hai…besaram aurat!" was the typical reply she received. They could not stop themselves from replying with a taunt.

"We do not want our women to turn out like you … you shameless woman!"

Kamla would turn a deaf ear to such criticisms.

Now, she had a bigger issue in her 'arms'.

Checking frequently whether the baby was still breathing or not, Kamla hurried towards her modest hut. She was greeted by her seven-year-old son Ramu, who was playing with marbles.

"Mai what is that..? Oh, a baby!" He ran after her, inside the hut.

"Shushh do not shout..." Kamla hissed at him, but not before her quarrelsome and dangerously notorious neighbour Putli, overheard her.

"No…No you cannot hold her, she is very small."

Kamla placed the infant on her cot with a thin blanket underneath. There was barely any milk left. Ramu would have to go without milk today. She tenderly washed the baby with lukewarm water and Dettol soap. The girl was beautiful, brown, and tiny with soft curls. . Warm touch, soft bed and a full belly was enough for the little one to sleep peacefully. Kamla's heart went out to her. She was sent by *Chhath Maiya,* she thought, thinking that the goddess worshiped in their village had intervened just in time to save the girl-child. She bowed to the imaginary deity, and slumped on a mat next to the bed. Her mind overran with thoughts.

Was the mother pinning for her newborn?

Was she forced to abandon her, just because she was a female child?

Is she born out of wedlock? Such thoughts clouded her mind as she attended to her household chores during the day while waiting for her husband Rampravesh to return by sunset.

Rampravesh had to cycle 10km from the District office of Madhopur, where he worked as a peon at the Literacy Mission in order to reach home. He was honest and hard-working, a good man.

With the opening of the Literacy Mission and with the arrival of its programme head Shakuntala Deb, a lot had changed. It became their sole window to a different world, a ray of hope for the village. She and her husband were the only literate people in the village. Kamla could not pass her 10th grade, her greatest regret, while Rampravesh was a Class 10 pass.

It was past 6 pm and Rampravesh would return any time now.

Excitement at times gave way to trepidation. Would he consent to what Kamla had just done? Kamla had already decided that she would 'keep' the girl. Society was her main concern. She did not expect much objection from Rampravesh. He was a kind man. But an extreme reaction couldn't be entirely ruled out after all, Rampravesh had also grown up with these villagers. She took the necessary precautions and asked Ramu to go to bed earlier.

When Kamla heard the 'cring-cring' of the cycle bell, she knew that her husband was just entering the courtyard.

She let him settle down and served him an early dinner.

She broke the news. The infant was sleeping in a small heap, on the bed.

He neither threw a tantrum nor did he praise her actions.

There was neither any joy nor any remorse, in his expressions.

"Give me some daal", Rampravesh pushed the plate towards Kamla.

Serving the *daal* on top of the heaped rice, Kamla gently prodded her husband, "You did not say anything, are you totally mad at me?"

"What should I say?" Rampravesh spoke after a long pause, his face grim and tired. The dim lantern light cast a deep shadow on his downcast eyes and slightly trembling lips. After some more time lapsed in complete silence, he addressed his wife in a calm voice, "You acted as any kind-hearted woman would do in that situation, but you failed to foresee the consequences. The villagers will not accept this. As for me and you, we can manage and feed another mouth." Saying so, he looked up at Kamla. She had tears in her eyes, tears of gratitude and love for her husband.

"What will they say...? They will but taunt and sneer which we are used to anyway," Kamla said as softly as she could, heaving a sigh of relief.

"We have one and we will raise her as the second one. You wanted another child, didn't you?" Kamla hesitantly asked Rampravesh.

Their eyes met. She lowered hers and continued, "I will speak to the Collector saheeb to get her adopted legally. He will come next month for the inauguration of the new Mission Office," her voice sounded happier and more confident than before.

Ramparvesh stood up saying nothing, he raised the mug and without touching its rim, gulped down the water.

"Eat and go to sleep Kamla, don't get over-excited," he said to Kamla in a tired voice and moved on to make arrangements to smoke a *bidi* (cigarette) outside.

"How can someone leave an infant on a heap of garbage to die?" *Kamla's* voice trailed off as Rampravesh stepped outside in the courtyard.

The night passed. Kamla slept with the infant by her side and Ramparvesh slept with his son.

The baby recovered overnight. While her bruises remained, her movements and overall appearance appeared much healthier.

Ramparvesh took the infant girl in his arms and smiled.

They named her Radha.

"They'll pay me an extra 150 Rupees for Radha as she is a girl child," Kamla informed Rampravesh as she cleaned the stove, and set the milk pan atop. For every girl child, the local NGO gave a paltry sum of Rs.150 as an act of encouragement to keep the girl child. Greed and money went hand in hand, as the daughters of Madhopur limped towards life. Kamla continued, "At least the cost of extra milk will be taken care of."

"I don't know...", said Rampravesh with some uncertainty in his voice.

'"You don't have to worry", replied Kamla gently, as Rampravesh peddled his cycle out of the courtyard to work.

Little did Kamla know what was in store for her and Radha in the future.

An abandoned infant girl rescued and sheltered by Kamla' - this rumour had spread like a wildfire in the little hamlet of Madhopur.

"Ram...Ram, god only knows from where she picked up this evil child," Putli's shrill voice was heard outside Kamla's courtyard.

"Who knows? Maybe 'she' is her own child, a result of some sin she is very much capable of committing? Collector saheeb cannot be so generous with her without a reason," said Gita with sarcasm.

Kamla quickly picked up Radha and went inside her hut, her ears burned hot and her cheeks were flushed.

Few women even dared to peep from the open door. Kamla was unnerved. This was not what she had expected. So much animosity! That too for someone who had just rescued a child?

"Is this the girl you picked up, Kamla?" Parvati *mausi* strolled in, later that very afternoon, uninvited,

Mockery in her tone, *gutkha,* in her mouth, she seated herself comfortably on the *charpai.*

"Yes *Mausi*," replied Kamla.

"Well…You did a good job *bahuriya* but of what use? We as a community will not accept her." Fake concern laced everything she just said.

"You will have to give her away, or face ostracism. *Pata nahin kiska paap hai*". Her words hung in the air, dripping poison, no one knows whose 'sin' she is. Kamla was shaken.

"Here… let me see her face. I can read what's in store for her", Parvati was a self-proclaimed fortune reader. She also practised some kind of black magic, her claim to fame. The villagers were more scared of her acidic tongue than the actual practice.

"I am telling you Kamla, go and put her back where you found her, she must have brought bad luck for her mother and will do no good for you either," she tried to anathematize the newborn with her diktat.

Kamla hesitantly picked up Radha from the makeshift swing of sari and lowered her on the outstretched arms of Parvati, when she exclaimed, *"Hey Ram!* What bad signs I see!" and she pulled her hands back at the right moment, intentionally, and Radha fell down! Kamla cried out in anguish, "*Mausi* what did you do? Get out of my house! You wicked woman."

"I will drag you to the Panchayat and will put a hex on your family," Parvati warned her before she left.

Radha, by the grace of God, had fallen on the haystack and was unhurt. Ramu had picked her up and was pacifying her as Kamla stood where she was. Rooted to the spot.

She was unable to comprehend the ire, and the animosity the villagers had developed for Radha, an innocent life unaware of the hornet's nest that she had stirred up. Tears flowed down her cheeks as she hugged Radha and thought that indeed what a difficult life she has been 'blessed' with. Twice in 24 hours, she was nearly killed! This made Kamla more persistent. Ramu hugged her, afraid yet assuring Kamla of his support, in his own way.

This incident made the three of them shaky. Kamla decided to keep herself and the baby confined in the house till Shakuntala Didi returned.

Kamla's hope further crashed when she heard of the Collectors' transfer. She was worried.

A sense of an impending danger loomed in the horizon. She didn't want to leave Radha alone and go to the local police office to register a complaint.

Unknown faces peeped inside her courtyard; unsolicited visitors called on her, local women visited her on the pretext of silly things. An unknown terror gnawed at her.

A week passed.

Radha needed the mandatory vaccinations and a visit to the doctor. Kamla was getting impatient. One day as she was about to fetch the milk that was usually left for her outside her courtyard, in a mug, she saw Jamil sprinkling some white powdery substance into the milk! Kamla froze with fear. She was horrified. Jamil quickly vanished round the corner but not before completing what he had intended to do. The smell was unmistakably that of bleaching powder.

So, this was a well-hatched plan to kill Radha or to let her starve. The consequences could have been fatal for the family. She decided to register a formal police complaint, and also get fresh milk from the bazaar. Leaving Radha at Ramu's care she ran to the police post to seek help. The officer-in-charge was not present and the policemen, who were hand-in-glove with the locals, refused to register a complaint and sent her back saying that they would look into the matter when time permitted and insulted her with derogatory remarks.

Angry and frustrated Kamla met Rampravesh on her way back and was witness to yet another horrific scene being enacted, right inside their courtyard.

Ramu and Radha were being attacked by Bihari, a drunkard, along with Gitia and Putli. They were trying to snatch Radha while Ramu was trying his best to hold on to her. Kamla screamed and lunged at Bihari with the bamboo stick that lay nearby. Taken aback by the unexpected return of Kamla, Bihari paled; and tried to hit her back but Kamla was quick; he was caught off-guard by a blow from the *lathi*. He yelped in pain and jumped the fence. Kamla ran after him. Rampravesh in the meantime took charge of Radha and, pushed Ramu inside the hut and locked it. Gauri and Gitia had fled by then.

Kamla remained outside, howling and roaring like a lioness.

"Come on…Come you rascals, come… Dare touch my children and I shall make sure you are dead", she shouted, standing in her courtyard with tears streaming down her face.

Kamla was raging like fire, ready to take on anyone who dared to harm her children. By now a small crowd had gathered. But no one spoke or came to her rescue.

"Impotent! Son of a bitch! Trying to kill an infant… Come and fight me…*tohar lash bhejbau tohar baap ke…*" She threatened to send the dead bodies of their attackers to their fathers.

She sat down in a heap in the middle of the courtyard. Her hair dishevelled, her sari almost loose, moving to and fro crying like a mad, possessed woman. Rampravesh took her inside, lit the lamp and made her change her sari. Kamla sat down and stared at the flickering candle, petrified at what would come next.

Silence descended upon the house…But fire raged within.

They understood the gravity of the situation, assessed the pros and cons and decided the inevitable. Her courage was not failing her, but somehow she found herself out on a limb. Then and there they decided that they had to leave…Not flee, but leave their home, for the sake of their children's lives. Kamla hugged Radha, her daughter. She would not chafe under any pressure.

Radha and her husband packed a few of their belongings and left for the mission office. It would hopefully provide them with a safe place to retire for that night. She looked back once, at her deserted home, from the far end of the empty, narrow, dusty lane and walked away without any remorse.

It was late evening, and most of the villagers were inside their home. No one bothered.

The distance of 10 km was covered by cycle as well as on foot. It was late night by the time they reached the mission office. Kamla was elated to see that Shakuntala Didi was back in the office. She welcomed Kamla with open arms and congratulated her for her act of bravery, after hearing her out. She gave them a small room to spend the night in and provided some food and drinks for all.

The very next day they went to meet the local MLA. After hearing the whole story he took out a five hundred note from his pocket and gave it to Kamla, saying, *"Rakh lo, bahut hi aacha kaam kiya hain tumne, bachchi ko bacha ke. Hum iska upaye kar dete hain."* Pressing the money into her hands, he urged her to keep the money while assuring her that she had done a commendable job.

"I will arrange for a berth in the local orphanage," he said, "This way you can go and meet the girl whenever you want to." He eyed Kamla lecherously, chewing vigorously on this paan. The local orphanage was a living hell. It was rumoured that the MLA trafficked female inmates from there. Kamla's heart sank.

"You cannot keep a child, that too a female", he informed them authoritatively. "You can be jailed". His intentions were clearly not good.

"Why didn't you inform the local police?'' he tried to coerce Kamla, upon seeing her reluctance.

"So, it seems that you cannot help us Yadav Ji. Let me see. Maybe, I have to request help from the High Commissioner." Shakuntala intervened, "You know we are linked with them for the projects that we work on for the betterment of your *Zila* , and I am sorry to say, I don't see much progress as promised by you. In a month's time the Central Govt. will send their representative, and it is me, who will give the 'go ahead' letter as the Mission head." Shakuntala's professional approach made the MLA's step back. She spoke in 'his' language of browbeating. The message was loud and clear. He hesitantly had to draft a letter to the local *Panch*, directing them to extend support to the family.

The very same day their home was set on fire. Everything burned down to ashes. A chill ran through Kamla and Rampravesh's spine when they heard about it. Kamla did not shed a single tear. She was saving her energy for the fight ahead. Rampravesh was heartbroken and angry. Kamla's relation was getting soured with him. He at times blamed Kamla, but she ignored it knowing what they were going through was a transition, and she had to remain calm and strong during this phase.. She was steeling herself for the worse. Her eyes only welled up imagining being separated from Radha.

It was her fight for her daughter's life, her right to live, and not merely exist!

"I will continue fighting for Radha Didiji', she told Shakuntala.

"Do not worry, nothing will happen to her, I have already spoken to the concerned people,." she said softly patting her back.

Jamil was arrested and was bailed out within 24 hours, whereas Parvati Mausi, Gitia, and Putli were warned and let off in absence of a woman police in that area.

A letter addressed to the CJM was drafted by Shakuntala on behalf of Kamla and her husband to adopt Radha legally, with an application to the local Bal Bikas Kendra.

Pressure from the top level made the files move fast. Kamla was directed to keep Radha in care of the local

NGO, while they would do mandatory house and financial check of the applicant. It was a safe place and Kamla decided to stay with her till they formerly got Radha's custody.

An illiterate, small, frail woman who could not even make her both ends meet, was now in the news and support was pouring in for her, from several sides. Three months passed.

It was a new morning, and Kamla was looking forward to the day.

Today, she would get the legal custody of her daughter. As she emerged from the house Shakuntala came forward and hugged her. With Rampravesh by her side, her head held high, Kamla walked out of the gate. Her tiny hands reached out to touch Kamla's cheek as both mother and daughter looked at each other and smiled.

Glossary

Marad: macho/hunk/stud
Ladki: girl
Aurat: woman
Besharam/besaram: shameless
Samjhen: do you follow/ understand
Chhath maiya: worship related to Sun God.

Ladki bachao ladki padhao- save girls educate girls
Anchal: part of the sari which hangs from the left shoulder
Baloom/baloon: a colloquial term for condom
Daal: lentil
Sabzi: curry made with vegetables
Saheeb: Sir

Bidi: coarse and raw tobacco rolled
Gutkha: tobacco and broken beetal nuts in a powdery
mixture of lime stone usually flovoured.
Charpoi: a wired bed of coconut fibre in wooden frame
Bahuriya: daughter in law
Mausi: maternal aunt
Panchayat: comprising of five headmen of the village panch
(is five)
Lathi: a thick stick usually made from bamboo
Zila: district
Didi: elder sister/ ji added to show respect.

New Zealand and Australia

Shades of Amara

By Sindhuja Manohar

Amara was a misnomer in every sense of the word. Her mind blossomed in Southeast Asia, but her blood flowed with Indian pedigree. Her heart was captivated by the liberal "American dream", but her body danced to traditional Indian tunes. Her tongue perked up at Italian cuisine, but she could never cheat on her first love – ghee roast *dosai* with coconut chutney and tangy *sambar*. Her eyes glittered during her adventures around the world, but they shed happy tears when she was nestled between the blue mountains of her grandparents' tea estate in India. She groaned every time her family embarked on their annual visit to India, but was enveloped with an undeniable sense of protection, care, and belonging as soon as she stepped out of the bustling airport in Chennai and into the sweaty arms of her aunts and uncles.

Her cousins called her a coconut – "brown on the outside, white on the inside" – and she proudly did not deny that. And yet, she believed, somewhere deep inside, that she wasn't very different from them either. Amara was of the opinion that she was a 'good' Tamil girl; she obediently spoke Tamil with her Tamil family, she dutifully visited claustrophobic Hindu temples during her trips to India, she never complained about the overindulgence of Indian sweets and snacks when they visited their Indian friends, she responsibly stayed away from "the white boys", she did not bare her shoulders or wear anything above her knees, and she always obeyed her ridiculously-early curfew. She would always make her traditional Indian parents proud – coconut or not.

Until she met Akash.

Until she dated Luke.

Until she married Anand.

Akash

"So, what have you decided?" Amara's voice faltered, exposing a twinge of doubt that hinted she wasn't quite as ready for his answer as she wanted to be.

Akash pulled himself forward, gently rubbing his knees against hers, both elbows on the tiny table at the crowded Starbucks on the corner of 36th and Madison. He looked right into the dark brown pools of her eyes, glinting with anger, and yet glittering with hope. His hand reached across, palm up, inviting, welcoming, tempting, as always.

Amara sighed, then slid her sweaty palm onto his, and he clasped his fingers around hers.

"Amara, this isn't easy for me, but-" he started, when

Amara swiftly pulled her hand away, almost knocking over her tepid chai latte.

"I knew it," Amara clenched her jaw tightly and turned her eyes toward the stream of pedestrians out on the chaotic New York street. She willed her tears to slide back inside, but they threatened to overflow any minute now. "I knew it, Akash!" she spat his name out with undisguised devastation.

"Come on, Amara…" Akash frowned and tried to reach across for her, but Amara crossed her arms and moved her legs away from the warmth of his body. "Look, we knew this wasn't going to have a happy ending," Akash started again. "I have been hesitating all along because I know we don't have a future."

"But why don't we?" Amara's shining eyes challenged him. "Akash, listen to yourself. You're too busy saying no to even give this a chance."

"You don't understand," Akash leaned towards Amara, and casually slid his arm around her shoulders. He laid his head against the curve of her slender neck, closed his eyes, and took a deep breath. "You smell like a bed of lavender."

"I thought it was a bed of roses?" Amara couldn't help but smile at the top of his head, turning her face and gently kissing the crown of his wavy raven-black hair. It was hard to believe they had only known each other for a year now, having crossed paths in a Creative Writing class on campus – a course both had selected as an elective, as it had nothing to do with

Amara's degree in Biochemistry or Akash's degree in Engineering. It always felt quite serendipitous to Amara that they happened to meet this way, in an environment that they had self-selected, a mutual interest between two opposing trajectories. Sparks flew from their first argument over the legitimacy of spelling of color/colour, with Amara insisting that British English was the original while Akash was convinced everything was better the American way. This made sense, she supposed, because her childhood had been coloured by Malaysian crayons and Australian markers as she straddled a mix of South-Indian-Malaysian-and-Australian homes for the last 18 years of her life, but Akash had grown up under the star-spangled banner, American in every sense, and yet cooped up within a strong Gujarati identity.

Amara couldn't get enough of Akash's teasing dimples and sparkling eyes; looking into their endless depths made her feel like she was falling back gently into an expansive ocean that was going to hold her up and help her stay afloat, forever. She couldn't help herself; she had grown up with visions of Prince Charming and beautiful fairy-tales where two people met, fell in love, got married, and stayed together forever. She had had her share of middle-school crushes and high-school fantasies, but never a boyfriend. Akash was her first; her first real spark, first mutual attraction, and her first kiss. In her mind, that kiss sealed everything. The beautiful feelings that grew out of their many meetings, within their young hearts... They were the very reason for lifelong commitment, weren't they?

"Okay, stop being so distracting," Amara mumbled somewhere into Akash's warmth, slightly turning her head to check if anyone was watching their obvious display of affection. This was their usual meeting spot, where they would sit together for hours on end, his coffee going cold and her chai being refilled multiple times, chatting, laughing, caressing hands and playing footsie under the table. It was their private bubble within a public hideout, somewhere they could stay away from prying eyes and pretend to be a real couple, boyfriend-and-girlfriend, in an actual relationship.

"That's your fault, not mine," Akash's lips lightly grazed the edge of Amara's ear before trailing a path down to the side of her mouth, lingering on the precipice.

"No, stop it," Amara shifted away from the warm burn of Akash's touch. "I need to know. Are you serious about this or not?"

"Amara..." Akash's voice trailed off, as his eyes lowered and rested on the slightly chipped beauty of Amara's polished nails pressing hard onto the top of the table. "I think we both knew when we started this, this friendship, this connection, that we could never really be a real couple."

"So what?" Amara interrupted, her eyes flashing with defiance. "That was months ago, Akash, when we thought it was a mindless crush, puppy love, whatever you want to call it. But we aren't that anymore. We care so much for each other. We could have a future together! Why won't you even try? Why are you quitting before giving it a proper chance?"

"Because my family would never accept you, that's why!" Akash blurted out, focusing on her now clenched fists, still pressing into the table. "And you know that, Amara. I've always told you. I'm Gujarati. You're Tamil. My family wants me to marry a Gujarati girl. I'm sure your parents want you to settle down with a good Tamil boy."

"Sure they do, but you are at least Indian!" Amara retorted, now crossing her arms across her chest and leaning back into her chair, creating a noticeable chasm between Akash and herself. "You might not be Tamil, but you're Indian, Akash, and that's good enough. That's good enough for both of us! But, unlike you, I am willing to fight for this. I'm ready to talk to them about you, about us, and I will make them see why you mean so much to me. They might not be happy, but I think they will want me to be happy at the end of the day. Wouldn't your parents want the same? Wouldn't they be happy enough you're not running off with a white girl? Come on, you grew up here, in the multi-coloured States of America, and you're telling me you have to marry within your community! It is just ridiculous."

Akash looked up, stared into the pools of fury in Amara's eyes, those almond-shaped eyes he felt he could drown within, and felt something draining out of him. It was hard to keep up with this fight; in recent times, this was all they talked about. Their proposed relationship. Their possible future. Their desired commitment to each other. If only Amara could understand how much his heart ached for her, if only she could see that he wasn't like her, that he has had his share of complicated relationships and a trail of broken hearts, that she would be the last person he would want to add to that multi-colored list of failures. Akash was an American citizen, a red-blooded American boy in many ways, but he was trapped within his traditional Gujarati identity. His parents were already matchmaking him with all those eligible Gujarati girls, introduced to them through a well-meaning aunty or uncle, and coerced upon him as appropriate partners for his Gujarati future. Amara never understood his stubborn loyalty to his family and his community, persistently asking him what was wrong with her: were her Tamil roots inferior, was her darker skin a disadvantage, were her Malaysian childhood and Australian influences evidence of impurity? He couldn't explain to her the impenetrable allegiance to his Gujarati community, and how moving away from it would break his parents' hearts. His American passport was not a ticket out of his ethnic identity.

"I think it's better we stop seeing each other for a little while," Akash hesitantly offered. His eyes were cast down again, while his fingers fumbled with the zipper on his jacket.

Amara felt like she had been punched in the gut.

"Stop seeing each other?" she echoed him uselessly. "How can we stop when we never really started?"

"You know what I mean, Amara," Akash replied. "All we do is fight about our proposed future, you know, the one that will never exist. We don't get together for fun anymore, we don't go to the movies like we used to, and we can't even enjoy a cup of coffee without it going cold and us ending up on opposite ends of the table."

"Because our future is worth fighting for!" Amara snapped back. "Or I thought so anyway."

"We can remain… friends?" Akash offered, quietly.

"That's all we have ever been, Akash," Amara said, staring out the busy window again. "I wanted more, you wanted more, and I'm ready to fight for it, but you're not." She paused. Then she looked him right in the eye and said, "You're such a coward."

Akash flinched slightly. "You don't understand," he tried again. "I just don't want to put you through all these challenges. You think it would be easy to come into my family, when they would reject you even before meeting you? If we decided to stay together, you would spend every day of that future defending yourself to them, justifying why they should accept you. And I don't want you to have to do that. It wouldn't be right. You're too good for that."

"That's for me to decide, don't you think?" Amara asked, turning back and looking at him. "It's my choice to take on those challenges. It's not for you to tell me I won't be able to handle it."

Akash stayed quiet, while his eyes locked onto Amara's. "I'm sorry, but…" his voice cracked, as he slowly pushed back from the table and stood up. "I can't do this anymore."

Amara's eyes widened, her arms clasped tighter around her chest. "Where are you going?"

"It's done, Amara," Akash mumbled, looking at his feet. "I don't think we should see each other anymore."

"Like, ever?" Amara's strangled voice let out the desperation that was thudding inside of her.

"Yes," Akash replied forcefully. "Let's end this chapter. It was never going to have a happy ending anyway. I'm sorry."

Amara slowly staggered to her feet, holding on to the edge of the chair. "Fine," she stated in a crisp, clear tone, while her legs wobbled and her heart beat furiously.

Akash inched a bit closer and leaned in for a hug, but Amara stepped back hastily, bumping her knee against the table and wincing with the shooting pain.

"Hey, are you okay?" Akash frowned, reaching out to hold her.

"Don't touch me," Amara said through gritted teeth. "Of course I'm not okay!"

Amara grabbed her bag, and dashed past Akash, her eyes focused on the swinging doors at the Starbucks entrance. She shoved open the door, and stepped out into the throbbing current of New York human traffic. Without a glance behind her, she crossed the street and hailed a cab.

Luke

The sun peeked through the muted grey-blue curtains in Luke's corner of the brownstone apartment nestled in a quiet corner of Brookline, Massachusetts. Amara opened her eyes and gazed at Luke's sleeping form with a sense of wonder. She was huddled against Luke's warm form, his arms wrapped tightly around her, her body's curves melting instinctively into all his arches. It felt like the most natural place for her to be. He looked so calm, so peaceful, and so very handsome. It was hard for her not to be constantly enchanted by his ocean-blue eyes, dimpled grins, and golden-boy charm. Her finger lightly trailed the slight blonde stubble along his jawline, down his neck, and rested on his chest. She gently pressed her palm against his beating heart, watching her hand move up and down with his breath, and smiled.

Amara's phone buzzed on the cluttered nightstand next to Luke's bed. She turned and searched for her it under an avalanche of her crumpled clothes, Luke's sweatpants, an array of his law school papers, and used coffee cups. The buzzing continued while Amara kept digging within the comfortable mess of their existence, finally extricating her iPhone from inside her purse that was lying on its side at the edge of the table. It was her dutiful roommate calling, checking why she hadn't come back home after last night's party. Amara thought the answer was pretty obvious, considering she's been sleeping over at Luke's place for the last few weeks.

She tossed the phone back into her purse, and turned back to Luke. She could stay like this forever, just staring at rise and fall of his sculpted chest, the golden hairs on his arms against the chocolate brown of her skin, the very perfection of this moment. And the many moments they have been sharing together, just like this.

Amara had to admit she never thought she would find herself in the arms of Luke, not after that humiliating first meeting at Venu. She had been dragged out for a wild night of drinking and dancing with her well-intentioned college friends, but she was in no mood for frivolities after her heart had been tossed aside by Akash. She figured the drinks would help drown her sorrow, if anything, and wasn't quite in the mood to be hit on, even by someone as strikingly handsome as Luke. He had sauntered up to her at the bar, where she was still sullenly nursing her first drink, and casually asked, "How's that drink of yours?"

"Fine, thank you," she had absently replied, her eyes vacantly staring out into the throbbing sea of writhing bodies in front of her, their currents moving up and down to the thunderclaps of flashing light and relentless bass. Her ears had tuned out the incessant thumping of the music, and her body was slumped on the bar stool. She hadn't made any efforts with her makeup, her hair, or her clothes. She wasn't even aware Luke was still trying to talk to her until he leaned in closer and said, "What is it?"

"What is what?" Amara had eyed him suspiciously. Luke had pointed at her drink, and smiled, that irresistible dimple magically appearing as if on command.

Amara had closed her eyes and sighed deeply. "Listen, I don't really care to talk to you. Or to anyone here for that matter. I just came out because my friends forced me to. I didn't come out to meet a guy, no matter how hot he thinks he is, and I definitely didn't come out to dance and get drunk and end up in your bed tonight. So will you please leave me alone and go find some other girl to rub up against?"

Luke had laughed, a full-bodied warm laugh, that had deliciously enveloped her, slightly thawing out her iciness. He had smiled again, deepening his dimple, and said, "Nah, I just wanted to know what you're drinking, because I'll make sure not to order that. You've been sipping the same drink for the last one hour! It really can't be that good."

"So you've been watching me for a whole hour?" Amara had quipped, a small grin slipping out. "Okay, so like that isn't creepy. At. All."

Luke had laughed again, and settled into the bar stool next to her, a little too close for comfort. Or maybe not. Amara had realized she wasn't resisting as much as she was pretending to.

Luke's gentle stubbornness in keeping her talking,

no matter how much she resisted, continued the conversation for the next couple of hours. They started sharing silly stories, loud laughs, and intimate smiles. Luke's presence was calming for Amara's frazzled nerves, and before she knew it, she had ordered another round of drinks. And Luke ordered the next. The night that had started on the bar stools ended up with them intertwined on the dance floor, their bodies giving in to the mounting temptation, apparently drawn together by magnetic attraction.

They were inseparable after that night. Days were spent having mimosas for brunch on Newbury St, taking lazy strolls within the Boston Commons, and cuddling next to each other on park benches. Nights were spent out with their friends, fancy drinks and sweaty dancing until the rosy hues of dawn peeked around the corner. Luke introduced Amara to his family and she was surprised to see that she fit in like a glove. Thereafter, weekends were spent road-tripping to Luke's family home in Connecticut, Amara delightfully cushioned inside Luke's fire-red Audi as he sped down the highway. Weekdays were spent studying together in the library, their feet playing footsie while their noses were buried in their textbooks. There was something so familiar, so comforting, to lock ankles with him, mindlessly rubbing against his denim-clad legs and breathing in every bit of his wholesome presence.

Luke was a breath of fresh air for Amara. The simplicity of his expectations made their relationship feel like the most natural development in her life. She had come happily undone by his pleasurable persistence in being a part of her life. Everyone knew they were in a relationship – their friends, their professors, his family – except Amara's parents.

It wasn't that she didn't want to tell them. She did. But she couldn't ignore that gnawing feeling inside that they would think what she was doing was wrong. She was in a relationship with a white man, and that, well, it just wasn't expected. Her parents had nothing against members of other ethnicities, but that didn't mean they were willing to welcome one into the family. Her Tamil roots called for strict codes of behaviour, cultural norms, and matrimonial expectations. And none of that could include Luke. No matter how badly she wanted it to.

Amara continued to gaze at Luke's sleeping body, his face as innocent and clear as a child's, his heart as open and vulnerable as the day they met, and sighed softly.

It wasn't fair to him. This couldn't go on any longer.

In that moment, Amara made the decision to break Luke's heart.

And, as she had done before, she pretended her's wasn't breaking too.

Anand

The rain was pounding hard against the bedroom windows as Amara slowly lowered a swaddled Nikita into her crib. She stepped back and admired her lowered lashes, chubby cheeks, and a rosebud mouth that was puckered in deep sleep. Amara had been lifting her in and out of this crib for the last few months, and she still couldn't believe Nikita was their own. A part of her and Anand. How had they managed to create a being so beautiful, so delightful, so perfect? Well, she had certainly been a surprise. A most delightful one, of course.

Amara checked that the baby monitor was turned on, then tiptoed out of the room and into the hallway. As she glanced at the photos lined against the wall, her eyes rested on her wedding photo. She walked a little closer and lightly touched the gold frame, looking at her and Anand dressed in their wedding attires – she in a deep red silk *saree* and glittering diamonds while he was wrapped in a white and gold *veshti*. Anand's head was bowed towards her, his face inches from hers, his sparkling eyes admiring every bit of her, while her eyelids were bashfully lowered, a shy smile playing on her lips. It was a quiet moment of tenderness, a slice of intimate happiness, a snippet of their togetherness, that was nestled within the hundreds of Tamil marital rituals that were performed during their busy three-day wedding function.

It was unsettling the number of emotions that bubbled up within Amara simply by glancing at the photo. So much had happened since that moment. After their glorious wedding festivities in Chennai, where they had been joyously flanked on both sides by their respective families, Amara had moved to Anand's residence in Singapore as his shiny-eyed bride, his newly acquired jewel. She moved into his condo behind Orchard Road, comfortably cocooned within all the luxuries he afforded her. Her wish was his every command; all she had to do was ask. Their first chapters were exciting, spontaneous, and filled with extreme pleasures. They honeymooned in Bali and vacationed in New Zealand, shopped at the ritziest stores and dined out at the classiest restaurants, revelled in 7-star stays and squealed down highways in fancy cars. Despite his demanding investment banking hours, he would sneak away from work earlier just to be home with her. He would surprise her with bouquets of fragrances, random gifts, and constant displays of affection. He would whisper sweet nothings into her ears as they drifted off to sleep, bodies wrapped around each other, his touches making her feel like his goddess. There was nothing Amara could ask for that Anand couldn't provide. He was her permanent protector, her faithful provider, her life partner.

It had initially surprised Amara that it could be this easy to love a Tamil man. Their shared mother tongue, their love/hate relationship with India, their liberal upbringing, their traditional expectations – all of this paved an easy path for a growing camaraderie. They enjoyed Bollywood movies, Tamil melodies, and English comedies. They had eclectic friends from all corners of the world, mutual family members from near and far, and a growing circle of local company. Amara's parents were impressed not just by Anand's outstanding professional progress, but also by the obvious affection and care for their daughter from the day he set eyes on her; they were satisfied she was in good hands. How could she not be happy when a man who was treating her like a queen?

Amara snapped back from her reverie, suddenly missing her parents fiercely.

She took a deep breath in, looked at the photo one last time, and tried to remember the woman she had been in that moment, the man Anand had promised to be. But it was difficult. They looked like strangers to her now.

She walked down towards the kitchen and rummaged inside the cabinet for her favourite cup. She could drink coffee anytime, and these days she noticed she enjoyed it more at night after her long, tedious day was over, and she had safely tucked Nikita into her crib. And of course, before Anand got home from work. Her half hour of uninterrupted, caffeine-indulgent, self-induced coma.

As Amara stirred in her generous spoon of sugar into the steaming coffee, she thought back to Nikita's arrival. Their baby girl's birth had been celebrated with much fanfare; both sides of the family had been present for the delivery, all their friends had bordered her bedside at the hospital, even some of Anand's co-workers had turned up. Everyone had been there. Well, everyone, except Anand. He later said he had an important meeting he couldn't get out of, and that he hadn't expected Amara's water to break on the most inconvenient day of his work week, or that Amara's labour and Nikita's birth would have all been over in a matter of a few hours anyway. It had just been all too sudden for him. Amara hadn't pressed any further, deciding it was easier to accept his rambling excuses than to actually investigate the truth.

Settling into her favourite armchair by the sprawling living room windows, Amara took a sip of her coffee and looked out absentmindedly. The storm had not let up; the glass panes were streaming with rivulets of rainwater, and there was rumbling thunder to add to the cacophony. It made her feel like she was at sea, swaying on her restless boat, deceptively unmoored, and yet oppressively anchored.

She was a married woman and had been for three years, but she often felt like she had been doing this for a very long time. Cooking, cleaning, housekeeping. Ensuring there was the right amount of milk to sugar ratio for Anand's morning coffee, that had to be served to him piping hot before he got out of bed. Ironing his work pants so they had the right lines, hanging up his silk ties in a particular order, colour-coding his suits from light to dark. Anand enjoyed her spicy chicken curry, fragrant lamb biryani, and all versions of her homemade *parottas* and *chapathis*. He liked her dressed in traditional sarees, her hair pulled up and away from her face, with a bright red *pottu* right in the middle of her forehead. He was happy to parade her to his work colleagues, and was even more impressed when they complimented her beauty and, sometimes, her brains. She often felt like she was a delicate piece of jewellery safely tucked inside a beautiful vault, an exquisite bird locked inside a golden cage, who had the key to let herself out, but not the right to do so.

It's not that she didn't go outside – she did take Nikita out in her stroller for morning strolls around the neighbourhood, and before Nikita, she was often seen window shopping along Orchard Road, but these days, something had changed. She felt the invisible shackles on her feet, the shadow that followed her everywhere, the suffocating feeling that she was physically able, but emotionally arrested.

It was a sinking feeling that had crept up on her in the last year, and it had only intensified after Nikita's birth. Anand's many missing nights at home and lingering musky perfume on his work shirts certainly did not help. Not to mention that hurriedly scribbled phone number on a restaurant napkin that was stored carefully within the folds of the dollar bills in his wallet. Just thinking about it reminded her of everything she never was and never wanted to be, and yet found herself becoming as time went on. Jealous. Possessive. Insecure.

She had become the Indian housewife she said she never would be – the one who waits obediently for her breadwinner of a husband to come home and pay the bills, while she cleaned the children's bottoms and put hot food on the table three times a day. The one who is paraded in front of others dressed in silky fineries and surrounded by flamboyant dinner conversations, but reduced to mono-syllables and sweatpants back at home. The one who is expected to stay loyal, and trustworthy, and dedicated, while Anand got to live different lives between the time he leaves his office in the evening and gets home for dinner late at night.

This married life, to a Tamil man, who was supposed to be everything and more, as explained by her culture, as persuaded by her parents, as upheld by Indian society, turned out to be Amara's biggest heartbreak.

She knew she was living a lie, but she continued, because, at the end of the day, she believed this is what was expected of her. This was her marriage chapter.

Unless, well, she was allowed another chapter.

Glossary

Dosai - South Indian crepe made from fermented rice flour
Sambar - South Indian lentil based vegetable stew made with tamarind broth
Saree - Elaborate garment made of cotton or silk that is draped around the body; traditional attire of Indian women
Veshti - Garment made of cotton or silk that is draped around the waist; traditional attire of South Indian men
Parottas - Layered Indian flatbread made from flour
Chapathis - Flat unleavened Indian bread made from wheat flour
Pottu - Traditional coloured dot worn on the center of the forehead

Khushi

By Tania Basu

A lady with a husky voice finally announced the boarding time and everyone waiting patiently and helplessly to reach their destination, shuffled, almost all together, to load themselves - with their hand luggage and jackets and laptops - before they joined the queue.

We gradually moved on into a huge A380 and as I snuggled into my seat with my laptop and a packet of lollies, I could feel a gentle tap on my shoulder from the seat behind followed by my name. A bit surprised as to who could call me Trish here, I looked back and was greeted by a couple of smiling faces.

"Priya and Shubho," I exclaimed!

"What a wonderful surprise!"

Seven years had gone by and a host of memories from Bali visited me in a flash. Steve and I had gone for a holiday and so had Shubho and Priya. We met at a Yoga class as strangers, and as the universe sometimes transpires, a magical connection was established between the four of us, just in seven days.

Much happened in those seven years and eventually we lost touch. But as they say, if people are destined to meet again and things are destined to happen, all the positive and negative forces launch a battle against each other and make sure that they happen!

Shubho and Priya were flying to Kolkata to share their little bundle of happiness, Khushi, with family and friends and celebrate her first birthday with them. Born against all odds, Khushi was a miracle child and Auntie Trish was invited to spend a few days with them and be the guest of honour on her first birthday. The twinkle in the little angel's eyes, her innocent smile and the warmth of her parents' invitation were more than enough to draw me like a magnet and I certainly could not refuse their invitation. Little Khushi had won my heart.

After spending a few days at Bodh Gaya, which was my first destination on this trip to seek for peace of my troubled soul, I arrived at Kolkata, the City of Joy. Like most Westerners, my knowledge about the city was highly biased and filtered through the eyes of Dominique Lapierre. My initial reaction, needless to say was an overwhelming high dose of sensory overload. Having grown up in a quiet country town of Australia, I was pretty numbed by the riot of colours, hordes of people, lack of traffic rules, unlimited rickshaws, taxis and buses honking to get their way past each other and the rat race. It was the first time in my life that I was out of my comfort zone. I was stunned for the first few minutes. But then, gradually as our car meandered through the chaos, I could feel that pulse of life which seemed to have been submerged in the depth of my sorrows. Kamala, who had come to receive me at the airport seemed to sense my feelings. With a few Hindi words that I had learnt in Bodh Gaya and a few English words that she had learnt from Priya and some sort of a sign language, we managed to engage in a broken conversation to communicate with each other. I had heard so many stories about Kamala from Priya that although we were meeting for the first time, I seemed to know her pretty well.

Kamala was in her mid-30's and had come into their family some 28 years back due to a twist of fate. When she was a little child, a deadly tornado disaster had struck several villages in the Eastern part of India and had taken away everything from them. A social organisation assisting in the relief work, helped several children to relocate and find new homes where they could be of some help and shape their new lives. Kamala was one of those lucky ones to survive the calamity and find a new home. Ever since, she has called this, her new home and family. A highly efficient young lady with a curious mind, with a zeal to learn and a heart full of love, she didn't take long to carve a special place in the hearts and minds of every member of the family.

After a good 35 minutes' drive, the white Pajero came to a halt in front of a beautiful three storeyed bungalow with huge iron gates and sprawling manicured gardens. The evening sun was on its way to retreat and in that mellowed light, I could see a woman in her mid-60's clad in a light blueish cotton saree, waiting at the door next to Priya. Kamala must have announced my arrival on her mobile. As I stepped out of the car, even before I was introduced, I knew that the lady in the saree was none other than Priya's mom,whom Kamala has been fondly referring to as *Mashimoni* throughout the drive. *Mashimoni*…I preferred to call her too.

An exchange of warm hugs and smiles, followed by an interesting ritual wherein *Mashimoni* welcomed me into the household, blessing me with some *dhan durbo* and *pradip*. It was a way of saying 'Stay blessed'. I felt so special by the love and warmth with which I was embraced into this family.

Under the supervision and management of Kamala, warm cups of *chai* and homemade sweet and savoury delights followed in a few minutes - all tailored to my taste. In between sips and bites, I was introduced to other members of the family, some of whom came and went as per their varying shifts of duties with household. It was interesting to note how the face of India was changing through the outlook and effort of the strong female influence in all stratas of society, as compared to what it used to be earlier.

After polishing off the snacks and chai, Priya and Shubho took me for a little tour around the house and the garden. That is when I met *Dimmamoni* for the first time. A grey haired woman clad in a white saree wrapped around her frail body in a different style from that of *Mashimoni,* the octogenarian lifted her eyes as she heard footsteps entering her cosy and well-ventilated room on the second floor of the house. As soon as we entered her room, she greeted me in clear English, "Hello dear...How are you doing? I am so glad to meet you." I was bowled over by her impeccable English and was almost stammering to find an answer! I was under the impression that women of that generation in India were not much exposed to the English language. Priya smiled at my amazement and pointed at the bookshelves, full of books in the room. I was in total awe for this woman when I came to know more about her background, history and life. A convent educated lady of the 1930s, *Dimmamoni* had a vast knowledge of English and Bengali Literature and current affairs of the world. Despite her poor vision and hearing capacity, she read two newspapers on her iPad everyday and listened to audiobooks in both the languages to keep her thirst for knowledge satiated.

Born at a time in history, when society, family pressures and expectations demanded her time more than anything else, *Dimmamoni* despite being an extremely bright student had to give up school at a very early age. Intellectual pursuits meant more freedom and more freedom meant demanding equal rights. So responsibility took over a higher hand and throttled her desire to enlighten herself and belong to the world. Being the eldest daughter of a clan of twelve, she had almost single-handedly raised some of her younger siblings and had been not an aunt but a mother to *Mashimoni,* who had lost her mother from typhoid at a very young age of two. No wonder she was so much honoured and revered in this household.

During the next few days of my stay, I was fortunate enough to have some very interesting and enlightening discussions with this erudite lady on various topics including history, anthropology, culture and spiritualism. I came here with a narrow and tunnelled vision about so many things but gradually I realised that one cannot judge a book only by its cover; there are innumerable layers and treasures hidden around every corner.

Three days were left for the birthday and the house was gearing up for the grand event. After all it was Khushi's first birthday. She was such a precious little baby. Born into the family after years of struggle, this charming child brought unbounded happiness to all. Priya and Shubho were completely besotted with her. Throughout the day there were streams of organisers flocking in and out to cater to all the aspects of the event. Decorators, electricians, caterers, photographers, hired car services for pickups and drop-offs; everything had to be coordinated and taken care of. Catalogues to choose from, colours to be matched for chairs, tables, balloons, flowers and a thousand other things. It all seemed chaotic and scary. Everything will fall into place on the final day, assured the organisers.

The day before the party, *Mashimoni* wished to visit Dakshineswar temple and Belur Math with the whole family to seek the blessings of the *Goddess*

Kali. And, I must thank her for that memorable trip. I was absolutely stunned by the philosophy of the organisation, which functioned with the combined efforts of monks and disciples, who were engaged in social work round the year in the fields of healthcare, disaster relief, education and culture.

During the serene boat ride on the river Hooghly from Dakshineswar to Belur Math, I came to know how *Mashimoni* had lost her mother when she was just an infant. She was nurtured and brought up by her grandparents, uncles and aunts, some of whom were very close to her in age. She was the apple of her father's eye but he was gracious enough to watch her grow up into a beautiful young lady from a distance. Mashimoni had survived rough times but *Dimmamoni*, her late mother's sister and other members of the family, always ensured that there was no dearth of love and care in their modest household.

Sitting on the banks of the Hooghly, I just could not hold back my tears anymore. I felt the divine presence in that place, in that moment. God seemed to have plans for every soul that breathes in this Universe. One does not have to be always related by blood or by birth. It is the love, the trust, the faith in each other, that binds hearts together to form inseparable bonds.

Last four years of my life has been like a roller coaster ride, with several challenges, and recurring questions that I have asked myself,about existence and the meaning of life. The separation of my parents, who were the anchors of my life and had protected me like a cocoon for all these years, all of a sudden exposed me to a world where everything seemed vicious and unsure. To top it off, Steve, my partner of so many years whom, I thought I could lean upon to share my distress, also decided to desert me with my baggage of worries and move on with my best friend. I was a shattered and miserable soul who wanted to live and love but hardly had the strength to do so. In an effort to pull myself together, I decided to travel to the land of peace to do a soul-searching journey. And here I am today sitting on the banks of the Hooghly river, with people who were strangers to me until a few days back, pouring my heart and receiving unconditional love from them. Somewhere deep inside me, I could faintly feel the pulse of life which I had lost in the depths of my sorrow for some time.In this far far away land I could hear Nietzsche whispering "That which does not kill us, makes us stronger". *Dimmamoni, Mashimoni,* Priya, Kamala, Khushi - all have their stories of joy, woe, struggle and sacrifice. But sometimes accepting them and weaving our way through them may lead us through an interesting journey.Maybe one needs to seek peace not only in shrines but within and around one's self. Was it a total coincidence that I had bumped into Khushi (joy) and her parents on the plane or was this meeting predestined….I do not know! But that troubled soul that landed here a few weeks back definitely takes off rejuvenated….liberated….. empowered and connected!

Glossary

Mashimoni: An endearing way of referring to aunty
Dhan durbo and Pradip: A mixture of grains of rice and grass and a kind of candle used as auspicious articles to offer blessings
Chai: Tea
Dimmamoni: An endearing way of referring to grandma.

Languages: An Expat's Confession

By Ekta Sharma Khandelwal

Prologue

Languages had always intrigued Ira. Learning different languages always fascinated her and resonated with her in a distinct way. They seemed to bring out a hidden part of her character. Born into Punjabi surroundings, her grandparents and extended family conversed in Punjabi, but Hindi dominated the conversations with her parents and neighbours. However, the third language Ira acquired, English, which she learnt in the school, in time, usurped the Hindi and Punjabi spaces in her expression. When she looked back, she realised that she had taken the ability to speak more than one language completely for granted. It wasn't until she got married and joined Amol, her husband, abroad that she started thinking consciously about her love for languages.

Ira built an expat life, around speaking and hearing at least three foreign languages every day. At this point, so many questions suddenly rose to the surface of her mind – What made certain languages so influential around the world? Why did some countries take such great pride in speaking their native language, while others seemed embarrassed by theirs? Was there a hierarchy of languages in the world and if so, what was the hierarchy and why did it exist?

One really acquired a taste for real language experiences when one travelled a lot. Eleven years, six countries and three continents later, having dabbled in with very many languages, Ira nonetheless felt bewildered by these questions that were popping up in her mind. Living around the world, while trying to learn new languages, and simultaneously scrutinizing the ones she had grown up with, had brought forth many personal revelations for her and had started many a discussion around the family dining table.

Ira was born to a Punjabi family. Uncles, Aunts and Grandparents communicated with her in Punjabi. The national language, Hindi, came to her naturally, with the course of time. Then Christian convent education system brought English as a medium to communicate. This one, the final one was like a public-transport network that took her far and deep, but at the same time it made her realise that she is growing in an era where only English worked properly. Punjabi and Hindi spaces in her expressions were easily expropriated by the new 'important' language.

Her school days had opened the windows to two more languages. Then she had to take an additional language in school. She chose Sanskrit. It enabled her to study and understand mythology and scriptures. More significantly and perhaps, it kept her grounded.

She used to visit her maternal Grandparents during the summer holidays when Urdu embraced her life as the fifth language. This language came in the form of a blessing from her *Nanaji*.

He used to show her his diaries full of beautiful Urdu poems, saying *"Beta* there is no language that is more beautiful. It will envelop and protect you within its world." Ira used to find the poetry mesmerising. Even now, it transported her to places that remained inaccessible to the other languages. Ultimately though, when she lived in her parents' home in New Delhi, the unspoken rule was "speak English outside the home and Hindi or Punjabi inside".

****

It was the year 2007 when she got married. She was getting married to Amol. It was an arranged marriage. Her wedding date had been brought forward as Amol had to move to Tokyo for work soon after the wedding. Her marriage was precisely thirteen days old when she received a phone call from Amol. He was very happy because the paperwork was going well. Soon she would be on her way to Tokyo! And he had more to say besides.

"Learn Japanese before coming," Amol said. "You will make the most out of your expatriate adventure".

Ira already spoke five languages but she felt daunted. Perhaps, she reasoned to herself, her fear came from the fact that she was soon to make her upcoming first international flight.

"I will try," she had said. She had been polite but inside, her mind was all in turmoil.

I have never deliberately made an attempt to learn any of the languages that I know, she thought.

I have heard that it is also tougher when you are an adult. With just a month before my travel, my full-time job and a new family to contend with, will the classes be enough? Questions and self-doubt flashed through her mind.

All of her education, upbringing and modern views were fogged with the thought: what if her husband thinks less of her, if she fails. Ira's head was bursting with quick fixes and thoughts. She had just a month to sort out the language issue as well as a million other things.

"You have to mask your accent too and I think, instead of learning, use translation apps. It is all high tech now," advised Tia, her sister.

"Politely ask people to speak in plain English," said *Maa*.

"Spend some time with your in-laws now that you are married rather than wasting time in learning," bullied Nitin, her younger brother. "Learn to use chopsticks too", he laughed sarcastically.

"Speak calmly in Hindi, it will keep you humane," her father compassionately advised. She was close to him. He happened to have a doctorate in Hindi language and also had a lot of experience in dealing with people of different backgrounds, due to his real estate business.

"Daddy," Ira said confidently, "Thank you, but I think I better survive with English. I will have a smoother transition".

"You never learnt how to read or write Punjabi all these years. It's your mother language", said *Maa*. "How will you work around Japanese in a totally new environment and away from all of us?"

The realisation that she was leaving behind her established network of friends and family support suddenly hit Ira hard. She began to struggle with separation anxiety. Now that she was going to leave her comfort zone, it did not seem like a good idea to take the leap, and move abroad. After all, she thought, didn't many people choose to stay in one place and not move?

Anyhow, Ira did make an effort to learn Japanese. One month flew by and she hopped on a jet, and landed in Tokyo. Oh my, she thought, wasn't it the cleanest of all the cities in the world that she had ever visited? At the airport she exchanged currency at the bank and received a piece of origami. She would soon find that she collected origami everywhere; they were dispensed freely with the random things that she bought. Interesting, Ira thought. They are just like shopkeepers in India, who hand out éclair toffees to small children when they don't have change.

Ira was very excited to meet Amol. Their last goodbye flashed before her eyes. He had left for Tokyo in the first week of their brand new marriage. They hadn't known when they would reunite. After a drawn out cappuccino, exchanging irrelevant comments about work and the food, they had stood rooted to the spot by the security queue at Indira Gandhi Airport, Terminal 3 for at least fifteen minutes, desperately clinging to each other, as if this would somehow mean that Amol didn't have to go. Afterwards, when she caught a glimpse of herself reflected in a window, she thought that she looked like she'd run a marathon in the rain. The goodbye had been awful.

She walked and walked, looked ahead ... Again walked some more...Looked right... And finally, there was that moment of memorable eye contact with Amol that would remain in Ira's mind forever. The handsome and attractive guy standing there was her husband now, Ira thought, when she saw Amol waving crazily at her. Ira ran and hugged Amol tightly. People were rushing and walking past her, while she stood there in the arms of the person who meant the most in the world to her, tears welling up in her eyes.

Never mind the language lessons she had buried herself in the past month before her maiden international travel, all she could manage at that moment was to squeak a simple 'Hello' to Amol.

On her second day in Tokyo, she thought she would give Amol a surprise by visiting his office. She cooked his favourite *moong dal halwa*, packed and rushed out. Their apartment was close to the train station.

So many people took trains, thought Ira. It looked as if 70 million people lived within an hour's commute of Central Tokyo! Everyone seemed to be carrying a transparent umbrella – that's invented in Tokyo, wondered Ira – they probably came up with it to help people walk without bumping into one another. She smiled at the thought. On her way to the station, she went about speaking to everyone in English even if they didn't respond much.

Once on the train, Ira's thoughts continued to dwell about the country she now called home. Japan was a mono-ethnic country and more than 98% of the population was Japanese. It was not hard to imagine that the culture was therefore heavily centered around Japanese and not on foreign languages.

For the Japanese people, being able to speak English wasn't a necessity but rather an optional skill, one that's nice to have but isn't indispensable. It was wonderful to see how the Japanese society took pride in their language unlike others who lapse into English during everyday conversation. That's not the case everywhere, thought Ira. In some countries, and India too, even people who do not speak much English try their best to sneak in a sentence or two, considering it pertinent for their acceptance in the 'cooler' crowd. Sadly, society judges a person as well brought-up and educated from the amount of English he or she speaks. Ira realised that unknowingly and unconsciously she too had somehow got sucked into the trap by not speaking the language true to her roots.

The lady in front of Ira, opened her lunch and Ira snapped out of her thoughts. The Japanese woman ate exactly five spoons of rice, wiped her mouth nicely and put on her headphones. Ira was shocked and thought to herself, I eat that much just to check if the rice is cooked or not! No wonder Japanese women stay so slim, even during their pregnancies, or at least return to their slim selves quite quickly.

Not to be deterred by her co-passenger's eating habits, Ira pulled out Parle-G biscuits from her bag. She even offered them to the man sitting next to her. It was practically part of the staple diet in Indian homes! She was surprised when he grabbed three of them.

"I remember them from my visit to Nepal", he said. "Great biscuits", he added.

Ira got down at the right stop. Mission accomplished. "I will survive here", she thought proudly.

However, it became quite clear in the first month that learning Japanese was mandatory if she wanted to more than just 'survive'.

Learning a new language was a humbling experience. When living abroad and forced to speak that country's language on a daily basis, the language mishaps just keep on coming — some were more embarrassing than others. After all, when our words fail us, it can not only result in confusion, but very often laughter, shock and even anger.

Ira started self-learning tutorials and at one point she thought she was ready for basic communication. She went out, ready to try her new language skills. She met a lady with a young child while walking in the market.

"Kowai desu ne", Ira said. The child was cute.

The lady looked at her and ran as fast as she could. Ira was shocked.

May be she is in a hurry, she thought. She tried this phrase plenty of times that day and it backfired with a look of shock and panic every single time. She came back home and asked Amol, what does it mean.

"You're scary, aren't you?" he replied while changing the television channel.

"What do you mean?" Ira came out of the kitchen.

"What?" he asked.

"What do you mean, I am scary?" she said.

"No, no. The Japanese sentence, you said, meant 'you are scary, aren't you'? Why what happened?" Amol asked.

She gasped and sat down quietly, embarrassed. She was supposed to say *"kawaii"* and not *"kowai desu ne"*.

Learning Japanese also meant understanding the Japanese way of thinking. This is what she put on her study wall as she learnt more.

Yes = yes.

No = no.

Will think about it = no.

Give me time = no.

Next time maybe = no.

*I like you or your idea or your attitude or your food BUT....
= No.*

She kept reminding herself, life will be easier in some months and the opportunities will come.

"If nothing works, I can always teach English", she thought.

Ira and Amol lived five beautiful years in the city of Tokyo before moving to Australia. In those five years, every single party they went to, this exact conversation (in Japanese) occurred, word for word, which she used to translate into English and came to refer to as the 'Template Conversation'. She would come to laugh about it later but at that time the monotony killed her.

"Ah! Juice!" This was replaceable by beer, wine, soups, coffee…

"This juice is delicious!"

"Yes! This juice is delicious!"

"Quite delicious"

"There's nothing quite as delicious as a cold juice after a hard day of work!"

It reminded her of those trees in the Hollywood movie 'Lord of the Rings', who sat around in a circle for an hour making low sounds just to say 'hello' to one another. That's what this was like.

Ira kept at it by trying out the broken Japanese that she could manage but it didn't always help. In some ways the Japanese shops reminded her of New Delhi, back home. She noticed shop employees in Japan scream all the time, and sometimes with no reason. With sales person screaming all the time, it felt like 'Palika Bazaar', a market in New Delhi, she thought.

"What are they saying?" She asked Denia, her neighbour who happened to be fluent in English.

"Very seldom are the words actual words", Denia said, letting her in on this secret.

"You know, aside from *'Irasshaimase'*, they're not using actual words, most of the time", Denia added.

Apparently, some stores actually demanded that employees *'enlisted as barkers'* absolutely refrain from using actual words.

Weird, Ira thought.

Next day, Ira and Amol were in J'antiques – a vintage store that sold chic American clothing and furniture. She was looking at a vintage chair, standing near the salesperson.

"Irasshaimase", he yelled at them. He kept on yelling repeatedly.

Irasshaimase in English meant 'come into the store!' He must have yelled it maybe a hundred times. They were the only customers in the store.

"Why is he telling us to come into the store if we're already in the store?" Ira asked Amol.

"He is driving me crazy" Amol said.

She later found out that it's a Japanese thing. Like, one says the word 'Hello' in English, 'Hello' doesn't mean anything. If its dictionary meaning is sought, it says: *'used as a greeting or to begin a telephone conversation'.* Many of the words used perfunctorily in the Japanese language have both useful purposes and cold, hard semantic meanings.

That kind of bothers me, thought Ira. She couldn't think of the reason, perhaps, it is because of the fact that it is a foreign language.

With more shopping came more opportunities to communicate. Like every new expat, Ira initially converted everything to Indian currency, a habit that she eventually stopped. She couldn't help noticing that the country was quite expensive! She was vegetarian. It was so hard to find vegetarian food and poring over the ingredients in everything she was picking up had almost become a new hobby over the past months. It was disappointing for a vegetarian when even potato chips had extract of beef or pork and bread included lard as an ingredient. Talking about it, Ira could rattle off for hours about how the 'Indian' curry powder she liked to use, later was advertised 'now with Beef extract' on the can.

Let's settle with a regular Cappuccino now and I will cook at home, thought a dejected Ira. So, Cappuccino it was. The gentleman at the checkout gave her a receipt for 400 yen which amounted to about INR 253. It was almost more than double of what she used to pay in India in 2007.

"Bhaisahab mein aap ko bewakoof lagti hu kya?" Ira yelled spontaneously without realising that she responded in Hindi. Really, she wondered, did she look like a fool to him?

Pondering on her outburst, Ira realised it had felt so good and liberated talking in Hindi rather than English. Next day, in the city with Amol, not bothering with Japanese or English, *"Do mango shake de dijiye"*, Ira said to the man at the fresh juice corner shop, asking him for two mango shakes. She pointed to the correct photo in his menu card. He made them delicious, fresh mango shakes.

"Dussehri," she then said to him. He didn't bother to react or respond but she felt good.

"Ye scarf to Made in India hai," Ira told the man selling pretty scarves that the scarves were made in India. In response, he offered to beat the Indian price. He won.

After a few stressful months masking her accent to try to make herself understood, she realized that speaking calmly in Hindi actually led to a better communication and indeed kept her humane. As time passed and till she learnt to communicate effectively in Japanese, she chatted in Hindi wherever English was not the bridge, especially in hotels, supermarkets and the streets of Tokyo. She ignored the fact that nobody understood

Hindi. Sometimes she used translation apps on her smartphone, which were quite efficient but she managed to get the point across and communicate. This was a high point in her relationship with Hindustani, a language she thought she owned but had lost somewhere in the labyrinth of her adolescence.

A year of living in Tokyo passed and one day she received a call from India, her home. It was Tia. Their mother was seriously sick. *Maa* was struggling with advanced stage of cancer. The very next day Ira boarded the flight to New Delhi. Little did she know then that within the span of next six months both her mother and her grandfather would pass away. The latter was shattered beyond repair at the thought of his only daughter, the twinkle of his eyes, going through so much pain.

After seven months of staying with her family in India, she boarded the flight again to Tokyo, this time to reunite with Amol who had been an enormous source of support. He had tried his best to help her bear the loss and nurse her broken heart in the past few months.

Music was Ira's soul, a consistent presence in her life. As has been quoted from the famous musician, Frank Ocean, 'when you're happy, you enjoy the music. But, when you're sad, you understand the lyrics'.

At this time, '*Tu naa jaane aas paas hai Khuda*', a soulful composition sung by sufi singer, Rahat Fateh Ali Khan caught her attention. It was in Urdu of course and the song told her that God was everywhere; Ira recalled her grandfather's words that Urdu touches unacknowledged grief and nameless pain. The beautiful composition flew like river water, breaching the dam that she had constructed in her mind. It flooded her mind with peace and acceptance.

When one loses a language, it's like forgetting a familiar route in a forest. One wants to explore parts one used to know, but can't seem to find the way. There is a dull ache for something intangible that one seeks to recover - distant memories and echoes of laughter that beckon.

As she grieved for all she had lost, Punjabi came back to Ira in the voice of Surinder Kaur, through the song *'Chan Kithan Guzari Aayi Raat Ve'*. The legendary singer's question was simple, where were you last night? Punjabi was the language Ira had ignored most as she had never bothered to learn to write or read it, yet it was also the one that yielded the most laughs in her adult life and would one day prove to be very helpful in 'yelling' at her children.

Ira and Amol moved to Australia after five years of living in Tokyo. It was a big move and she was excited.

They embraced parenthood soon after moving to Sydney.

"It will be twins", disclosed the nurse excitedly on one of the prenatal visits to the clinic.

Ira went through a rollercoaster of emotions while Amol danced with joy. Time passed and two gorgeous charmers, the twins Eva and Vir filled their hearts and home with joy.

One day, visiting the new additions to the family, her neighbour happened to mention that she spoke to her three cats in Sinhalese, her native language. Ira couldn't imagine talking to her fish, her only pet, in Punjabi, a language more familiar to her ears than to her tongue. She stuck to Hindi.

For Ira, the pieces of her disjointed, broken worlds were woven back by Urdu and Punjabi words intertwined in poetry. She felt at home in Urdu. She used its vocabulary to express hospitality, show respect and love. Hindi immensely contributed to restoring her sanity and it worked fabulously in Japan. It was the language of her emotional expressions. Majority of the Japanese people didn't speak or understand her English or the Hindi and as there was no other language to connect with them, it was best to use the one her emotions were most fluent in. She was a better person, smiling and being affable with everyone. In Hindi, she was more talkative than usual, commenting on wonderful food and telling people her personal woes. Nobody understood her words, but she felt her emotions were understood.

Sanskrit would one day help Ira to pass the religious scriptures and mythological stories of her childhood as bedtime stories to her children, a time that was precious to Ira, Eva and Vir. She would read and they would listen with their mouth wide open, sometimes in awe and sometimes in disbelief. She felt proud as a mother, pride deep down within her, when she heard them reciting shlokas and mantras.

****

Epilogue

There are languages that one knows how to speak and then there are languages that speak to us. Languages that one understand and those which understand us.

Ira wondered if Eva and Vir too will have multiple language compartments in their soul. One for the warmth of the languages they were growing up with, and the other for the vocabulary of the rest of the world.

****

Glossary of Hindi, Urdu and Punjabi words

Nanaji - Mother's father
Beti - Daughter
Maa - Mother
Moong dal halwa - A popular dessert from North India
Parle-G - A brand of biscuits manufactured by Parle Products in India
Bhaisahab me aapko bewakoof lagti hu kya - Brother, do I look like a fool to you?
Do mango shake de dijiye - Two mango shakes, please
Dussehri - A sweet and fragrant variety of Mango fruit
Palika Bazaar - A market in New Delhi, India famous for electronic items and clothing

Ye scarf to Made in India hai - This scarf is made in India
Tu naa jaane aas paas hai Khuda - You don't know the God
is near you
Chan Kithan Guzari Aayi Raat Ve - Where were you last
night?

Indonesia

Gari

By Poppy Choudhury

The sound of the early morning rain falling gently on the terracotta tiles of the house woke Sheen up. She tossed and turned lazily, stealing a blurry glance at the alarm clock by the side of her bed; it was 4am. She began to feel the familiar rapidity of her heartbeat and the old sinking feeling which always accompanied the unwelcomed panic attack. Her throat was dry, but she was not thirsty, the early morning attack as usual was making her palms sweat.

Veer and the kids were fast asleep beside her, all huddled together on their large bed, which she called their football field bed. At the start of the attack her heart would beat fast and erratically; a strange repugnant sensation would then move down her chest and tighten her stomach muscles and then bounce back upwards, jerking and paralyzing her torso, numbing her mind for several minutes. In those moments she would try to calm herself and gasp for breaths.

Sheen hastily fumbled for the emergency paper bag. She had been taught to breathe in and out of it. For the next several minutes as she lost control of her body and lay motionless, she knew all that she had to do was to push herself to silence her mind and focus on her breathing. Like the eerie calm of a wave swept beach, long after the hard, rapid, and strong waves of a stormy night had given way to peaceful silent waves, normalcy would return for Sheen too. But, it would take time. The attack would slowly retreat; her heart would again beat with a regular pace; calmness would return to her mind and body, accompanied with a feeling of being drenched, exhausted, and despondent, like a shipwrecked traveler on a lonely, unknown island.

Curling her fragile body, Sheen thought of the packers who had arrived that morning. The usual sight of boxes as well as the frenzy of bubble wrap, tape, scissors, the male chaos, the whole unsettling feeling of leaving, had left her feeling flustered, possibly triggering the panic attack.

In her two decades of marriage she had moved six countries, across four continents, and lived in ten different houses. The excitement of an impending adventure of discovering life in a new country, had long faded. By now she should have been a seasoned expatriate; comfortable with the idea of being a foreign resident with limited permits who would move and leave at short notice, yet she was not. Leaving behind the houses she had called homes, in each country, had become increasingly difficult. When strangers in foreign lands asked her, "Where is your home?", she still got rattled, and wandered off in her past.

With every new place, her mind would warn her to maintain a dispassionate approach; her reckless heart yet would unchangingly forge deeply tangled relationships with the food, the people, the language, and most importantly the home of their fleeting and professionally brusque stay. This last entanglement always irked her the most.

During those long, lonely afternoons when Veer was at work or traveling and the kids were at school and those silent nights when everyone had fallen asleep; Sheen would walk tirelessly steering her watchful eyes from wall to wall and room to room of the houses she lived in. She always had to familiarize herself with each spot and curvature of her homes. She had to always know all the exit routes, the secret corners, the distances to places from the new houses, as well as the sturdiness of the doors and windows. Her mind would fuss over hundreds of small decisions. At times, she wondered if her obsession bordered on neurotic behavior.

As the panic attack retreated, Sheen pulled herself from the bed, and limped towards her little patio. The early morning blue and white tropical sky was streaked with different hues of deep red and orange, the sun peeked through the palm trees on the horizon. Sheen feebly raised her arms to greedily feel the golden sunrays slip through her long slender fingers. As she touched her face with her sun kissed hands, she felt vibrant and hopeful.

Closing her eyes as she rested on the cane chair, her mind wandered off….

Sheen was now a nine-year-old restless girl, transported back to her own beautiful *Gari*, the home of her parents in the by-lanes of the old part of the busy mountain city of Srinagar. Everything moved in slow motion as she floated in and out of her *Gari*, nestled in the valley, surrounded by the rugged Himalayas and deep blue skies with pristine fluffy clouds. Several images flashed through her mind; little Sheen carefully perched on her grandfather's shoulders tenderly holding the new kaleidoscope bought from Lal Chowk entering the enormous traditional mud and wooden house. Sheen could feel her fingers gliding over the rugged carving of the enormous walnut wooden doors with copper knobs of their home, smell the gentle brewing of the early morning *Kahwa*, and hear the soft grinding sound of the walnut seeds. She could see the huge windows of her house facing the majestic mountains patiently waiting for the last ounce of the winter snow to melt away. She would catch the glint of the oscillating golden *atharoo* fastidiously fixed to the long dangling *dijhor*, on the long earlobes of her wrinkled but eternally beautiful grandmother, Babi. Sitting on the upper floor of the extended balcony of her wooden stilted home, she would monitor the hurried walks of the neighborhood children to the local baker to buy the early morning *roti*s in their colorful *pherans.*

The comforting panorama of the familiar images of the past scrolling down the screen of her mind's eye would slow down Sheen's breath; she loved this ritual usually after these panic attacks. Most of all she loved to imagine stroking the long shining hair of her beautiful Zooni and gently running her fingers through the edges of her face. It offered a strange steadfastness to her otherwise unpredictable life, which seemed to be constantly on the go.

Sitting on her patio, Sheen gently opened her eyes, they wandered over to the favorite pink and red bicycles of her children, which they had long outgrown, lovingly parked in the corner of the patio. This time these bicycles were to be left behind. The sinking feeling began to gnaw again. Every move demanded, choices had to be made, what to leave and what to take.

The bitter cold night of January 19th, 1990, in Srinagar was no different. Religious and communal tensions that had been brewing and disrupting peace and relationships between the Muslim and Hindu Kashmiris over the last few years had intensified during the cold winter months. Life had been stressful for the close-knit Kashmiri Pandit community, who as Hindus, were the minority. At home, Sheen constantly sensed a pensive mood and anguish of her family elders. But her life otherwise had rolled on with normalcy. Afzal and she were still best friends and she still loved to wait for him near the mosque as he went in for his afternoon prayers. It was together that they had decided to name her new beautiful Bombay doll with golden long hair and white satin lace frock as 'Zooni'.

That night, as her family was finishing a late dinner, the street outside had begun to reverberate with the overwhelming noises of thousands of people, marching, shouting, and chanting, demanding that the Kashmir Pandits leave Kashmir or be prepared to die. Her father suddenly had leapt to the front door, speedily placing the double long wooden beams on the door and bolting it securely. One by one all the large walnut wooden doors of the house were speedily shut, and the thick heavily embroidered white woolen curtains with deep red and orange flowers were quickly drawn. Her ten-member household had assembled in their large central living room. As the heat from the large *bukhari* ferociously burnt the coal, they had held onto each other with deep fear etched across their faces. Babi had pulled Sheen closer to her, and as she buried her head against her chest she could hear her old grandmother's heartbeat bursting through her frail chest and the pale green eyes cloud over with worry.

The family conversed in hushed tones that were punctuated by rapid and animated exchanges. All that she could grasp was that it was time: time to leave their home; time to leave Kashmir. A lifetime of a decision, to finally flee their own home, built by her great grandfather on the land, which for centuries had belonged to her ancestors was an overnight decision spanning over a couple of hours. All their Kashmiri Pandit neighbors and friends too had finally decided to leave, and it was going to be a very dangerous journey ahead.

Why were they leaving home? Who were these strangers outside her home? Where were they going?

When would she return home? Could she quickly run across the street to inform Afzal? What about the new seeds they were to plant in their orchards once the snow had melted away? Many thoughts troubled her. In the darkness of the night, the family hurried to pack their essentials and busied themselves closing and locking all that was important.

Sheen pulled herself from the warmth of the *bukhari* and silently hurried to see Zooni, who was fast asleep in the corner of her small *Kaieni*. Her beautiful eyes with their deep long eyelashes were tightly shut. How often Sheen's heart had swelled with pride stroking her smooth, white cheeks with their red glow and luscious golden hair. Not wanting to risk her beloved doll, Sheen lovingly wrapped Zooni in her old warm worn-out pashmina shawl and hid her in the inner panels of the secret old wooden chest, making a mental note to write to Afzal, asking him to take Zooni away with him for safekeeping until she would return to Srinagar. Everything after that forever remained blurry for her, except the patches of memories of the dim torchlight that had guided them through the secret wooden staircase of the house, to the brook, where her father's small white Maruti car had been waiting to take them away to safety.

That night twenty-five years ago, Sheen had left her home in Srinagar. Home, where her grandmother had arrived as an eleven-year-old new bride, where her father was born, where her grandfather's ashes rest peacefully scattered in their apple orchard, with the small brook behind the wicket fence of the orchard gargling, beneath the pure cerulean sky. With that she had left Zooni, Afzal, and a long list of many more things. That night she had carried the wooden boathouse toy which has now become old, the *Samavar* which has since broken, and a few black and white pictures of their house, which has since become patched and faded. She had also carried a deep sense of recurring panic, an indescribable pain, and a sense of loss which one gains with losing one's *Gari* and homeland.

Note: January 19, 1990, is Indian Kashmiri Pandits' Exodus Day. On this day, several hundred thousands of Kashmiri Pandits were forced to leave their ancestral homeland of Kashmir, pushing them into a difficult and painful exodus and destroying the rich Kashmiriyat of the valley people. The diaspora of Kashmiri Pandits today scattered all over the world still waits to return to their homeland, while many of the older generations have passed away, waiting.

Glossary:

Atharoo: A golden pendant hung at the bottom of the dijhor, a traditional Kashmiri Pandit women's jewellery
Bukhari: Traditional furnace in Kashmiri homes, given the tradition of long and hard cold winters
Gari: Home
Dijhor: Traditional ear jewellery made of long gold threads, uniquely worn by traditional Kashimiri Pandit women, usually as a symbol of being married.
Samavar: A Kashmiri kettle for brewing tea

Kaieni: Top most floor of the house, usually used as a playroom for children

Kahwa: A popular Kashmiri tea, gently brewed accompanied with almonds

Kashmiriyat: A kashmiri way of life which is reflective of their rich traditions, culture, language, art , food, life philosophies and belief systems.

Pheran: Long woolen winter robes

Rotis: Kashmiri flour bread loaves which are sold in local bakeries and available in several shapes and types.

Paksh (For) and Vipaksh (Against)

By Munmun Gupta

The city of Jakarta, heavy with early-morning traffic, buzzes with the rush of people headed to work.

In the car, Maya's new husband turns to her, noting the anxiety lining her face as she sits beside him. "Are you nervous?" asks Jai, looking at her fondly.

"Oh, it's no big deal," Maya replies. "After all, I'm just a debate coach."

"What do you mean? Don't say that. Your new job is important!" He touches her chin, turning it to look directly into her eyes. "It's a prestigious university, Maya. I'm so proud of you."

Maya has been in Jakarta for only one month, and she has landed this job on her own merit in a strange, new, metropolitan city. Her love for the art of debate had brought her to a new phase where she felt the need to share this passion of hers with others as a debate coach.

Maya wonders why she is so lucky. She has a husband who adores her and a job she has always desired. She feels as though the city of Jakarta has welcomed her with open arms and bestowed her with unconditional happiness.

In just one month, she has grown to love everything about Jakarta, so full of life and color — from street musicians to motorbike taxis to *nasi goreng* to corporate skyscrapers! She loves it all; it's her new home. And Jakarta, is where the most important chapter of her life is about to begin.

"All the best, M!" Jai nods an affectionate goodbye as she gets out of the car and walks toward the school and her new job.

Ibu Wahyuni, an elderly woman from Human Resources, greets Maya at the university entrance. "Miss," she says, "allow me to give you a quick tour of the premises."

At the end of the tour, they walk toward Maya's classroom. She is excited to meet her Debate Club students and wonders if they will like her. "This is Room 304, the Debate Club. I will leave you with your students," Miss Wahyuni mutters as she turns away and walks toward the elevator. Maya enters the classroom.

"Good Morning, everyone," she says to the waiting students. "My name is Maya. I'm originally from India but I moved to Jakarta a month ago. I have a Master's Degree in English Literature, but my one true love is debating. I've had people tell me that I am shy in person but quite the opposite when I debate. To me, the power of debating is being able to discuss a subject passionately, even if you know nothing about it or, in reality, completely disagree with the position you're taking. Debating, to me, is fast and furious — just like the movie!" Maya smiles, hoping for a positive response from her students.

Their reaction is cold. A girl with an angular jaw and bleach-blonde hair, her black roots still visible, stands up. "I'm Jenna, the Debate Club President," she announces importantly. "You should know that we are all here to improve our GPA's — not to debate anyone."

She smirks, looking at her peers and they grin back at her.

Maya, nervous now, is taken aback. This is not what she signed up for. Is she really expected to coach students who have no interest in debating? This is not how she had imagined her first day as a debate coach !

Mustering up some courage, Maya says confidently, "LEET, LEET, LEET."

Maya got the attention of her students as she repeated those words again,"LEET, LEET, LEET."

A boy with heavy braces and pale skin blurts out, "What is LEET?"

"That's a good question. And what's your name, young man?" Maya smiles to herself. *She knows she is going to get through this difficulty.* If debating has taught her anything, it is about the power of words, and she is about to use all her debating skills to turn her students around.

"Vincent. My name is Vincent," says the boy, playing with his pen.

"Label, Explanation, Examples and Tie-back. That's what LEET stands for," Maya begins. "Every argument requires a structure, and this is where we apply LEET. Label is a short and simple sentence about what your argument is. Explanation is why your argument is true while your opponent's argument is false. Examples are what convinces others that your argument holds conviction. Tie Back shows how the argument supports the case being discussed."

She continues, "Tomorrow, using the LEET structure to convince me, each one of you must come up with an argument that supports the notion, Debating is a waste of time. I will rebut and oppose each of your arguments. May the best debatee win!"

Maya knows she will have to convince her students that they can really benefit from learning the art of debating to earn their respect. She thinks a lot about this on her way home.

Later, when Jai joins her at home, she is delighted to see him. Jai asks, "How was your first day at work, hon?"

"It was really challenging. The students were hard on me, but I'll get through this."

Jai hugs her and says, "I believe in you. You're a prize!" Maya appreciates his love but feels anxious. She doesn't want Jai to doubt her capabilities.

The next morning, Maya puts on her power suit. A black suit and white shirt is a timeless formal look and perfect for debates, Maya thinks. She is determined to win over her students today.

At the university, she greets everyone enthusiastically as she rushes to Room 304 in her black power suit. She finds her students waiting for her and greets them with excitement.

"Good Morning, everyone! I hope you've all prepared some strong case arguments," she begins. "I'm excited to hear them, even if you are only doing this for better GPAs. Now, who would like to go first?"

Patricia, a girl wearing thick, black-framed glasses, volunteers. She starts by saying, "Debating is obviously a waste of time as it teaches us to argue, and arguments affect one's health. For example, a couple that argues often have higher stress levels. This pushes them to addictive habits like smoking or alcohol consumption, and this ties me back to my case as to why debating is a sheer waste of time."

Maya is relieved and impressed that Patricia at least got the structure right. Even though her case needs more research and a better explanation, it gives Maya hope that her students can build their debating skills.

Jenna who seems nervous, decides to go next. "Good morning friends," she begins. "I believe that debating is a waste of time as it results in half-truths, distortions of reality and personal attacks. How can anyone explain their stance on a subject when the information available to them is fabricated and distorted? Will Jokowi fix health care in Indonesia? I don't know because the information available to me on various media outlets is fake. I believe debating is a waste of time as most of the information available to us is false."

Maya claps enthusiastically and the rest of the students chime in. "*Jenna*," Maya exclaims, "you have passion! Obviously, you care about social stigmas and nuances, and your argument represents what you stand for. Debating is a wonderful platform for you to address issues that you strongly believe in. This passion will help you put forward your arguments without any fear. Good job, Jenna!"

Jenna blushes as she didn't expect favorable feedback,especially after how she had behaved the previous day and sits down quietly. A boy, sitting next to her, pats her back gently as a sign of support.

Maya's surprised at how much time had passed, bringing them to break time .During the break, Maya checks her emails and finds one from the Dean of the University. It said:

Dear Mrs. Maya,

Congratulations on your new position as a Debate Coach with State University of Jakarta.

We hope you're settling in well in your new role. We have huge aspirations for our Debate Club and you as the new mentor.

Our dream is for our debate team to be represented in different states and countries as one of the strongest. We will be assessing the performance of the Debate Club at the end of each semester.

All the best to you and the Club!

Best Wishes,

Prof. Dr. Raharjo Hermawan, MM (Acting)

The break is over and the students file back into the classroom. Maya feels warm sunlight radiating through the classroom windows. She's ready to rebut the arguments she's heard so far.

"Greetings, fellow debaters!" Maya begins, facing the class. "I will be speaking against the motion that Debating is a waste of time. My opponent expressed the opinion that debating results in poor health. This statement is flawed. Debating is a sophisticated way to put forth arguments and follows a strict code of conduct. I remind you that in debating, we rebut the argument and not the debater. Personal arguments can impact health but not arguments presented while debating. Our job is to attack our opponent's argument, not the opponent personally. Debating, in fact, teaches us valuable life skills on how we should conduct ourselves with discipline while putting forth an argument."

Maya has the attention of the class now and continues affirmatively, "Another argument presented today was that debating is a waste of time because most available information is distorted and fake. I would like to point out that we as individuals can evaluate information and thus should be able to distinguish legitimate from unreliable sources. For example, news published by Jakarta Daily may not be news. However, that does not make it fake news. It is our job to assess information and to ensure that we don't spread fake news. A study conducted by Brown University proves that students who debate score better on ACT and SAT tests. This is why debating is not a waste of time. In fact, it provides debaters with valuable life skills."

The class is silent, and Maya asks, "Would anyone like to rebut my arguments?"

When a few hands go up, Maya sighs with relief. She knows this is the beginning of many sophisticated debates that will take place in Room 304. It will be a long journey for her and her students, but together, they will argue and conquer.

Glossary

Paksh : For
Vipaksh: Against
Nasi Goreng : Indonesian Fried Rice

USA

A Journey to Remember

By Sumona Ghosh Das

2001, in the month of May, the air in Kolkata was hot and humid. Jhilik's *ma* and *baba's* face was moist, even in the temperature controlled Netaji Subhash Chandra Bose International airport. It was hard to tell whether they were marks of sweat or traces of tears. Their only child, their daughter, was flying for the first time to an unknown land, alone. Heart pounding, head dizzy, ears ringing, tears on the verge of breaking out, that pang of leaving her parents far behind in the visitor's area, all rushed into her senses like a gush of boiling water. But Jhilik stood strong, clenching the handle of her suitcase, ready to board British Airways. She looked at her passport and boarding pass. Her itinerary read, 'Final destination-Chicago, USA.'

She met many interesting co-passengers on the plane. The gentleman sitting next to her was from Bangladesh. She chatted with him that her grandparents were from Dhaka, from undivided India. As she spoke, her mother's face caught in that moment when Jhilik had spotted her waving from the wall-to-wall glass window of the airport, before the flight had taken off.

Her mother had told Jhilik stories about her ancestors. She taught her to be grounded, and be proud of her Bengali heritage and culture. Jhilik thought of her grandparents who migrated from Bangladesh to India during the partition of 1947.

Today Jhilik, was the migratory bird, flying over seven seas. History was in the course of repeating itself.

Mistaken identity

The flight landed in Chicago O'Hare airport. Jhilik's heart started throbbing again. She was going to see her husband, three whole months after their wedding. Why was she nervous? He was no stranger. She had known Akash for nine months now. They had chatted for hours on the phone, crossing timelines between Chicago and Pune. Their family friends had introduced them to each other and they had had an arranged marriage.

Maybe the newness of the place gave a subtle novelty to the person. Determined to make a good impression, Jhilik saw her husband eagerly looking for her at one of the arrival gates. But Jhilik had already emerged from an adjacent gate and now she was standing right behind him!

Jhilik decided to surprise him.

Softly, she crept behind him and was about to hug him, when she saw a familiar face waving at her from a distance, and that man looked like Akash!

Perplexed, she dropped her hands next to her, realizing just in time that she was about to grab a stranger.

Blushing red, Jhilik decided to curb her romanticism at that very moment.

Phew! Arranged marriages can be elusive, initially you run the risk of mistaken identity!

She thought and turned towards Akash-her husband.

A whole new world

Akash opened the door to the apartment for her. She saw a 'Welcome' balloon floating in the middle of the living room. It warmed her heart. She entered her first household in the United States. The hallway had a closet on the left and a kitchen to the right; it led to a decent sized living room. She opened the blinds and looked out, over the balcony. There was a line of weeping willow trees swaying in the breeze and a small pond overlooking the balcony. Jhilik took a deep breath and immersed herself in the surrounding beauty. There were going to be many introspective days spent on that balcony. There would be plenty of rendezvous with those weeping willows while her consultant husband traveled to other cities for work....

Jhilik was a little hungry so she opened the fridge only to find that it was fully loaded with... *Nothing*. A gallon of milk and half a dozen eggs were in conversation with a strange looking wrinkled object.

Following his wife's gaze, Akash glanced inside the fridge and exclaimed "Oh! That's the mango I bought to make mango lassi....err....three months back!"

What is in a name?

Jhilik lived in the Midwestern city of Columbus for a year. Their apartment was right next to a sprawling mall that had stores like the Ralph Lauren, Gucci, Coach, American Eagle, Michael Kors, Nike and alike. Now, Jhilik came from a small town in India and just the idea, that she was living next to all these 'big' brands, all within one roof amused her. Her days as a marketing major from a management school kicked in. She started to observe keenly: the brand designs; brand placements; target market; store presence; product quality and concepts she had spent hours learning. All the 'case studies' revolving around these famous brands suddenly seemed to come alive in this shopping mall! She saw a glittering computer store called 'Compusa', so she mentally pronounced it in that same manner and thought that's a funny name.... Later Akash told her it was pronounced Comp-USA and not Compusa, with a tight-lipped grin she did not find amusing; in her head, she was already mortified at her own ignorance. As a former marketing major, she saw the misunderstanding as a travesty.

Back in the mall, her eyes caught a glance of her favorite chocolate shop. Godiva! She stealthily walked inside and devoured the smell and warmth of cacao. She picked up a box of assorted chocolates and went to the cashier. Jhilik noticed this young girl in her twenties had purple streaks in her hair, multiple piercings, and tattoos. Her eyes were loaded with kohl. She had a gothic look. As Jhilik noticed her, she realized that she too was being observed!.

The 'Goth' girl glanced at her forehead.

Finally, she couldn't contain her curiosity and said, "I hope you don't mind me asking, but what is that on your forehead? Have you been physically abused?"

Jhilik blanked out at the suddenness of the question.

"What? My forehead is abused?"

"There is a red mark in the middle of your head! Please don't be scared, I am here to help you. You tell me what happened?" The girl insisted.

Jhilik whispered, partly in shock, partly not knowing what else to say, "Marriage happened."

Then, she explained that the red mark was vermillion, that Indian women proudly decorated their hair-parting with this vermillion, which sets them apart from the rest, as a married woman. She explained that in her culture, the red mark denoted social prestige, dignity, grace, and respect for a 'married' woman.

Myriad of sentiments revolved in Jhilik's mind at that moment. It was more than just a question, *Are you physically abused? What is that red mark?*

While she was trying to understand the girl's purple hair, the girl, in turn, was trying to make sense of the red streak rising from Jhilik's forehead. Even within the realm of misunderstanding, there was a momentary connection between the two women, worlds apart.

The Universe in a University

Columbus had a lot to offer. Good friends, memorable gatherings, local sightseeing, and good universities. Jhilik wanted to continue with her studies, she had Akash's support as well. She joined the local university for advanced courses in Management. The country where Jhilik came from, the one defining trait of a good student was his or her ability to memorize. Memorize subjects, topics, paragraphs, letters, pages, and diagrams even numbers in mathematics! Students with a sharp memory were often bestowed with high marks. But then, for Jhilik, mugging up textbooks had never been her forte. She needed to understand in her own terms. The definition of the population by Adam Smith, as she had studied at college looked very different than the original, when she wrote. Although she believed her concept was correct. She didn't care that it was supposed to be word-by-word. As a result of her 'self-analysis' and saying no to copy-pasting a concept from a textbook, a perfectly round circle sat on her test paper, popularly known as a zero. That one 'zero' made her believe in high school that she was no good in economics.

Then, fast forward few years; she got a four-point grade average in Organizational Behavior! What happened? What changed? Perhaps the country and its education system? Perhaps it was just her time? She finally found that her learning style was not flawed after all. In fact, it got appreciated for its content, originality, and uniqueness, by her faculty and peers. For bringing a fresh idea on the subject, her professors applauded her. For the first time, she didn't have to imitate a famous author or quote a famous personality to make her point. 'She' and her 'original ideas' were enough. Her originality was encouraged, new thoughts were welcomed and her faculty supported independent research. Jhilik thrived in an unconditional, unrestrained environment.

The power of Control

Driving was an elusive subject for Jhilik. Being a single child, her protective parents never let her drive. Forget about a car! Not even a *scooty*. Because the whole town would crash down upon their child, if she ventured out on a two-wheeler, was their constant worry. This conspiracy theory was a slap in the face from the past when Akash put her behind the steering of his black SUV and said, "Jhilik, drive."

She had driven many race cars, rocket ships, cruise ships, cool bikes...But only in her dreams.... Never in real life.

It was a desperate cry from a husband who was adamant about teaching his wife how to drive! For Akash, a hundred grid spreadsheet was easier to decipher than a shopping list and frequent grocery trips! In hindsight, his plan failed after fatherhood brought countless diaper and formula shopping expeditions into his life.

But on that particular day, Jhilik fancied the idea of independence that driving could bring. She was scared, but on board with this plan. And that is how 'Sardarji Driving School' came into the picture. Sardarji taught Jhilik how to change gears, how to hold the steering, rules of the road, forward, backward, maneuvering, acceleration, and all the car driving and 'controlling'. Jhilik thought, *yes control is important, after all, we are driving a car at an average of 50 mph.* With some acquired confidence from the first lesson, she took to the steering, with her trusted teacher Sardarji in the passenger seat and Akash in the back seat. Jhilik drove down the Golf road on that chilly Sunday morning.

She was going fast, so she asked, "Sardarji control karoon?" (Sardarji, should I control?)

Confused, he asked, "Madamji kya control karoon?". (Control what, Madam?)

She said, "The car. Aur kya!" *(The car, what else?)*

Sardar said, "Usse control karna nahin, usse brake lagana kehte hein" (It's not called 'control' its called hitting the brakes).

Jhilik frowned at him for a moment because she thought she had used the right terminology for the situation.

Staring at the rearview mirror Akash's amused look didn't help either, who was mouthing the words, "Yes, control Jhilik, control."

Stop at the STOP sign

Jhilik basked in the aura of newfound confidence. She

knew how to drive and she was good at it. The whole town was not crashing down upon her as predicted by her loving but protective parents. All she needed was a driver's license now. She found out that there was due diligence before getting the license, unlike in India. She had to study hard, there were rules for driving as well as rules of the road. She had to give a written test and a driving test before she could get that coveted driver's license. It is an important piece of acknowledgment in the United States. Passing and excelling in exams was never an issue for her, then why was she nervous this time? Perhaps she was trying to anchor her new roots, she would firmly put her feet and build a new foundation in this alien land. This driver's license meant more than just driving a car, it was her identity.

Jhilik passed the written test easily. Now it was time for the driving test. The examiner, a lady from the DMV (Dept. of Motor Vehicle) appeared in front of her. To Jhilik she was no less than her elementary school principal, who had the power to make or break the system. Diligently she buckled up, started the car and started driving with the examiner by her side on the passenger seat. She diligently followed all the 'rules of the road' and finally came to a stop sign. She 'controlled' her car and made a right turn from the stop sign. They finally came back from where they started.

The examiner got out of the car and announced, "Thank you for taking the test. You did a rolling stop at the STOP sign, hence you have failed the test."

Jhilik FAILED! She had never failed a test in her life and yet, she failed a driving test! "What on earth is a rolling stop? And when did I do that? She thought."

Akash silently added, "Perhaps you needed to 'control' more."

Jhilik purposefully ignored the hilarity of his statement at that time. She was too miserable looking at other women getting their license; it looked like 'Olympic medals' to her. She vowed to come back, pass the test, STOP at that dreaded stop sign and get her rightful license.

She did that just a couple of months later.

A proud father

A few years later Jhilik and Akash had their first born, Maya.

Jhilik still remembers the look on her husband's face, she had never seen before. Pride, joy, happiness, calm, and contentment, all the emotions were melting together in his eyes. She realized at that moment that even *he* was alone in many ways after he migrated to this country for work. Now he had a wife and a daughter who were there to stay. He now had his own family. After a year, their joy knew no bounds when Jhilik's parents came all the way to Chicago to celebrate their granddaughter's first birthday and their son-in-law's graduation. One night, while Akash was on a trip to Europe, Jhilik took her parents and daughter to a friend's house in Palatine. It was midnight when they returned. Maya was fast asleep; she had her grandmother to keep her company in the back seat of the car. Jhilik's father sat in the front passenger seat. Jhilik carefully drove through the long dark roads, a half an hour drive, while chatting with her parents. Out of the corner of her eye, she got a glimpse of her father's face that seemed to glow in the dark.

She asked, "What happened Baba, why are you smiling?"

He said, "At this hour of midnight my daughter is fearlessly driving on these dark roads and I am sitting beside her. My heart is swelling with pride."

The moment paused, Jhilik remembered that moment for the rest of her life. Her *Baba* was not scared that his daughter was driving, he was proud of her.

Have a great summer

Fast-forward eleven years, Jhilik never missed a chance to volunteer at Mira's first-grade class. Mira was her second child. Volunteering offered a window into her child's outside world. Mrs. Wisely greeted her with a smile. Jhilik finished inserting all the papers inside each folder for the students. A bunch of first graders helped her without being asked.

Jhilik thought, *kids learn from what they see, not just what we tell.*

At last Mrs.Wisely gave the students their report cards.

Tagging along Mira, Jhilik finally approached her car. The school buses had already started lining up, she wanted to get out of the school zone fast, secretly competing with the bus driver who was about to block her way. Hence, in a desperate effort to get out she pulled out the wrong way and sure enough a cop was standing right there. Like a very good citizen, Jhilik turned her car immediately into the parking space, only to find she parked in the handicap parking spot… She instantly turned on the emergency lights in order to let the cop know she was parking temporarily.

She got off the car to speak to the cop if there was a way out of that area, and sure enough, she found Mrs. Newmann, the school principal staring and had possibly watched her recent acrobats.

"You can't leave this place until all the buses are loaded and gone", she said, as if she could read her mind.

Jhilik nodded and gave a pleasant smile, wishing that this moment would fast disappear!

While waiting in the parking lot, Jhilik looked at Mira's report card. She had done well in all of her subjects. Her spirits soared and she smiled at her, in the rearview mirror. There she also got a glimpse of some upbeat teachers passing by to stand on the sidewalk by the school exit. As the buses exited one by one the windows were filled with clusters of hands waving bye-bye to all the teachers. The teachers joyfully waved back.

Jhilik thought, this system doesn't teach you to fear; this system sets you free and gives wings to fly and achieve your dreams. This system creates students like her child who says that she likes EVERYTHING about her school. This system gives such principals and teachers who stand on the sidewalk to bid goodbye to their students and say, 'Have a great summer'!

A journey to remember

The café is dimly lit. The red wall has a beautiful mural of the metro cities of the US. It has the landmarks of Hawaii, San Francisco, Los Angeles, Denver, Dallas, St' Louis, Chicago, New York, Niagara, Washington DC and so on…All connected with lines on a map. Jhilik puts on her glasses and admires the mural. She is now fifty years old; she has lived or visited almost all of those cities marked on the map. Every city has memories and she left behind a piece of herself in each of those places. Jhilik runs her own boutique Marketing and Advertising firm, 'MirMaya Creations'. She paints, writes and picks up the camera in her free time. Maya is a senior in college studying engineering and design. She loves to sing and play the piano. Mira is a freshman, majoring in English Literature. She has mastered the Indian dance form of *kathak,* and loves to perform. Jhilik takes the last sip of the coffee and exits the café. A man in a blue sweater is placing his golf clubs in the back of his car. She taps him gently on his shoulder, there is no mistake this time. It is Akash. Jhilik smiled.

From '*Jana Gana Mana*' to the '*Star Spangled Banner*', life has taken her on a journey to remember.

Glossary

Baba: Father
Scooty: A light version of scooter
Sardarji: Men who follow Sikh religion, and wear turban on their head.
Mph: Miles per hour
Kathak: Traditional Indian dance form.
Jana Gana Mana: Indian National Anthem
Star Spangled Banner: American National Anthem

Sour Apples and Hot Peppers

By Suparna Basu

The apple trees were laden with apples and each one of them competed with the other for sourness. The pepper plants she had planted in late spring were now loaded with hot peppers, although her wish to raise them from seeds had failed miserably. She went around, proudly inspecting her plants, sharing her pride with Dad, explaining to him how each of her green babies was special. Megha even shared her concerns with him when she noticed her green babies had issues and required extra love and care.

Years ago, during a trip to Gaya, a sacred city in India, Megha had witnessed a young couple performing the last rites or *pind daan* for their young son who had recently expired. When the priest urged the parents to release the departed soul from the confines of the world, the mother could not hold back her tears and wept, "But he did not experience life. He was only five. He hadn't gained lifelong friends yet, did not learn to mount his bike, did not....Had not.... I cannot allow him to go. He needs to come back, experience, enjoy the beauty of our planet, live a full life. I cannot let him go." She was inconsolable.

Many years had gone by, yet Megha experienced an intimate connection to the emotion the mother had shown that day in Gaya. Letting go was extremely hard. Whenever her mind was idle, her thoughts would return to Dad. He too had missed out on so much; her home, her kids and the fact that she had become a teacher. Megha's father had barely been fifty-five years old when he died. He had spent a pleasant evening that day. Megha's parents had enjoyed the company of their friends at the Bengali Library, *Surith Pathagarh.* They did their groceries on their way back from the *Pathagarh*, ate dinner together, watched a Hollywood movie before retiring and he died soon after. Their neighbor, a doctor, confirmed he had suffered briefly. "It was a massive heart attack Megha. There was nothing we could do. He never gave anyone any time. Transporting him to the hospital would have been futile. He indeed did not suffer much," he repeated. "He was gone in a couple of minutes."

Her marriage was new. She had recently moved halfway across the world to join her husband to embark on a life together. Her home far away from Patna was a quaint midwestern, slightly rural town that did not show up on any printed map of the United States.

The news of her father's death never sunk in.

Even when she called home, she refused to let reality sink in. She always imagined him to be on his grocery trips therefore reasoned why she never got to talk to him on the phone. Her Dad's imaginary grocery trips were so therapeutic. They allowed her to breathe whenever she felt suffocated. This imaginary world, that she had created exerted a calming effect on her.

Dad was very much part of her life. He had been an extremely affectionate father. They made so many memories together from eating *puchka* a spicy water ball, to harboring secrets from Mom, to buying endless school supplies and stacks of storybooks. He patiently explained each chapter when she performed miserably in a history test during her fifth grade. They went shopping together when they visited Kolkata. They had spent many Saturday evenings enjoying theater together. He was her driving instructor and even took the blame when she hit a cow and a rickshaw during those early days of driving in India. Her Dad was someone whom the community looked up to, the man people came to when they required help. He commanded respect and love from everyone he was acquainted with.

He was no longer over here, but her memories with him seemed like a prized treasure. Her biggest treasure of all comprised of the hundreds of letters they had sent each other during the first eight months of her marriage. Her 'Dad, did you know' letters were his treasure. "Dad did you know we do not require anyone to scrub our car?" As she wrote, she imagined his response, "Then how do you do it?" She resumed the conversation on paper. "We just drive into a car wash and sit back and watch an automated machine do it."

"Did you know we drive to Atlanta, 180 miles away, to buy Indian groceries every month?" She could virtually see his eyes pop in surprise and ask, "One month? Won't they rot?" At the international market in Atlanta, she bought *ilish maach,* the famed hilsa fish which was a traditional Bengali delicacy that had been packed in Chandpur, Bangladesh. She also bought mustard oil that had the 'Made in Dhaka, Bangladesh' written on it. She knew it would have made Dad nostalgic about his own childhood before the partition. She sent him video diaries in VHS cassettes once they bought their first video recorder. Megha literally recorded everything. Her fridge, her microwave, her dishwasher, her answering machine, her computer, her walk-in closet, the mustard oil and anything that mattered to her in her world were recorded. It was her new toy. Her world though was distinctly different from the one she left behind in India, yet he understood things easily. He was a Hollywood movie enthusiast. He had seen it all in the movies. "Dad I am practicing my driving skills at incredibly high speeds. It makes me nervous and it isn't as easy as it looks in those movies. I get on the interstate and get out at the following exit and keep doing it as if in a loop. The speed and the number of cars zooming past me make my legs feel like jelly," she wrote.

Now she does not write anymore. Instead, she talks to him every time she is alone. She has mastered the art of soliloquy. She shared all her triumphs, her failures, her battles, and her dreams. She shared it all as she walked, checking her lilies, her iris, her towering rose-of-sharons, and those wildflowers she admired that kept coming back year after year for the last twenty-two years since she threw a bag of seeds she got from somewhere as a gift.

Life has been interesting. Megha raised her boys well. "Dad, you would have been proud of them. They play the violin and don't need to be pushed to practice unlike…," she trails off, chuckling under her breath. "This lawn care company is doing nothing," reality intrudes upon her most private of thoughts. "Look at those weeds along the flower bed. I need to call and talk to the company owner today." Anyone could tell, it wouldn't be a happy conversation.

Almost eight years had gone by since she had last talked to her Dad on the phone. Megha was now a teacher and did not have much time to talk to her father. She knew her Dad would be extremely proud of her. She was doing what she loved and felt passionately about. Megha pushed hard on the gas pedal. She was late for work almost every day. Dropping her oldest at school, the baby at the babysitter's before braving the downtown traffic posed a challenge every morning. Her biggest worry each morning was parking. "I hope I find one quickly." She was always late for the meeting, but her colleagues never seemed to mind. They were always delighted to see her. Most teachers at her school quit very quickly. The work environment wasn't like any other school. The teachers here were all exceptional, resilient, thick-skinned and compassionate people. They all noted a sense of relief when they saw each other daily because that meant no one had decided otherwise the night before and stayed home looking for a different job.

Dad, she remembered, always maintained an engaging way of teaching worldly lessons. "If you have satisfied 25% of the people, you were trying to work with, you can claim success!" His lesson resonated with Megha. Dad would be immensely proud of her for achieving what she did. He knew his baby girl was a rebel, headstrong and cared very little about criticism. Every time she was criticized it made her more determined to undertake whatever she had in her mind. This day she was not just a teacher; she was playing the role of a mother to many of her students who had enormous trust issues. The language, anger, and attitude she encountered would deter most from coming back the following day but those things did not bother her. She went on to not only gain their respect but their love too.

The personal stories of the children changed Megha emotionally and transformed her. It altered the way she looked at the world, people, and everything. It developed her into a new person. From being just a mother, she became a mom who developed a passion to love and enjoy kids just the way they were.

Almost all the kids she taught came from incredibly complex backgrounds. Most did not come from stable homes. Many were unaware of their paternal identity. Some lived on the streets, or with friends, relatives, anyone who would give them a couch for the night. Many young adults lived on their own in housing provided by the government, in neighborhoods called 'projects', where gangs were part of their everyday life. Some students were monitored by electronic devices, had parole officers they reported to and were in and out of juvenile detention centers commonly referred among students as 'juvies.' Her inner-city students were all under the age of twenty-one. The personal stories of these kids have always been shoved under the rug. What people generally hear as stories on the news are their stories about gangs, their failures, their deaths, and their drugs.

Antwan was her student two summers back. Kids like him made her job as a teacher mean so much more to her. Antwan had not come to school for a whole month. It worried Megha. Administrative office wasn't exactly aware of his whereabouts. There were rumors among the students. Some said he ran away from home. While others thought he was shot but survived. Believing a rumor wasn't the smartest thing for a teacher but they kept her awake at night and Megha decided to do a house call and she learned Antwan was at the Children's Hospital.

Megha's oldest turned twelve that weekend and she had organized a birthday party. The thought of Antwan admitted to the hospital occupied her mind. She felt she could not have a party, watch her son cut a cake, sing a song and pose for the perfect picture. She would contact her guests to inform about a two-hour delay. She rushed out that Saturday morning to assemble a care package, a box of chocolates, a box of assorted cookies, a bag of chips, nachos and a cheese dip, some bananas, some apples, and a 'get well' card all put safely in a tote .

An hour later she was at the inquiry desk with a visitor strap in place, looking for the room number. Antwan was shocked. "Mam, you?" A smile and then a tight hug let Megha know the kid needed assurance that he was loved. A goodie bag made his day. SpongeBob on TV reminded Megha he was still a kid whom society had asked to grow up faster than he wanted to.

"What happened sweetheart?" she questioned anxiously.

There was silence.

"I did not come all the way for this silence sweetheart. I want you to share with me. I need to know."

"I got very sick," he replied while looking the other way.

"How?" she softly asked.

Antwan started telling me his story.

"I don't want to live there. I want to be 18 and move out. It's so hard to live, sleep, function in that house. There is traffic at all hours of the day, especially at night."

"Drugs?" Megha asked.

"And more…" he replied.

"There is traffic at home. I sometimes feel scared. I want to sleep. It's so hard to sleep when it's so noisy."

Megha found herself hugging that boy and crying with him. She had children of her own at home. She could feel that lump stuck in her throat. She wished she could take him home, let him shower, eat dinner and have a good night's rest; give him some peace from this adult or rather this adulterated world where he was being forced to live. A child did not need to encounter this, struggle and accept his circumstances daily. Megha could feel why Antwan needed to run away from home. She knew he would not further open up. He had learned to bottle things up in his heart.

Antwan was found shot, injured and breathless in some alley ten days earlier. Maybe he was selling drugs. As a 17-year-old he was trying hard to survive alone. The police found him on the streets and admitted him to the children's hospital. He was getting the best care anyone could imagine but soon he would be back, alone on the streets once more living in that unsafe environment.

Megha lived in two worlds. During the day she dealt with kids and their extraordinary circumstances that were almost unreal for suburban moms, and in the evening, she was living her suburban quiet, peaceful life. Her two worlds were so far apart that by design they would almost never cross paths.

She came home and found it hard to explain her day. They weren't just stories; she was witnessing human lives, complicated worlds in which children lived and had to deal with adult problems. Megha wondered what Dad would say had he known about this. Talking in her mind was so much easier than putting words, and her father remained her best friend. "You are doing an awesome job," she was sure he would have whispered in her ears. "You are getting the opportunity to learn so much about this real world."

Every time she socialized, wore nice clothes, she felt that growing guilt. At parties, everyone cooked so much, ate so much, and partied even more. She often wondered why did they not volunteer in the communities that needed their help? Even when they did, she remained disappointed. Once or twice a year people with whom she associated would get together to cook for the hungry. The children were asked to play music for the elderly or volunteer in the hospitals to earn middle/high school credits which were points earned towards a college admission application. The takeaway from these events was always the name, the credit, and the non-profit status. It was fun to cook with friends and volunteer with them. She wondered if they would go to an inner-city school to read a book, volunteer to help with homework or teach math or help cut paper. Most of her acquaintances were horrified to hear the routes Megha drove to do house calls for her students. She could see it made them nervous and question why she needed to do what she did. Most volunteered an opinion, "Can't you find a different school to work in?" She felt disconnected from them and their conversation. Megha found most people she knew equating organizing a day of feeding the homeless as a year's worth of volunteering. Most of her acquaintances had never experienced asking an inner-city child if he had eaten his breakfast or asking him if he had slept peacefully the night before, a very basic necessity that almost everyone Megha knew from her suburban life took for granted and did not even consider a blessing.

Most people when they see tough kids on the streets doing drugs and gangs are terrified of them. They are thought of as rough, street rogues, emotionally very strong people and just don't have a softer side.

It had not taken Megha long to realize that her students needed something way more than just an education. They needed an adult who would listen to them, believe their stories, accept them just the way they were and love them unconditionally. Megha realized her phone calls to India, and Dad's pretend grocery trips, her daily soliloquy with him were not any more pretend than another human being who was living in this world pretending their worlds were all perfect, ignoring the world around them and pretending it did not exist!

Megha had plucked most of the pepper for that season. She was used to freezing the excess. It was getting chilly and there was frost on the ground. It would ruin all her harvest if they weren't removed. Her vegetable garden was almost bare, and the lawn care guy had winterized her lawn. The fall colors on her tree leaves were vibrant and were slowly settling on the ground. The squirrels were long gone and weren't running around the oak tree for acorns any more. The flowering plants almost pretended they were dead.

The yard looked lifeless but Megha sat in her sunroom sipping her morning tea with a slice of buttered toast and wondered how her 79-year-old Dad would look today. Yup, it was his birthday today. Would he still be as handsome as she remembered him 24 years ago? Would he recollect all the cool things they did together and everything about her? Would he be using a hearing aid now? Would he be as active as he was, would he still make tomato-orange juice like he habitually did whenever he was in town? Megha could almost taste the morning breakfast of toast, eggs and fresh tomato-orange juice her Dad made. Would he suffer from Alzheimer's and not recall her, like many his age? A million questions ran through her mind, and they haunted her. Dad was a young man when he passed away. It was hard to imagine him as an old man.

Megha welcomed each season, anxiously waiting for spring when she could walk around her yard with Dad again. She was always excited to reintroduce him, her enthusiastic green babies who usually broke ground and popped out even when the ground was covered in snow. Megha looked outside at the early morning sky that had all the hues of the midwestern morning Sun. She smiled and said, "Happy Birthday Dad, make sure you have fun and I will grab an extra bite out of that cake I got for you last night." She walked into her home to get ready for school again. She did not have those usual chores of dropping her kids at school or baby sitter's anymore. They were both grown up and took responsibility their own lives. As she got older, she wondered if her boys would ever walk around their yards talking to her and sharing their lives the way she did with her Dad once she was gone.

Solitude

By Sujatha Ramanathan

It's a bright sunny day. Birds are chirping, flowers are blooming in the nearby shrubs and a gentle breeze is spreading the fragrance evenly across her first floor window. With a cup of coffee in hand, Sneha is standing by the window, in a reflective mood. Ironic as it may appear, if someone had even mentioned a few years ago that Sneha would find solace, comfort and happiness in 'solitude'; she would have definitely bitten their heads off and walked away.

Life events, time and experience have the unique ability of transforming and moulding individuals; just like waves hitting a rock's surface alter its shape and presence over time. The element common to both transformations can come only from an inherent willingness to give up control, let go and just go with the flow.

Sneha had enjoyed a normal upbringing and childhood in India.

She grew up in a close knit family and lived in a middle class neighborhood in Mumbai. Sneha's mother was a homemaker and her father worked for the state government. Sneha spent a lot of time with her elder sister Kusum. Not only was Kusum her sibling, she was also her friend, teacher and guide. Sneha often had the pleasure of hearing stories from her mother, about the incessant rain on the day of her birth, which was accompanied by terrible thunderstorms. Transport services had ceased to function and it was nothing short of a miracle that her mother had managed to reach the clinic to deliver. After a few hours Sneha had arrived - a shrieking but beautiful child - warm and cosy in her parents arms.

It was obvious and noticeable from the very beginning, that both sisters were different in their personality and behavior. Kusum was mature but shy, reticent and calm. Sneha was childish and gregarious, and more talkative than her sister! Kusum conserved her energy and used it only when needed; Sneha seemed to dissipate it at the very first opportunity. Nervousness even manifested into nightly episodes of incessant teeth grinding for Sneha, which became a concern for her parents. As was the situation with children coming from the families that grew up in that neighbourhood Kusum and Sneha went to the same school as all others. Both girls were intelligent, hardworking and competent. They both excelled at school, teachers adored them and both girls genuinely enjoyed going to school. Extracurricular activities for Kusum included the arts, while Sneha excelled in public speaking and sports. Kusum stayed away from the public eye as much as possible, and even started writing poems as a hobby. Sneha participated in events that got her an audience, claps and cheers and that was the way she liked it. Kusum doted on Sneha, protected her as an older sister would and always watched out for her. Sneha on the other hand was blunt and sometimes rather rude to Kusum. She bore a grudge and was competitive, which is common between siblings. Sneha complained to her mother about how unfair it was, that success always came so effortlessly to Kusum. It angered and irritated Sneha that her own outcomes required so much more from her and even then the results were just average. Kusum had always excelled in Mathematics at school, so it didn't come as a surprise when she decided to pursue accounting related options in college.

Sneha's sentiments regarding her sister persisted. In college, as Kusum excelled, it just got more worse. Her resentment manifested in displays of intense anger and even aggression towards Kusum, and this put some serious strain between them.

Kusum and her parents tried their best to comprehend Sneha's feelings and even intervened to make her understand, but nothing changed. As Sneha got ready to graduate from school, she tried to be as different from Kusum as possible. Kusum during her school and college days had cultivated a close circle of trustworthy friends. Sneha, although more popular in school, instead could only boast of a fickle circle of acquaintances. During this time both sisters also faced personal tragedy when their mother was diagnosed with cancer at an advanced stage and passed away within six months. This loss was hard on their father and he became aloof, silent and reclusive. As the older daughter, Kusum rose to the occasion and took on more responsibilities at home including caring for her father as well as balancing her college responsibilities. One would have expected, that this tragedy would also dissolve all resentments within Sneha and bring both sisters closer. Instead, sad as this may be, this loss only deepened Sneha's irritability and outbursts and she personally chose to distance herself from her elder sister. Childish and immature as she was, in her mind, Sneha was always the victim and Kusum was the reason for all the wrong things that were happening in her life. Kusum, however continued to remain calm and displayed amazing maturity in her interactions with Sneha. She helped and guided Sneha in whatever way and extent she could.

Kusum graduated from college in accounting and then completed her Chartered Accountancy course. This landed her a lucrative job in a successful CA firm, which for a fresher, was an excellent opportunity. Sneha pursued her studies in Life Sciences and did well in college.

As a child, Sneha had always expressed a desire to pursue graduate studies in the US. Sneha got admission in a good University in New York State with full scholarship. This was a godsend for the family, as without any financial aid, there would have been no way to fund Sneha's education abroad.

Five years had passed since their mother had passed away, and as time heals all, the family slowly started recovering from the trauma of loss.

Kusum was thrilled and excited for everything Sneha had managed to accomplish till now. After all, Sneha was the first member from their immediate or extended family to ever go abroad. The family was very proud of Sneha's achievements and they firmly stood behind her and bid her a fond but sad bon voyage. Sneha had, in her own mind, deduced that the Universe was rewarding her for being better than Kusum and she felt proud and validated. Kusum though aware that Sneha's merit and performance had secured her this wonderful opportunity also silently and patiently hoped that this experience would open frontiers for personal growth and learning in her younger sibling.

Sneha boarded her plane in Mumbai on a full moon night eager to begin a new chapter of her life. The girl who had always been surrounded by a loving and protective family, was moving continents and oceans away..

Sneha landed in New York on a Monday afternoon and decided to unwind and settle down. Jet lag hit her hard and she went off to sleep for a couple of hours. Once awake, she decided to familiarize herself with her surroundings and walked over to the nearest grocery store. Sneha noted that public transportation was easily available and so were University shuttles that ferried students to and from the school campuses. Sneha was excited to start her University life in NY and meet new friends. This was after all the start of something new and adventurous and promised lot of fun in her life. She had been looking forward to this and had been lucky to find a friendly roommate in Sonal with whom she shared common interests. They spent a lot of time in each other's company. The school's International students association had also been of immense assistance in facilitating her adjustment in a new country and culture and making the move more manageable.

We are all aware that it is perfectly normal and natural for someone in Sneha's current situation to experience feelings of uneasiness, nervousness and apprehension. She too had been experiencing these emotions. Once the semester started, courses and assignments kept her busy with less and less time for thoughts of sibling rivalry or resentment. Sneha pushed such emotions away and hoped that they would soon disappear. As the semesters passed, the feelings just got more intense and took its toll on Sneha. She became more angry and got irritated at the drop of a hat. Common sense here would dictate that an intelligent girl like Sneha would seek some assistance. One would also have expected her to speak with Kusum who had never missed a single opportunity to support and assist her even when her own behavior towards her was far from acceptable. But Sneha's inability to admit that she was overwhelmed and really missed and needed her elder sister, was never expressed. School work kept her busy and being competitive by nature, she kept going at it doggedly. It was as if for that part of her Life, a different part of her brain was at work. This was not however the case with her social and personal interactions. Hiding behind school work and busy schedules, her contact with her sister waned over time. In the past, Sneha had always managed to extricate herself from difficult situations with her confidence and positivity. Now that those inherent skill sets were compromised and not optimal, she changed from an enthusiastic and cheerful individual with ample social skills to someone who was rather aloof, grumpy and secretive. Sneha's personal and social interactions suffered and her social circle which included Sonal and other school mates shrunk in size. Her health took a toll and she fell sick more often. Sneha became quieter and shunned company and was basically unhappy.

At school, Sneha kept performing well by burying herself and finding comfort in books, courses and study material. On the personal front, she slowly became aware of changes within herself and this concerned her. As Sneha was slowly becoming someone she could no longer identify with, at the same time she was also growing by displaying fortitude and courage to let go, self-introspect and open up her mind to welcome new experiences.

After nearly a year had passed by, as a first step, Sneha reached out to her sister and had a long and real conversation with her. It soon became obvious that as an older sibling, her sister was not competing with her but just looking out for her. After many such conversations in which her sister advised her to be compassionate, mindful and joyous to both herself and others, Sneha felt a sense of relief and comfort. The invisible wall that she had built herself between them was slowly beginning to crumble and disintegrate. Kusum advised her to drop her ego, practice gratitude and humility in everyday life. Lately, Sneha had also begun to enjoy moments of solitude and her own company in which her mind was still and calm without the incessant background chatter. These moments were proving to be therapeutic and helped soothe and heal her. In such moments of quiet solitude, things were clearer and Sneha's mind, got more focused. A new blissful self was slowly revealing itself to Sneha and she was excited to be part of this transformation. On Sneha's next birthday, her father sent her an email with the following words, which struck her as very true. Sneha was changing and her father's words were acting as a catalyst. Her father wrote:

My dear Sneha,

I wish you a wonderful birthday, may God's blessing always stay with you and Kusum. I am happy to see your progress and wish you well as always. We live in an amazing world full of wonders and opportunities. Wise men have often remarked that the human mind is the most wonderful and powerful thing in the world. Its powers and how we choose and use them decides our sorrows, happiness or solutions. The landscape of the mind has always been a mystery for ages and will continue to be so but one aspect is definitely clear. An uncontrolled mind is like monkeys riding on your back. Its landscape is dotted with constant chatter, chaos, unfriendly terrains, hostile mountains and inhospitable deserts but alongside and amidst all this disorderliness is an abode of inexplicable calm. This deep seated dwelling of inner peace and harmony is ours to discover and claim. It however requires us to be introspective and delve deeper into ourselves which often happens in moments of solitude. On your birthday, I wish you not only moments of great joy but also such precious moments of solitude, which I hope will prove to be your best birthday gift ever.

Yours lovingly,

Daddy

Europe

The Remains of Goodbye

By Agomoni Ganguli-Mitra

Bathroom: bathrobe and night cream.
Kitchen: clay teapot and coffee mug
Bedroom: cupboard check, winter coat(?), rucksack, etc.

A simple list helps keep the mind focused. Taking too much seems petty; leaving too much appears cruel, or worse, ambivalent. She sits on the roll-top rim of the bathtub and contemplates the bathrobes, side-by-side, shades of beige and cream, hanging behind the door. *You two make a lovely couple.*

Her toothbrush is gone. She can't remember having taken it. She tiptoes on the wooden floor, although she knows the neighbours have heard her come in. She doesn't want to disturb the silence, the smell. Every house has its own smell. It lingers for a few weeks after you move in, disappears once you have made it your home, and it greets you again, after long absence, just as it greets her today.

I love you.
Hold me close.
Go to hell.
We need to talk.

Kitchen. The teapot is a handmade wedding gift from her cousin, Jui. She runs her fingers over its smooth curves, remembering how pleased she was when it had arrived, that it matched the kitchen tiles. She takes off her boots and lets the cold of the kitchen floor seep into her bones. Opening a window, she takes a deep breath. The air of the Alps is strangely reminiscent of Christmas holidays in Kolkata, and suddenly, unexpectedly, childhood memories come rushing back.

Getting on the plane, furious that her parents had yanked her and her younger brother away from the first snow of the year, from the snowball fights yet to be waged with the neighbourhood kids, from the sweet smell of pine, oranges and chocolate. The anger would dissipate the minute she saw her cousins at the arrival lounge, eyes red from having waited until the early hours for their flight. From then on, it would be a whirlwind of noise and laughter, sunny days punctuated by eternal meals, rhymes in a mother-tongue that was both familiar and foreign, and sweets, mountains of sweets. Her favourite time were the winter afternoons. A knock on the door as they finished their late lunch, and Jui appeared, smiling, still wearing her school uniform. Together they would climb the stairs two-by-two, past the *thakurghor*, all the way to the rooftop.

Carefully curling their toes to clasp their Hawaii sandals, they would push a broken brick behind the corrugated iron door, as an additional safety measure against the spying eyes of younger siblings. Safe, they would lay out the bamboo mat, inside the triangle created by the drying clothes, hidden away from the workers from nearby building sites, and partially shaded from the glare of the sun, but not from its warmth. Once settled, they would each produce their offering of the day: she, the oranges and coffee-flavoured sticky toffees stolen from the larder, and Jui, a cassette tape of the latest Bollywood film soundtrack. This was a hard earned treasure, the tape smuggled from Jui's older brother's own pirated collection, itself slowly, and painstakingly built by bribing the staff at the music shop on the corner.

Stretching out on the mat, they would nestle the recorder in between themselves, listening, humming along, and discussing love. Jui was a couple of years older and seemed to have a wealth of wisdom she herself hadn't yet acquired. She would talk about the boys in her tuition classes, giggle about a special boy who always seemed to look out for her, the one who had slipped her a poem in a borrowed book, and who a couple of winters later, would become Jui's first and only boyfriend.

At four, the siren of a nearby factory would mark the end of the working day. Soon, both mothers would rise from their afternoon nap and loudly enquire about their whereabouts. But the girls still had a few crucial minutes of freedom. The builders would have left, and the window panes from neighbouring houses would soon be closed in preparation for the evening. With meticulous carelessness, they would edge towards the corner of the roof that looked onto the street. With heightened awareness but without directly looking downward, they would nonchalantly lean out and make themselves partially visible to the world. As if on cue, the bicycles would slow down, and a hoard of teenage boys, on their way their afternoon games of cricket, would find themselves immersed in urgent discussion right in front of the house. The girls would continue to chat, as if quite distracted by other things, just as they imagined the protagonists in their favourite movie might do, those who fell in love despite their feuding families, and who eloped a few minutes before the interval.

The rooftop romances rarely flourished beyond the few smiles exchanged from great heights. In real life, eloping at sixteen only happened to girls already considered far beyond redemption. There had been a boy once, she seems to remember. A few smuggled notes, an early Valentine disguised as a Christmas card. But this was almost fifteen years ago, and she can't remember whether she had dreamt it all.

A school bell rings nearby and she can hear the children running out, shouting greetings to their parents, screaming goodbyes to their friends. She closes the window and stands in the middle of the kitchen. She had stood at this spot three months ago, having just smashed a wine glass on the floor. The gesture had been accurately timed, the element of surprise being key to having the upper hand in any argument, especially one laced with stale spite and regret. She hadn't quite expected the sudden surge of elation however, as the glass had left her hand, and it had her almost laugh out loud. Later, once he had left, violently slamming the door behind him, she had spent a long time studying the broken pieces, wondering whether she could run her fingertips along the rough edges, a quick nick to release the little red worm throbbing in her veins.

Wake up
Leave the bed
Get dressed
Take train to work
Eat-cry-sleep. Repeat.

Lists were good. Lists, and patterns, and protocols. These were the good things in life. Not expensive wine, and luxury travel, and fine dining. Patterns anchored you to reality, to sanity, to life. Bedroom. Neatly folded silkwear. *Another woman?* No, she remembers buying it a few weeks before she left. *The lies we tell ourselves.*

She takes out the purple *Benarasi* from the top shelf of their shared cupboard. She remembers sweating profusely in the sweltering Indian summer, entwined in six yards of silk and gold jewellery. *From this day, I take on the responsibility to provide for your rice and clothing.* No dialogue scripted for the bride. Only protocol. Look beautiful and subdued. Appear grateful not gleeful. She remembers being hit with a wave of nauseating humiliation, and anger at herself for playing along with tradition, pretending she belonged. Had she not realised that the girl on the rooftop only lived for three weeks over the winter holidays? What had made her think that she could be that girl for the rest of her life?

She brings the soft silk to her face and inhales deeply. Handwoven with threads of pure silver, for his grandmother's trousseau, the sari is dotted with geometric patterns considered stunningly modern at the time. She carefully examines the fabric that has wrapped three generations of brides in silk and naphthalene.

Get married.
Play house.
Fall out of love
Arrange to pick up your things

She slips her coat on and reaches for her boots. The remaining tasks belong to others. Manage the paperwork, the rumours in the community. As she glances around the apartment one last time, she thinks she sees a gleam on the kitchen floor, in between two tiles. A moment of hesitation, before locking the door behind her. That piece of glass must have been nesting in the crack for months. It hadn't looked sharp enough to wound. If it did, it wouldn't leave a scar.

Glossary:

Thakurghar: a room for worshipping (Thakur is God, Ghar a room)
Benarasi: a silk sari woven in Benaras, India, popularly worn by the bride.

Five Half-Lives

By Abhilasha Kumar

The high, mid-July sun was beating down on them that evening as they set out for the fields on their bikes. Iris trudged slowly uphill, out of breath, but determined to show Matthew that she could do it. Sweat trickled down her brow and her neck, transforming her brown Indian skin into foamed espresso. Her sunglasses hid the physical effort apparent in her eyes and her mustard yellow strappy top could not prevent how hot this biking endeavour had made her. Clad in shorts and sneakers, she looked like she was dressed for a picnic. Matthew biked ahead of her, trying not to show the strain on his forty-eight year old knees, a good fifteen years ahead of Iris.

A day before, Matthew had asked her to bike to the fields with him, after work. "Let's lie in the fields of gold" he had said, referring to the stretch of corn fields that grew as far as the eye could see, just a few kilometres away from the city of Basel in Switzerland.

They reached the hilltop, and let their legs rest as their bikes glided down the slope, effortlessly, towards the fields. Clearly, Matthew had an idea about where to go and Iris was happy to follow. Truth be told, she was just happy to be with him, even though it was just for an hour.

They turned left onto a dirt road through the fields, looking for a place to park their bikes and chanced upon a cleared circle amidst the corn. "Did you know it was there?" asked Iris, bemused at this chance discovery. Matthew shook his head in equal amazement. They lay down on a bed of dried corn leaves, the smell of corn around them, the sun ever so slanted in the sky now. An eagle flew overhead.

Matthew drew his phone from the rucksack and played Sting's "Fields of Gold". They both knew the lyrics and music by heart, being the musicians that they were. Matthew timed the lines, *watch her body rise, as you kiss her mouth*, with a deep kiss that inevitably caused Iris' small body to rise upward, meeting his. As he released her, she fell back on the cushy bed, the itchy feel of hay on her back and bare legs, sweat running down her neck and down her temples. They lay side by side, with the odd, curious fly hovering and disappearing, listening to the song in their golden circle.

Neither moved for sometime after the song ended; each caught in their own reverie, absentmindedly watching the eagle circle above them. Time lost its meaning during that hour.

The compelling ring of his mobile phone bolted their minds toward reality. Matthew let it vibrate without answering, saying he would answer it later. "By the way, by when do you have to get home", he asked, changing subjects. Iris didn't have a specific time in mind, but with her in-laws visiting, she had better get home soon.

Sighing, shaken out of their dream state, they sat up – two lovers in a serendipitous circle of gold. "Ideally", Matthew mused, "we would sit here till the sun goes down, talk, make love, cuddle, and leave long after the stars come out". Iris smiled at the image it evoked.

They parted ways when they reached downhill on their bikes, Matthew turning right for his home, and Iris headed back to her terraced apartment, to cook dinner for her in-laws.

Her husband Akash had already picked up their three-year old daughter, Maya, from day care. Maya was busy playing with Legos when she arrived. Iris knew her in-laws didn't like the idea of confronting their daughter in-law's legs and thighs, preferring her in long skirts and *kurtis* with jeans. Their poker-faced silence spoke more than vocal rebuttals. She knew everyone at home was unhappy that she had arrived so late. But today, she didn't care. She had felt free with a head full of dreams, as she biked back home that evening, a gentle summer zephyr in her hair, smelling of Matthew's cologne laced with his sweat.

Home seemed like a parallel universe to be plunged in, one in which her body reacted mechanically to routine chores. She changed into frumpy pyjamas and a cotton tee-shirt, washed her face, removed her make-up and tied her long black hair in a high bun above her head as she stepped into the kitchen.

Mummyji, her mother-in law, was sombre; a slight pang of guilt stabbed Iris' belly. Everyone was waiting for her to arrive home to cook dinner. Akash was a different man while they were visiting, more of a son to them than a husband to her. Mummyji explained that she had cooked *daal* and asked Iris what else needed cooking. Taking her cue, Iris metamorphosed into daughter-in law mode and politely replied that she would take care of everything. It was a well rehearsed dialogue they repeated on a daily basis, like actors who knew their lines.

Maya strolled in, wanting her mother's attention. After a day's work, the long, hot bike ride and the thrill of laying on a bed of hay with Mathew, her thoughts still dwelling on him – she didn't have much left to give Maya. As if sensing her mother's disinterest, Maya opened the nearest kitchen shelf she could reach and started throwing salad bowls and trays on the floor, then looked up expectantly at her mother for the inevitable outburst.

Her in-laws shook their head in disapproval. A daughter-in law who wore inappropriate shorts, arrived late from work, didn't care much about tidying around the house, and spent such little time with her family. What on Earth had Akash seen in her?

Iris longed to finish the business of cooking and eating dinner. She wanted to shower and retire to bed, cuddled up next to Maya's little, soft body and message Matthew on her phone. She found the mundaneness of every day work, drab routines and the relentless pace of her responsibilities and duties, stifling. Ever since Matthew had entered her life two years ago, life had become a roughly strewn-together conglomeration of many half-lives as a working mother, wife, home-keeper, daughter and now lover. Her physical body enacted her duties half-heartedly, whilst her heart and soul longed to be with Matthew. Her mind often shut out those pangs of guilt that ravaged her as she avoided Akash's hurt eyes and questioning gaze. He wanted to know what was happening to his wife, a vague cloud of suspicion casting a shadow on his mind. She was no longer the woman he had known.

Iris found it difficult to stop this direction in which life was steering her. She felt like a fly in a spider's web, unable to escape - exhausted, willing for something to change by now.

It would have been stupefyingly simple to call it an extra-marital affair. This reductionism would fall short of defining what it really was. To Iris, it was a union of two kindred souls.

Her life had never been empty, and yet, life had never been full. Life had been somewhat happy with many check-list boxes ticked. And yet, there was a diffuse hole she could never put her finger on, something unnameable, just out of reach. A hole the size of Matthew, she thought wryly.

If not for that concert two years ago, life would have been more linear for Iris. She had auditioned to give herself something constructive to do. Her lifelong passion for music never saw its heyday, as in India, university studies for "better career prospects" always took precedence over secret dreams of being a rock star. Her company's Centennial anniversary concert seemed like her chance. The audition was a breeze. Her vocals were strong; her range spanned a spectrum from high thrill to low melancholic; and she knew her perfect pitch. Matthew was the drummer in the band; other members comprised two guitarists. Older, stranger, sporting a perennial air of disdain, he stood out from the crowd. She had seen him around and known him as a familiar face around the office building, without paying much attention. But now, she found that they had the same taste in music, the same love of lyrics and melody, the same understanding of their favourite singers. She found his hazel eyes magnetising, his compliments to her generous, his long lithe fingers on the drum sticks intriguing, and his views on everything metaphorical and philosophical to be resonant with hers. It made no difference that she had grown up in India and he in Europe, that they didn't share the same birth place or generation or ethos. They spoke the same inner language. Their words held the same meaning. Their dreams conjured the same images.

Their bond grew as their playlist spanned genres - from classic rock to rock and roll to jazz. One evening after rehearsal, it seemed natural and oddly familiar when his hands roamed down her body. Mindlessly, she surrendered to desire, to the moment, as it seemed light, surreal, afloat. For ten years, since her twenties, when she had met Akash as a student in an Indian university to their journey together to Switzerland, their marriage and now parenthood, the thought of another man touching her hadn't crossed her mind. It was thrilling and yet familiar, like Iris and Matthew had known each other for aeons.

There was nobody she could confide in, nobody she knew who would understand, or help her understand this mad frenzy her life had become. She had tried to put a stop to this growing closeness with Matthew. It was terrifying that he filled her heart, her mind, her thoughts and this connection engulfed her tightly strung life. It was like being given a pearl on a spoon held between her teeth whilst doing a tight rope walk – either the pearl would fall off, or she might fall off the rope, tumbling into an abyss.

Iris' days were filled with longing for Matthew, talking to him, being next to him, discussing songs and their meanings, the nuances of musical notes and the aberrations that added bulk to a composition. Their conversations would drift to the natural world, their long walks investigated treasures of nature, their joy quadrupled by sharing with each other. Caught in this whirlwind, powerful gusts of emotion toppled over her normal life with Akash and Maya. She would finish dinner as quickly as possible, put Maya to bed, and spend the evening on the phone with Matthew.

She would try to sneak half an hour on weekends for a quick rendezvous. Iris found it hard to focus on daily conversations about bills and social obligations. She learnt to dodge her parents' calls from India, her foggy head finding it hard to face long conversations about family life in Switzerland. Maya wanted her attention, her job demanded her attention and Akash's eyes became a vacant waiting hall, waiting for all parts of his wife to come back.

Two years hence, Iris was a drooping figure torn apart by the demands on her physical self, her body being asked to attend a life she had been living, a heart traveling wherever Matthew went, her soul pining for peace and wholesomeness. It became harder to keep the right pitch when she sang and her voice had gradually dwindled into a whisper, unable to sustain the sheer abandon that music demanded. Should she feel guilty about having fallen in love with Matthew? Should she curse her fate that she had met her soulmate after all this while? Was she selfish and irresponsible in savouring each stolen moment with Matthew, knowing that each moment she spent with him was time spent away from Maya and Akash? If Akash had done this to her, she might have left two years ago. How could she? What could she do? Was she an infatuated girl naively overselling her connection to Matthew? And would this connection crash into a hundred pieces in the face of mundane living, were they to get together? Or would it be the culmination of each buried dream she had, coming true?

Matthew lived alone, though Jackie was a background presence in his life. To Iris, it seemed like a relationship born out of necessity, simmering on a back burner. They met occasionally and went on dates together. Matthew's affection for Jackie was reminiscent of old friends who had known each other in youthful days gone past. It didn't 'feel real' and he had said as much to Iris, who had no reason to disbelieve him. In the early days, Matthew spoke about Jackie, much as Iris spoke of Akash and Maya. Eventually, both refrained from mentioning their 'other' lives, as their time together became a precious commodity full of tenderness, intimacy and long conversations about music and dreams of an elusive, nebulous, Utopian future in which neither consciously mentioned the other.

That night, like countless nights these past two years, Iris woke up in the middle of the night. She knew from experience this was the end of her sleep, and grudgingly prepared herself for the nothingness of a black hole, tossing and turning, keeping thoughts at bay, waiting for the first hint of orange-blue to colour the sky. Her thoughts strayed to Matthew. Something deep inside her had stirred and woken up in that crop circle, surrounded by 'fields of gold'. Those vague, weak thoughts she always fended off in her mind, those thoughts of 'what if', now became factual entities and managed a foothold in her consciousness. Once ajar, that shut door opened with surprising ease. Matthew and I could start a life together. I'll have to fight the whole world as I know it. Mummy and Daddy will be shocked. There will be all that crying and lecturing. Maybe I can go to India and speak to them personally, try to make them understand. She paused, thinking of Akash and how it would destroy him. Her heart sank, thinking of what she had shared with him and how he loved her. Was it fair to him? But then, her heart retorted, was it fair to me? Is it fair for us to live like this, half in and half out, together but far apart? Akash was young and strong and would be able to move forward. As for Maya, she was three. Who said she couldn't have two fathers? Matthew was fond of Maya and Iris knew that they could grow to love each other. Didn't Matthew often say that he wanted a real relationship, stopping himself before saying more, perhaps conscious of the seriousness of her circumstances.

It felt right, destined, terrifying and courageous. It would mean toppling over her world. She would never know if she didn't take that leap of faith. Iris had fought with herself to keep this decision at bay for two years, not allowing herself to admit that she had to go one way or another. Now unable to sustain this protracted, long drawn, tightrope walk, she had to hurry to the other side, or drop off altogether. The thought of doing the latter seemed sacrilegious.

I have to tell him, Iris thought excitedly. Next week, he will be leaving for his summer holiday in the US, following music festivals around the country. How she wished she were free to go with him. Perhaps she could arrange for them to meet the evening before. Maybe those two weeks apart whilst on holiday will give him time to think and plan this next phase in their life.

Early next morning, Iris messaged Matthew. The week was agonisingly slow to pass. Iris' heart pulsated with the energy of relief when she allowed her true feelings to come to the fore. One afternoon, she went to the bank vault and fished out her most prized asset, a small gold coin that she had received in college for "outstanding singer of the year". The omnipotent Hindu symbol "Om" was engraved on one face, and Ganesha on the other. She still remembered the deafening applause and cheer when she had approached the stage as Father D'Silva announced her name. She was the only one who had received that coin, whereas achievers in other categories had received less valuable presents. To her, this coin held the promise of tomorrow, the smell of Destiny, and the pride of accomplishment. It was only right that Matthew, her kindred spirit, should have it as they embarked upon a whole new chapter.

The evening finally arrived. She had carefully laid out her plan, ensured that dinner was made at home; Maya was looked after and in a good mood. Thus far, there were no glitches in the plan. She showered, took extra care not to smear her eyeliner and put on her berry red lipstick. She dressed modestly but elegantly, wearing her black skirt with long slits on the sides, with a simple white, low cut, tee shirt under a stylish Indian, indigo, bolero jacket. The bike ride was deliberately slow-paced, allowing time for her heart rate to calm down and her sweaty forehead to cool. She had never done this before, and for the first time in her life, felt like she wanted to commit to someone, rather than just follow where life was taking her.

Conversation was easy with Matthew, who was happy to see her. They settled in bed with a glass of wine, watching the twilight sky from the window. She didn't know every single detail about Matthew's past. But did it matter that she didn't know exact details? She could feel it in his present, a constant ghost lingering over him. She had never pushed him to talk about it, sensing that he preferred not to anyway. All that mattered was the present moment and the promise their future held.

She couldn't hold back any longer and cleared her throat for the speech she had practised in her head this past week. She brought out the gold coin, encased in a little red box, and said, "This is for you. I want you to have it". She could tell Matthew was fascinated and wasn't expecting it. His kiss said thank you more than his words did. She took a deep breath and finally spoke slowly, holding his hand as he sat reclined on pillows and she lay on her stomach, facing him "I have wanted to speak to you before, but it feels like now is the right time. I have thought about it on and off for a long time, but have finally admitted it to myself. We belong with each other. I belong with you. I want to be with you, start a new life together. I know what I am saying, and the serious devastation it entails. And the battles that I have to fight, and perhaps you too. But we can get through this ring of fire to the place we both have in mind". She stopped to look at him carefully. His eyes were suddenly very still, his expression calm. He nodded slowly, "Thank you for telling me how you feel". Her heart sank; this wasn't the response she had expected. As if sensing it, he added "There is a lot to talk about. I will talk to you properly. Another time."

Iris left unspoken a whole other part of her speech about how they would approach this new chapter together. She had a feeling Matthew wasn't ready to hear the practicalities yet. They avoided further conversation and filled their thoughts with music and lovemaking; the evening hours slid closer to midnight, sooner than either of them wanted. Their goodbye was intense, pregnant with unspoken words, their faces betraying the cacophony of emotion inside that neither was able to articulate.

As she biked back under a cool, moonless, starry summer night, tears slid down Iris' cheeks, salty tears of pathos and confusion. Matthew's messages were waiting for her as she quietly slid her house key into the apartment door, careful not to wake the household. Safe in her bathroom, she read what he had written, "I am just emotionally exhausted".

His two weeks of vacation flew by, with Akash, Maya and work becoming a distant blur for Iris. She lay awake at night, just to be able to chat with Matthew, given the time difference across the Atlantic. They talked about the photos he sent, the bands whose live performances he attended and they talked of sweet nothings like lovers do. Thoughts of Matthew and conversations with him filled her days and nights like a little child in a large cinema hall for the first time – it felt larger than life and she was transfixed.

Matthew said on the phone one day that he had been thinking of her all the time. He promised that they would speak when he got back. That night, Iris found sleep after several weeks. Relief flooded her maudlin heart, her drained mind. It weighed on her that she spent little time with Maya and scarcer still was her laconic dialogue with Akash. It felt overwhelming, shuttling between the works of disparate lives, with no bridge in between.

When Matthew returned, she noticed that he had lost weight, his face looked drawn and his eyes were sadder than usual. When they met after work one evening, she asked him what was on his mind. He just shrugged and smiled, "I am not hiding anything". "I never implied you were", she quipped, suddenly feeling inexplicably nervous. He seemed distant that week in general, but she knew he had met with Jackie, who had become alert to Iris' growing, dominant presence in his life. She wondered if that had anything to do with how he appeared. Quickly changing the mood, he offered, "I realise I haven't treated you properly at my place. Somehow we never end up having dinner", he smiled at the memory of their entwined limbs on a summer evening. As if telepathically, she smiled at the same memory. They agreed to meet end of next week and Iris' heart lit up like a Diwali night, knowing that they would finally get to talk. The anxiety she had felt these past weeks seemed to vanish as she looked into his smiling eyes.

This next part of my life will be called fulfilment, she promised herself.

Butterflies flew in her stomach, as anticipation of the coming week paradoxically made her attentive at home. She played house with Maya, read her stories, cooked more often and more elaborately, and found her sleep was better. She started to hum again.

The day finally arrived, as days always do. And passed into evening, as days are meant to. Iris had the week's work under her belt, her desk tidied, her household chores under control. Akash couldn't complain when she left for the evening, although he had resigned himself to silence in general. It made her sad to think of how it must have been for him, enduring the slow motion farewell of his wife, stretched over two years. "I won't put you through this any more than necessary, I promise", she told herself as she showered, surprised to find a surge of positivity rush through her veins. Her selection of attire was careful, almost superstitious. Her favourite black top with a low back and a tight, red, knee-length skirt, with translucent stockings. Her usual red lipstick with her hair left hanging on her shoulders, straightened to the full.

As she approached his neighbourhood, Iris took deep breaths, feeling oddly free. It had been an odyssey, arriving at this brave decision, one that went against everything her Indian upbringing had imbibed in her. We don't divorce just to be with someone we fall in love with. We stick it out, if the marriage is functional in every other aspect. It takes serious abuse and victimisation to justify the end of a marriage. It was going to be a heartbreaking battle that weighed onerously on her. But it was going to lead to a new chapter, one that will commence this evening. Suddenly, the enormity of what might happen that night dawned on her.

Matthew was warm and loving that evening. More than that, there was a sparkle in him. He enjoyed her in a way she enjoyed being enjoyed. Hours flew by and Iris waited patiently, knowing that Matthew needed his own time to initiate "*the*" conversation. They caressed each other as music filled the room, Matthew drumming on her bare shoulders and back, her fingers strumming guitar chords on his chest.

It was a rude shock to realise that it was past midnight, and it was time for Iris to be getting home. She dressed hurriedly, feeling deflated and panicking that they had not talked. As if sensing her expectation, Matthew sighed and sat up, "I know we have to talk, and now it's time for you to go. There are things I have to fix first". She sat down next to him, pulling her top over her, "Yes, I know. But we can do that together". Matthew shook his head and didn't say anything. "It takes a while", he said. Unsure about what it meant, but sure that she shouldn't probe further, she got ready to leave. "Well, get home safely", he said, kissing her gently. "Will you be in touch?", she asked, surprised at her own question. "Yes" was all he said, and looked away. Something about his face when he looked away seemed reminiscent of the evening when he had said that he wasn't hiding anything. A faint sadness creeped into his eyes, which did not meet hers.

He said goodbye to her at the door downstairs. Suddenly, Iris felt embarrassed. She kissed him goodbye yet again and started to leave. A few feet away, she turned back to wave but found him busy on his phone, peering hurriedly into its white light in the darkness.

Her wave unnoticed, Iris slipped away, this time facing a crescent, autumnal moon, cold and still. Tears, those familiar friends, flowed freely. She didn't know why. Was it disappointment? Was it rejection? Was it her foolishness? Her legs involuntarily performed the task of cycling her home. Back home, she tiptoed into the bathroom, washed her face and changed into cotton pyjamas. Sleep didn't visit her that night.

The next day, fever gripped her. It wasn't just a seasonal infection. Since that evening in the summer, Matthew had not mentioned her proposal at all, simply referring to it as "I know we have to talk". Last night, he had not addressed it, and she got the feeling he kept putting off that conversation. And yet, it was one of the most memorable evenings she had spent with him. It seemed incongruous.

Matthew could not be reached that day. Perhaps he was busy or sleeping in late, she thought. By late afternoon, she started to worry. Finally, she received a message saying that he was spending the weekend somewhere in the middle of Switzerland. He was on the train with Jackie. Perplexed, she wondered why he did not tell her last night about this trip.

Hours passed by. Something inside her felt uneasy. Silly. Apprehensive.

She had to get out of bed. She folded laundry, played with Maya and watched a Bollywood movie that challenged her to keep watching to see how worse it could get. It did.

Akash made chai with ginger and cardamom. She freed herself from her self-imposed bedroom exile and stepped out, as the soft setting sun warmed the living room. A familiar, deep voice that belonged to Jagjit Singh piqued her ears. Akash smiled at her, remembering old college nights in India spent singing his *gazals*. It had been a decade since Iris had sung a *gazal*. "Let's make chicken curry tonight", he said. Akash's comfort zone always took on a culinary form. She met his gaze with steady eyes, not betraying her fragility. And smiled, "Yes, good idea. Been a while".

Inside her bedroom, Iris read another message Mathew sent, "Going to stay the night. Jackie's generous present. Nice hotel".

Irish washed her face and tied her hair into the usual bun above her head. She turned up the volume on Jagjit Singh's lugubrious voice and stepped into the kitchen to make dinner. Akash came inside to help dress the poultry. Maya set up her dollhouse near the kitchen door.

The heady smell of *garam masala* simmering in a ginger and onion gravy filled the apartment and the exhaust shaft, wafting into a cold, Swiss night.

Outside, the sun had set. It left behind a trail of whisky, orange-red flares in the sky, marking the trail of a blazing day gone past. Soon, an inky blackness would replace the memory of the day, inviting a silvery moon to shed a different light on the sky. The same, wholesome, expansive sky.

Glossary

Ganesha: Indian God with an elephant head
Gazal: Type of Indian song
Garam-Masala: Spices

The Half Ticket

By Ipsita Barua

7:00. The alarm that once heralded a routine is now a pleasant but inconsequent chime for Anika. She rolls over, and sinks deeper into the white HÖNSBÄR. It still smells of IKEA, like a mix of cotton and plastic, but so familiar.

It's October outside. The air is nippy and the trees, dressy.

I have to get the woollens out, she thinks.

Although it is her first autumn in Zurich, Anika knows the mercury could throw in a surprise any morning, because like her, it is on the cusp of change, too.

During her decade in Dubai with Vishesh, the thought of change never crossed her mind except for the few odd paycheck progressions in a not-so-illustrious career. She was happy, and content. With a job, home, friends and a much-happy married life, she and Vishesh were the picture-perfect example of 'settled'. And then it came. Change. Disguised as a promise to live the charmed Swiss life. Not much thought was given to this prospect of change. Caution was thrown to the wind and Anika found herself transported to newer, exponentially greener pastures. 'Camel land to cow land' is how she refers to their move. It's probably her last tagline before she quit her job in advertising.

It's been four months, five Netflix series, and countless comfort calls to faraway family and friends since she nestled into her new life. However, familiarity still remains a fable.

"Why don't you go say 'Hi' to the neighbours?"

"Try to be a bit more creative with your suggestions, Mr. Banker."

"I thought that's your department."

"It was. These days, it's spent on dinner and in saving the Francs."

****

Some days she feels so naked. Stripped of everything she has painstakingly accumulated over the years to mask her anxieties, fears and insecurities: work; friends; neighbours; takeaways; roads; signs; parties; picnics.

Poof all gone.

And there she is, exposed and vulnerable. Incapacitated in every mundane manner. Barely being able to speak the language. Read the signs. Find friends. Or even, chillies in the supermarket.

The coffee is cold with her new-found time and her inclination to dwell on profundity. She hardly cares and clutches the mug tight, wanting to hold on to the last remnants of warmth and comfort.

"Vishi, do you think there's an Integration for Dummies handbook?"

"Sorry, what?" He shouts, over the buzzing shaver.

"Never mind. Nothing. Omelette or fried?"

God, will men ever learn to listen?

****

18:15. The mellow Merlot swirls in the glass like a flamenco dancer. Teasing with intrigue. Enticing with passion. Anika holds up the glass to the open window and squints to see the fiery red leaves through it. Wine 'o' clock has to be her favourite time of the day.

She has made herself a cozy corner by the living room window, which opens out to a lush, sloping lawn. To her right is a three-storeyed apartment block, just like theirs. To the left of the lawn, separated by a hedge, runs the street that curves at the corner and leads to the main road where the bus stop is. Their second-floor apartment offers unobstructed views all the way to the end of the road, stopping just a few yards short of the bus stop.

Like a theatrical performance about to begin, Anika hurriedly rounds up her dinner duties, pours the red and takes her seat by window. Just in time for the 18:20

bus. She then plays a little guessing game as to who would emerge first from the bus at the far end of the street – *Gabbar, Mona Darling, Munna Michael, Chulbul Pandey, Chandramukhi, Hawa Hawai, Basanti, Mogambo* or any other unassuming regular of bus number 704 who was subject to a window-watcher's ridiculously twisted sense of nomenclature and Bollywood love.

Just then, in slow motion, with a bounce in gait and blazer thrown carelessly over the shoulder, *Hero Hiralal* takes the lead and waves out with victorious elan.

Vishi is early today. Anika smiles and waves out to him.

Later, over a plate of aromatic herb-baked salmon, Vishesh pulls out an envelope from his laptop bag.

"Here, for you. You don't need anything that's for dummies."

"It's a half-fare ticket for buses, trams and trains in the city. The zone map is printed on the back of the leaflet. And it's valid from tomorrow."

"Anywhere in Zurich?" Her brows lifted those tiny almond eyes in utter disbelief.

Anika fills his glass to the brim with the remaining wine. Vishesh smiles, because he knows what that means.

Men do listen. Sometimes.

****

8:00. The bedroom looks like a battleground. Pairs of jeans lie on the floor like wounded warriors.

Tops, shirts and dresses dumped and left to die. The scarves, limp and lifeless, hang on the bed frame, long forgotten. Belts, bags, scattered and screaming to be rescued. Amidst that bloody chaos, the teal blue dress with Peter Pan collars is chosen for victory. But not before being tested under the smouldering iron.

I'll come back and clean this mess. Anika reassures herself and hurries with catastrophic urgency, not to miss the 9:02. Swiss public transport is notoriously punctual, even when timings are as odd as 11:17 or 21:22.

She would always wonder why they couldn't just round it up.

She reaches the bus stop at a similarly odd time, 8:57. An elderly woman, probably in her 60s, smiles and nods at her with a perfunctory "*Grüezi*".

A simple 'Hello' shouldn't feel this awkward to say, she thinks. Anika hastily returns the pleasantry and immediately looks away, dreading a Swiss-German language firing squad.

She could sense the anthropophobia kicking in, a predicament as big as the word itself.

In the bus, she reflexively chooses the anonymity of the corner seat in the last row. Slightly elevated, the seats in that row, less preferred, offer the best views throughout the length of the bus, up until the driver's seat. Just how she likes it.

It's not her first time. But, her first time alone in the bus. She re-checks her route and the connections to

Bellevue, from where she's scheduled to go on a free, guided City Walk, the word 'FREE' doing somersaults in her mind with all the enthusiasm it deserves in a Swiss city. Twenty more minutes and five more stops to go. Thankfully, Google Maps and the bus route display are in sync.

Nächste halt Englischviertelstrasse. Each time she passes by that stop, she tries to imitate the flair with which the automated voice in the bus announces that tongue-twister of a sentence. So far, she hasn't moved beyond 'Englisch'.

Today, she doesn't try too hard. She's giddy with the excitement of having an itinerary in hand. One made by others. With those who speak what she's fluent in. To lanes she's never been to.

A little relaxed with the comfort of knowing where to press the 'Stop' button, Anika reclines to take in the sweeping views of the bus aisle and beyond. She knows no one. And vice versa. The motley crew looks fascinating enough to pull out a few more names from the *filmy* archives and she gets down to work immediately.

The commuters seem like route regulars. The atmosphere is exclusive, and tinged with the everyone-knows-everyone kind of vibe. They smile at each other. Exchange pleasantries and apples. Discuss the weather and grocery discounts. Share seats and recipes.

How many years here before I can be one of them. She wonders.

Far in the second row, Anika senses that the Asian lady with the pram is relying on pure instinct while replying in English monosyllables to the Swiss German-speaking septuagenarian next to her. But she doesn't look flustered. She listens intently and complements her replies with hand gestures and head nods. Few minutes into what looked like a game of dumb charades, they even share a laugh.

Anika feels hopeful. And a wee bit at ease, just watching them.

Her gaze shifts to an elderly lady, seated right beside the conversing couple, but so seemingly distant in her thoughts. The bouquet of fresh flowers look handmade, but uniformly trimmed at the stems and tied together with a white satin ribbon. Short, silver hair with not a strand out of place. Spotless white trousers and a loose paisley-printed shirt, neatly tucked in.

She must be one of those who measures the length of her spoons and pairs them according to the diameter of her plates. A picture of poise and Swiss perfection.

Anika finds the subject of her attention extremely intriguing in demeanour. Just when she readies her right brain for some more character and lifestyle assumptions, the lady in question gets off at the next stop and disappears behind a tall wrought iron gate. A park. Or a garden. Anika is left guessing.

Three more stops to go. People watching can take a break. She moves to the window seat in the same row.

Not particularly attentive, until 'Jewel of India' makes her sit up and take notice.

An Indian restaurant so close home, eureka!

She wonders if they have mutton biryani on the menu. Here, in this part of the world, there's no mutton, only lamm which is just lamb of course but somehow the sound of lamm biryani has been putting her off all this while.

Need to get hold of their menu. Note to self.

Near the big, bright bus window, the autumn sun is bright. Pleasant outside, but an irritant inside. She wipes the tiny beads of sweat threatening to ruin her kohl and BB cream. But then she realizes, there's absolutely no one to notice how different she looks without these facial crayons.

"Are you unwell?" They used to ask her at work when she had to skip her only make-up routine to catch the 8:15 Dubai metro. But here, she is just another face in the commute. Unrecognized. And probably, unnoticed too. A tiny wave of liberation sweeps over her. And her thoughts shift to the slightly worn-out grey sweatshirt, almost as old as her college degree but still just as comforting as those times.

This weekend, I'll fish it out from the rolled-up heaps and renew our vows of being together in mess and muck. Shrugging her shoulders and smiling to herself, she revels in the pleasure of this almost-forgotten privilege.

****

6:50 AM. She outsmarts the alarm. And snuggles up to the snoring spouse. He stirs and pulls her closer. The stubble always comes in between, but this has been her refuge for years.

"Remember, I told you about the tattooed boy on the bus, inseparable from his headphones? The other day I saw him walk into the Tinnitus Therapy centre, two stops away from us. I had to Google it to know about it."

He strokes her short, messy hair, half asleep, half in love. By now, he could sense when her voice was even slightly quivering.

"And that lady with the bouquet every Tuesday, she goes to a cemetery, not a park. The elderly man, who sits on the same seat, always gets an extra coffee for her. Isn't that sweet?"

"So you are Sherlock now? Write a book on your characters. Pepper them with your imagination."

She hates how casually everyone throws around that phrase - Write a book.

****

The pale grey sweatshirt is enjoying the attention it thought was out of its league. The distressed jeans, not too happy with the pairing. Her eyes are bare. Her cheeks, nude. But her face, beaming at the sight of the 9:02 bus, even after three weeks of the same routine.

She smiles at the crowd of three at the stop. Her Gruezi is no longer a hasty one. She now sits in the front, just a row behind the reserved seats. "Ich spreche ein bisschen Deutsch", an open declaration of her limited German-speaking skills makes conversations easier, she's noticed.

"'Nächste halt Englischviertelstrasse", she lip syncs with practiced ease and some bit of pride.

It doesn't feel like a journey anymore.

****

18:00. 'Bitte alle aussteigen!' This automated message to alight at the terminal stop always works like the snap of a hypnotherapist's fingers, bringing Anika back from the microcosm of her commute's vagaries and idiosyncrasies comprised of students, new mothers, bored elderlies, busy homemakers, confused tourists and the like.

She gets off. Helps Mia with her pram. Waves to Nicola. And offers to carry Uncle Daniel's grocery bag. The Bollywood naming is getting few and far between. And the bends in the route, all too known to reach out for the seat handle just in time.

"Vishi, would you like lamm biryani for dinner?"

"From Amrit ji's place? Why not!"

Weekend dinner sorted. Lamm or mutton is no matter now.

The temperature has nose-dived, but it doesn't catch her unawares. She pulls out her jacket and ear muffs from the bag.

Feels like winter is here.

And also home.

Glossary:

Gabbar, Mona Darling, Munna Michael, Chulbul Pandey, Chandramukhi, Hawa Hawai, Basanti, Mogambo, Hero Hiralal: Names of characters and titles of songs in some of the most popular and classic Indian movies

Filmy: Related to films

Nächste halt: Translates into 'Next Stop' in Swiss German language

Ageless

By Jyoti Kapoor

I stood there astounded, eyes widened in disbelief.

I have spent many hours in my life in front of a mirror but looking at myself in the flesh, in front of me, was completely freaking me out. What I was witnessing was not what I was expecting.

I immediately turned to read the date on the ultra-smart watch (USW) on my wrist, it read "17.08.2047", it was the 7th series USW powered by celltrons therefore unmistakably correct but I still had to ask the bot to tell me which year it was. Clammy palmed, I waited for the pin bootstrap to send the message to my network and get a reply. Crypto-magnetic field made sure that my messages are read, processed and replied to even while I am time-traveling. The voice crackled back at me, "Hello J, you are in the 47th year of the third millennium, it's the 21st century, and the time is 09:00:47 seconds".

So, the time machine didn't make any mistakes.

I had taken the time machine tour because I wanted to see myself at the age of 70; at 40 I wanted to see how I would look with lots of wrinkles and deep and saggy eyes. I had envisioned myself with short gray hair, spectacles and a tad bit plump but this woman in front of me looked exactly like me. Same eyes, same skin color, in fact, better, very glowing. Identical thick black Indian hair and the exact same height and I was looking fit! I am wearing a polyester type white dress with a neon green small badge on it as if representing an organization.

Same looks at the age of 70! How's that even possible? I was all bewildered and excited at the same time. I had only to touch my USW7 and say PIN-OUT and it would take me back to the year I had come from. But I had to find out more.

I was a shadow here and no one could see me, I could see everyone and everything but I couldn't touch anything or feel anything like temperature or wind. I had the possibility of traveling within 100 kilometers of my landing touch-point by using spatial displacement in the AI generated radiation paths.

I needed to find Robin, my geeky scientist friend, who had created the time machine. I needed to ask him what was going on. I looked at my USW7 and asked it to search for Robin and typed in the private key to send him the message. Robin got the message and confirmed meeting coordinates and time.

I had some time to look around and observe. I immediately asked my USW7 to send me to some people I had on my mental list, some friends and colleagues. To my utter surprise, everyone was still looking young. Darn! I was not supposed to take any pictures!

I saw everything was very hi-tech as expected; people were using voice and hash codes to get simple things done. The architecture had changed into very flat minimalistic lines and glass-buildings. At every gate or entrance of buildings I could see some glass-like screens displaying logs of actions that were happening all around; people entering a building, leaving or even those who were just passing by made the logs update themselves. Even in the parks, these log screens were updating all the time. In restaurants, people ordering a drink and many other actions triggered the logs to go up and get updated. So, data was being collected and used. Everything was digital and people were controlling devices and actions by a small screen that popped up from their palms and disappeared after taking some commands and executing them, but there was no physical device with anyone. No cell phone, earphones or headsets.

There were some drones flying around carrying parcels. Robotics and automation was always my field of specialization and upon reaching here, I could see many of the things that me and my team used to envision, were actually fully implemented and in complete action. This is the future we used to dream about. We were spending hours and hours in the labs, coding and testing recklessly. Sometimes we used to wonder if all this effort was even worth the outcome, but now looking at this world it all seemed justified. The future held the fruit of our hard work in the past. That was one point of relief in the middle of all the astonishment that I held at that point in time. I felt the slight burning of an upcoming tear in my eyes. I was thinking with a heart full of emotion, *I will never forget this moment.*

I kept flying around like a bird watching things.

Health didn't seem like a concern anymore. I couldn't find any pharmacies. And, people around seemed like they did not require them anymore because everyone looked youthful and fit.

Suddenly, my USW7 crackled again, "Robin reaching the meeting point. T-60 seconds" which meant I had one minute to reach the coordinates, in the spatial travel, enough time.

So I met Robin, the even younger version of Robin! "So what's going on, tell me," I showered him with questions and jumped around, pointing at things. He took the minute to see me and my astonishment. He was the holder of a copy of my private key so he was able to see me. Robin was shaking his head in disbelief, "I can't believe a person as driven like you made such a choice," Robin said.

"What do you mean, goodness, I am already very confused. Now, tell me what's going on" I was getting restless.

"Ok, let me show you," he gave some commands on

a map that popped up on his palm and our journey started. First, he took me to the front of a workplace, a big IT firm where I used to work.

People were going to work, some looked human and some close to them, but not really. Their clothes looked different; no one wore true fabrics anymore, I could see a new kind of textile on them, 3D printing was creating completely new fabric, I guessed. Then, I noticed one thing, people who were still going to work had no neon-green badges on their clothes while some people who were sitting in the garden and walking or relaxing had the same neon-green badge as my 2047 version.

Robin and I settled at a staircase in a garden, just outside the building. Everything had changed. We started to talk. He explained, "As you can see, some are humans and some are just Quorns - you call them robots in your year. In this era, sea water has been harnessed and there is no dearth of energy". He continued, "Most of the work is done by artificial intelligence. Humans only control systems and monitor incidents or simply innovate.

People don't get sick and they die only of heart attacks and even that can be avoided, by watching your health apps, up to quite some extent. Those who cannot go on anymore, just jump in front of the bullet trains or off the buildings, their bodies are cleaned within a minute by incident management bots. The suicide rate is very high; technology has left many people rendered useless. The pressure of social scores, lack of private lives, the drone-full sky and this technical dependence, all of this has created a society which is hard on most, if not all. Not everyone can handle it."

I was listening, this was disheartening. Was this the future we were shaping in our labs? I felt something sinking inside my heart.

"Work is a choice and the only thing one must work upon is keeping the drive and motivation up. As you can see there is not much to be done manually. How should one keep on going?"

The next place he took me to was an old age home. Full of young people. And, there was me, myself at the age of 70 looking younger than me at 40, sitting next to a window with a nice view; some strange looking food was being served to me.

"And that's you! The cosmetic and health advancement has made sure that sickness and age are not visible. Most people are healthy and young, only the mental state decides your age."

"When people lose their energy and drive they declare themselves, 'Old' and choose to wear the badge that you are wearing", he said. That neon-green badge!

This badge collects data about your heart-rate and blood vessels and keeps reporting it to your health systems, in case you need assistance or change in nourishment. Also from that badge, people can tell that you are the 'Old' ones and would treat you likewise because obviously people don't look old but they want to be recognized as Old.

"I cannot believe that you, my friend, in particular, you, chose the badge as well, already at the age of 60. As if you were just waiting for it to be launched. You were a person full of drive and energy and I thought you were one of those who would make a difference to the world. You had the spark and motivation in you that was almost communicable, and you chose the badge?"

I sank into a free chair in the room. I couldn't believe it either, is that my future? A lost woman who gave up and chose to be aged? Who succumbed to not making any more efforts and decided to be recognized as 'elderly' and out of the game? Was I done with the innovation? Was I done with the motivation, was I done with life? Did I have a life? '

The USW7 crackled again, *"Time to return, PIN-OUT, T-60 seconds"*.

Robin said, "So it's time, then all I can tell you is that, you did great and earned a lot of money and you can afford this fancy old age home. Not all old age homes are as fancy as this one and not all people invested as much money in cosmetics as much as your bunch" he added, pointing at the other residents around, "But actually in here, in this future, we wanted and hoped that some of us could maintain the drive and energy and could motivate people and make them laugh, create music and literature. Or make groups that foster love and maintain life and feelings in the middle of all this mechanical growth and that is a lot of work, which needs a person to feel and act youthful. You were surely one of those who could have done that, but then, you chose the 'badge'...."

10..9..8 ..7 .....

And I was back to the lab, the old Robin was there, it was still the year 2017. I was back in my world. I was supposed to do my vlog about the travel, but the look on my face implied that it would be done later, Robin understood. Heavy-hearted I went straight home.

I slipped into my home-office and slid into a chair. I thought about all that I had been through. I was really a person with drive and energy and I didn't want to care about how I looked in the future but who I was going to be in the future. The future needed me! Suddenly I realized the importance of the old people's yoga group. Their hands in the air and laughing hard trying to tell the brain we are happy and youthful. Indeed age had nothing to do with looks and the increasing number. It was more the question.. Do you feel OLD? Would you let your mind think and believe that you are aging? And would you pick up the 'neon-green badge' in the future?

…But thinking about it - that is nothing new. The question remained the same today as well and I didn't need to wait till 2047 to find the answer, I could choose it now. We all could.

I was sure of a few things - I would spend fewer hours in the lab, I would innovate responsibly, and I would get a life. And there was one more thing that I decided - that I wouldn't pick up that 'green badge', no cosmetic surgeries or procedures to keep looking young. My beauty or age would not be the perception of a beholder. It would be my actions and mindset that would keep me young….Keep me... How should I put it?

Yes - Ageless!

The Forgotten

By Rejina Sadhu

'A long and tough day!' Lavanya, thought to herself as she sat near the window, gazing at the gathering dusk.

He was no more.

She closed her eyes and saw Vinay's laughing countenance. She felt as if the young part of her 65-year-old self had just dried and withered with the news of his death. She tried to hold on to those tiny wisps of youth but struggled. She thought of her childhood.

Growing up with Vinay and his horde of siblings had given Lavanya a sense of the large family that she did not have. Being neighbors, they had flitted in and out of each other's households all the time. They were also good friends. As they grew older, Vinay's feelings for Lavanya started changing. Her kindness, her gorgeous laugh, helpful nature, beautiful voice–everything about her entranced him. He started weaving dreams of a life with her.

Lavanya dreamt of a life where she could travel around the world and see the places showcased in her beloved Malayalam movies. Her pursuits were creative and innocent. Going to the movies and escaping everything in a world of swirling colors and songs superseded all her favorite things. After her university classes, she helped her maternal uncle run their family's cooperative handloom enterprise. He indulged her movie madness by getting her tickets to the first day first show of most movies. After her father's death, her maternal uncle had become her father figure. As Lavanya continued to live this cosseted life, she had no inkling that things were about to change soon. A well-known family from the nearby city had approached her uncle for her hand in marriage.

The *Vazhathottam* family was well known in North Kerala for its scholastic family members and their vast acres of banana plantations. Lavanya's intended, 'Purushottam', was the eldest scion of this family. Purushottam was a reserved man who had to shoulder the responsibilities of his family at a very young age. His father was a Vedic scholar who spent his time with his scrolls and books while Purushottam took on the mantle of the provider.

Purushottam's work took him all over India and abroad. He bought a little house in Mumbai as most of his business dealings centered there. When the appropriate time arrived, his father broached the topic of his marriage. Purushottam, being an obedient son who was used to complying with his father's wishes, agreed without any objection.

Lavanya's mother and uncle were delighted with the marriage proposal. They gushed to her about her good fortune. The preparations for the wedding started in full swing. Lavanya was caught up in the enthusiasm and got swept away in a whirlwind of nuptial rituals.

Vinay's family also joined in helping with the preparations. However, Vinay's world had fallen apart. His Lavanya was getting married to someone else. He had just started negotiations with a factory in Mumbai to take on a project and had hoped to get the deal fixed before proposing marriage to Lavanya. Everyone around him was excited and happy for Lavanya. Amidst the entire wedding hullabaloo, he managed to speak to Lavanya. Her shiny eyes, innocence and zest for life shone through like radiant sunshine. He told her that he would miss her and that he did not want her to get married so soon. Lavanya looked at her best friend with so much love and grief that he could feel his own eyes glistening. She told him how much she was looking forward to a new life, but simultaneously also felt unprepared about leaving her protected world behind, filled as it was with love and affection from her family and from Vinay. She told Vinay that her mother and uncle had always put her interests as their priority and felt that their decision would be good for her like always. Vinay could see the different emotions conflicting and creating a turmoil in Lavanya's mind. He decided to not add to her tumultuous state and agitate her further by his proclamation for love. Lavanya told him that living in Mumbai would be like a dream come true for her, but she wished dearly to have at least one friendly face in this new city she would soon start living in! Vinay promised to be that face.

Lavanya and Purushottam moved to Mumbai after their wedding. Purushottam became very busy with his work as he was still developing his business and Lavanya had her hands full with household chores. She yearned to go out and explore the city but Purushottam forbid her from doing so. He did not want her to get a job or do any outside errands. He wanted her to focus on their home and hearth. Lavanya was a gregarious soul but day by day, she felt more and more stifled by the barriers put in place by her husband. The older ladies in her neighborhood took a liking to the friendly, helpful and soft-spoken girl. They reached out to her and showed her how to run a household in Mumbai. They took her under their wings. This unexpected blessing touched Lavanya.

Purushottam's taciturn and reserved nature continued to unnerve Lavanya. He took care of the household but was emotionally unavailable. He constantly reprimanded her for everything she did. Every facet of her personality and behavior was criticized and corrected. Her self-esteem withered and her romantic spirit slowly whittled down. At such a low point, her mother's letter brought the news of Vinay's move to Mumbai. Suddenly, there was a tiny ray of sunshine in her desolate life.

Vinay knocked at Lavanya's door with mixed emotions. He stuck a grin on his face as Lavanya opened the door with a big, wide smile. Seeing his friendly, affectionate face, Lavanya felt comfortable and happy in her own skin after a long time. She was back in her old Kerala avatar, coaxing him for news from home. He told her that his business was doing well and that he was thinking of expanding in multiple places in Mumbai. Her delight in his success was unbridled. He enquired about her life and she spun a mirage of a happy and pampered wife. Vinay felt appeased; at least his Lavanya was happy. He told her that his family wanted him to get married and were looking for a girl for marriage. Lavanya told him that she would whole-heartedly welcome anyone who was lucky enough to marry her best friend. She also told him that she looked forward to having a new friend (his wife).

Vinay's wife Sunayna came from a very rich family and her father helped Vinay expand his business further. Vinay became very successful but his sunny and fun-loving nature stayed the same. He focused on his relationship with his wife and a strong friendship grew between them. Although trained to be a microbiologist, Sunayna did not want to take up a career. She was happy to support Vinay and she helped him with his business by applying her meticulous attention to detail to his business presentations.

Time passed by. Purushottam and Lavanya were blessed with two children. Vinay and Sunayna also became parents to two adorable kids. Lavanya and Vinay became busy with their respective families. They met each other at family functions and visited each other's homes on special occasions. Lavanya's life rotated around her husband and children. As her existence centered around them she lost touch with her own inner spirit. Purushottam's drive for success consumed him. His kids were deferential to him but were never at ease. They picked up the condescending style adopted by their father while addressing Lavanya. Her husband never had a single kind word for her. Lavanya closed up within herself. She turned to books for solace. She escaped into the worlds traversing through the pages of the books. Life was a series of duties and responsibilities. Years flew by. The children grew older and went abroad to study in America. Lavanya was left with an empty nest.

Vinay watched from afar. He felt fortunate that though Sunayna was not the one he had intended to spend his life with, she had turned out to be a great life partner. He saw how Lavanya had become a frail shadow of her erstwhile radiant personality. He knew that Lavanya and Sunayna sometimes called each other and chatted about their families. He was thankful that he had at least a few shared moments with her via their families. He felt helpless but tried to ensure that whenever they met he gave her the opportunities to retrieve her old sunny self at least briefly by bringing in some humor and silliness to their family encounters. Lavanya noticed Vinay's kindness. His selfless and friendly nature reminded her of her childhood and adolescence in Kerala and brought some warmth into her life. These were her tiny treasured moments. Whenever she visited Kerala, she found that the number of familiar faces and places had dwindled. The bubbly Lavanya, who used to be full of song and mirth had ceased to exist in anyone's memory and no one remembered her anymore. Life had moved on. Lavanya was among the forgotten.

Meanwhile, Purushottam got the opportunity to head a business unit in Switzerland. He informed Lavanya and orchestrated the move quickly. Their kids were happy in America and did not want to move to Switzerland. They promised to visit. At the age of 54, Lavanya finally got the chance to see what another country looked like. Her dreams of travel had never materialized. Summer vacations were spent in Kerala reconnecting with family. Rest of the time, she spent in Mumbai. She called Vinay and Sunayna before she left India. She felt an unseen thread being tugged apart. Vinay tried to cheer her up with talk about snowy mountains, delectable chocolates and songs from Indian movies that had been shot with the gorgeous Swiss scenary in the background. She felt hope and enthusiasm stirring in her heart once again, thanks to Vinay and his playful spirit. She realized that she would miss Vinay a lot once she moved. He was the only reminder of her wonderful childhood.

Switzerland was a new entity for Lavanya. Everything seemed different from home, yet the snippets of memory from the Indian movies she had watched gave her a feeling of hope. She decided to use this opportunity for a new start in the best possible way.

Purushottam for once was happy to leave Lavanya in the hands of a relocation contact. While Purushottam worked with his team and explored growth possibilities for his company, Lavanya opened her eyes to a different world. The expat relocation package had provided her with an opportunity to learn German and the relocation contact put her in touch with local integration venues.

Her luck was about to change. With help from her relocation contact, Lavanya familiarized herself with the lay of the city, found the Indian supermarkets and established her new household. Her next step towards easing herself into the Swiss way of life was to learn the language. Lavanya enrolled in a German class. She was very apprehensive. It had been a long time since she had embarked on a new course.

On her first day in the German course, she met Ratna and Eleanor. Ratna was from Bangladesh and Eleanor was from the UK. Ratna was a widow who had spent most of her life in Switzerland. She had spent all her life taking care of her husband. Her husband's recent demise had left her stranded in every manner. A fellow neighbor had encouraged her to learn the local language so that she could keep herself engaged and integrate herself into the fabric of local life. Eleanor was a 45-year-old caregiver who worked in an old age home. She had joined to learn to communicate in German with the inhabitants of the old age home. This unlikely group of classmates became each others' confidantes.

After a long time, Lavanya was beginning to enjoy a sense of camaraderie and companionship. Her life at home was awash with strife and discord due to the disconnected feeling with her husband but hope was perking up in other parts. Purushottam continued to be immersed in his business and was hardly at home. Business trips, dinners and deadlines kept him busy. Lavanya found a lot of time on her hands. She decided to find a way to engage herself in a positive way.

Lavanya started spending more time with Ratna and Eleanor. They exchanged notes on how they had spent their day over a cup of coffee. They shared their favorite music with each other and sometimes met up for a potluck dinner. Lavanya discussed different possibilities of using her free time to help others. Her friends promised to look out for opportunities. The three friends thrived emotionally due to their strengthening friendship and companionship. Lavanya's chance to help out arrived soon.

One day, Eleanor turned up for the German class looking agitated. Ratna and Lavanya persuaded her to share the cause of her agitation. One of the inhabitants at the old age home 'Eugene' was slowly declining. He seemed to have given up his wish to live. Eugene had no family. He suffered from bouts of depression. Eleanor and the resident physicians believed that loneliness was the main reason behind Eugene's melancholy. Lavanya's heart went out to Eugene. She felt as if she could feel Eugene's pain and decided to do something for him. She told Eleanor that she had a lot of time on her hands and would love to volunteer at the old age home. Ratna volunteered to join too. They decided to spend time with the people at the old age home. As they slowly mastered German, they were able to chat with the inhabitants. Lavanya was drawn to the 78-year old Eugene and strived to bring a smile on his face. She painstakingly translated funny stories or narrated anecdotes from Kerala and Mumbai to Eugene. As his bouts of depression slowly subsided, Eugene slowly wandered back to the land of the living. Ratna and Eleanor would also join Lavanya from time to time to cheer him up. The three friends regularly helped out with the reading program, music hour and film extravaganza. The world was sunnier for the three friends and the inhabitants of the old age home. Many might have forgotten them but there was hope that some would remember them.

****

Eugene had spent all his life working. He had grown up in Sion, in the South West part of Switzerland. Born to poor Austrian immigrants in Switzerland, Eugene had endured a tough childhood. His parents had him in their late forties. He had no recollection of meeting his grandparents or anyone else related to his parents. His friends and colleagues had all moved on in life, and were busy with their families. Eugene had never married. In his early thirties, his long-time girlfriend 'Vivian' had succumbed to lung cancer. Eugene had a tough time reconciling himself to her loss. He had kept himself aloof from any emotional entanglements, thereafter. After retirement, his health deteriorated and he was unable to take care of himself. He succumbed to depression. His doctor recommended moving him to an old age home.

****

The old age home was situated on the banks of the Vierwaldstaettersee or Lake Lucerne in central Switzerland. The staff was capable and very friendly. Eleanor, his primary caregiver was a kind girl. She chatted with him and looked out for him. However, Eugene continued to struggle with his dismal thoughts. On one such bad day, Eleanor introduced him to her friends, Lavanya and Ratna. Lavanya started reading to Eugene regularly. Ratna and Lavanya volunteered at the old age home and helped the staff in keeping the inhabitants of the old age home engage themselves in different activities. Lavanya, particularly spent a lot of time talking to Eugene and they exchanged stories. The lonely clouds were receding for Eugene. Every day was brimming with possibilities.

Eugene woke up with a smile. He was looking forward to yet another lovely day. Like most days, he was meeting Eleanor, Ratna and Lavanya at the terrace restaurant of the old age home. He had friends who were just like family now. As Eugene busied himself to get a seat in the restaurant, Lavanya struggled to contain her grief. Sunayna had just called her to share the sad news of Vinay's demise. Sunayna's heartrending sobs and words had slashed through Lavanya like a physical pain. Vinay would no longer call to tease her. Her childhood friend and her last connection to her old self was gone. It was a defining moment in her life. However, she was not alone. Lavanya waited for her friends to join her. Today she had someone to share her grief with. Vinay would want her to move on and seek the brighter side of life. Eugene, slowly shuffling to their table, brought a small smile to her face. They were soon joined by Eleanor and Ratna.

The three friends sensed a sadness in Lavanya. They hugged her and asked if they could help her with anything. She hugged them back and shared the memories of her precious childhood friend, Vinay. They travelled down the memory lane with Lavanya. Their presence eased the heaviness that had settled on her heart. Linking arms with her friends she looked at the horizon. The view of Lake Lucerne from the terrace evoked memories of Kerala. Strains of a long forgotten Malayalam song about sweetening memories *'Madhurikkum ormakale.....'* played in her mind restoring a sense of peace in her mind. She had subconsciously knocked down a small brick in the fortress of anonymity….

The Goddess is Missing

By Nayana Chakrabarti

Shukla

The trees are gently losing their leaves and a crispy blanket of colour lies on the ground. Gazing out of the window, *Shukla* feels as if though there is a vacuum. Something gnaws at her. She would really rather that the unsettling feeling disappear; it disturbs her peace. This is the first autumn she has spent in England. She usually visits during the height of the Indian summer, escaping the heat and finding shelter in customary British drizzle instead. However, this year, Arjun has called upon her twice. Even though Shukla prefers to spend the festive season at home, she can never turn Arjun down or away.

Arjun had been flailing, drowning. He had no one to turn to, for shame. Naturally, he had called his mother.

Today, on the eighth day of *Navratri* - the nine days of the goddess - Shukla waits for Dolly, her daughter-in-law, to return. The latter left over an hour ago, banging her shopping trolley down the steps behind her. They have, predictably, run out of toilet roll, milk and bread and what a way to greet a guest is *that*?

Anyone would think that Dolly was trying to avoid the celebration. So far, so bad, because she truly has made such a meal of it. Shukla turns away from the bay window and rummages around beneath the coffee table for a magazine. She finds nothing that she likes. Shukla sighs, she doesn't know where to put herself.

Dolly is supposed to come back from the shops just in time for Arjun's friend's wife, Reshmi and her daughter to arrive. Today on Ashtami, the most special of all the nine days, the little girl is to be their *kanjak*. Dolly, of course, has failed to find a single friend! Excuses have poured from her mouth but then again, Shukla considers, her daughter-in-law has always been rather good at shirking her duties.

In Dolly's absence, Shukla paces the length and breadth of her son's house. She loves to do this when no one is around. Away from eyes, both curious and concerned, she likes to take stock of things. It is the only time that she can allow herself to imagine that this little corner of England, this sheltered cul-de-sac in the otherwise nondescript commuter town of Bramblebury is truly hers. The fact that she can equally stake a claim to its three bedrooms and modest garden goes without saying. Arjun has always said this. Whatever is his, is hers.

****

Shukla has basked in this comfort for years. One day, not long after Arjun and Dolly's twin daughters were born, Shukla had mentioned this in passing - this equal stake - to Dolly. Shukla had seen through the vigorous nodding of Dolly's head. She had caught that first look, the one that had flashed across her daughter-in-law's face before being quickly suppressed. The raised eyebrow, the sneering upturn of the mouth. How ungenerous she is, Shukla had thought, how unbecoming. This, then, was Dolly.

Dolly distilled.

Shukla had seen it on Dolly's face the very first time they met.

Up until he had met Dolly, Arjun had never been a disappointment.

After a daughter, Arjun had been the perfect son. Quick to walk, quick to talk, amenable at school and talented too. She had never been one of those mothers who had had to wait anxiously at the school gates and worry about how her child had done. Arjun always did well, sailing past every hurdle as if to the manner born. One year he even sold his maths notebooks to his classmates. He had brought her a sari with that money. Shukla had cheerfully and indeed faithfully accompanied him to all his tuitions. She would wait on the steps outside knowing that all that time the was spent outside in the sun or frantically seeking shelter from the rain was worthwhile. He was her investment. She poured herself into him, gifting him her life knowing that he would always keep her safe, keep her respected. She had no such hopes from her husband. Even when Arjun joined a rock band in college, she did not lose hope.

Every year, she had insisted on throwing a party on the day that Arjun's results were to be announced. She had no reason to be quietly optimistic. Arjun had always given her every reason to celebrate. Arjun applied to universities abroad and was accepted. In his final year, Arjun had asked if he could invite Dolly to the party. Shukla had, of course, said yes. She had never refused Arjun anything. He had had girlfriends before but none had been brought home. Delicately profiled, Arjun was a handsome young man and sometimes, she marvelled that her flaccid body had crafted him. His sister was ordinary but he was a god. The former had tried hard and was always striving hard to matter or reach the standard of her adored brother but she was a pleasant failure, destined to lead a life like her mother's. Ultimately, it was a successful marriage to a reserved businessmen several years her senior that made her. Once Arjun returned home garlanded with laurels from his studies abroad, she imagined the same future as her son-in-law for him. A quietly unambitious but well educated wife who would act as the ballast to his sails.

Shukla had not expected Dolly's naked adoration. She was a girl of no consequence. With her swarthy complexion, pockmarked face and her potbelly - her scrawny frame notwithstanding- Dolly looked ridiculous, like a fawning child. Shukla had every reason to believe that Dolly would not stay the course. But stay she did. After the wedding, her sister's words stung, "When she came, no? And stood beside our Arjun, I couldn't bear to look... Too shocking. Those fat lips of hers, I'd just love to snip them off with a pair of scissors I tell you. Snip, snip, snip." She had paused. "I thought Arjun had better taste".

It was the first disappointment.

Dolly seemed well meaning enough but then she had gone and fallen pregnant, with twins. Girls, no less. Like a limpet, Dolly clung on to Arjun as he soared; he was powered - and of this Shukla was sure - by the gift that she herself had made of her life. Degrees seemed destined to topple into his lap. And they did. But for Shukla, it was not enough. Had it not been for Dolly, Arjun could have done more, he could have risen higher than the University of East England. With its salmon coloured buildings ensconced in a verdant campus, it was too new and too middling to be Arjun's true intellectual home in Shukla's opinion. It was not Cambridge and neither was it Harvard and that was where Shukla had set her sights all those many moons ago. Arjun had settled in life but not in the way she had wanted him to. He had compromised for his girls. Unencumbered, he could have soared higher still.

Dolly had given the girls, Nisha and Tania, *filmy* names. They had been adorable enough and the novelty of twins had been intriguing at first. The fact that she saw them twice a year albeit for three months at a time allowed her to feel rather indulgent about them. Their mother spoiled them.

****

The house is, in fact, a shrine to the family that Dolly

and Arjun have created. For each photograph of Shukla and her husband, there are three more of the girls with Dolly's parents. Even the fridge has not been spared. Burdened by magnets and chimes and a hundred sheafs of craftwork and school notices, it jingles and rustles each time it is opened.

In spite of all that Arjun has given her, in spite of the life he has laid at her feet, Dolly lives in a disorganised shambles, populated by an overabundance of sentimentality and clutter. She fritters money away on key rings and pot plants, and of all things, pen holders. She visits the shops at least thrice a day, returning each time with nothing useful so that she makes the same trip again and again leaving Shukla to tidy the detritus she trails in her wake.

Shukla thinks ruefully about tea. She would like some now, but then she would have to make it herself and that in turn would mean entering Dolly's kitchen more than is absolutely necessary. The salt nestles up against the sugar. It is a travesty of organisation. The kitchen is a testament to Dolly's poor management skills. In the past, Shukla has tried to help. Now, she refrains because she knows that her advice will fall on deaf ears just like everything else has done over the years.

Dolly has refused to learn anything even broaching the subject of cookery and the kitchen -the heart of the home!- from her. Dolly regularly takes to her phone instead. Tapping away she seeks answers on YouTube, watches the food of her childhood cook in kitchens in New Jersey or New Zealand. She ferrets out her phone again, clicking away incessantly on Google, converting grams to teaspoons. She stores her spices in little pots, all uniform and silver-lidded. She throws away the jam jars that Shukla tries to frugally restore. She buys paneer from the store, she refuses to learn how to make it at home, she doesn't make ghee either, choosing to buy that from the supermarket too. She isn't concerned about quality. Things simply need to be done, after all. Boxes need to be ticked, *that* is her philosophy. Shukla is sure that there is no feeling behind any of her actions. For example, Dolly regularly purges her home of the sins of the kitchen. No matter the weather, she throws her windows open wide while the girls shiver inside.

Shukla takes stock of Arjun's house. Somewhere, her husband is snuffling away. His habit of falling asleep anywhere and everywhere has recently surged. The more Shukla seeks company, the more he sleeps. When he isn't sleeping, he watches people shout at each other on TV. Back home she doesn't feel the absence of company quite so keenly. There is the maid who comes to sweep and wipe the floors before washing the dishes and the clothes. There is the cook too, she comes twice a day. In the evening, she takes to the park in her white trainers. Together with her friends, she strides around her gated residential community , arms swinging, chests heaving, setting the world to rights. Back home in India- in the flat that feels temporary - she has a life that has its own direction. Here, in England, where her life really is, with her son and granddaughters, she feels as if she is simply treading water. Today for example, is a case in point.

She is waiting for Dolly to return. All she has requested is that Arjun and Dolly invite a little girl home -her preternaturally pubescent granddaughters will not do. On the eighth day of the the goddesses' celebration, she simply wishes to touch the feet of a girl who still has the touch of divinity within her, one whose inevitable mantle of worldly tasks and blemishes have not yet been settled onto her shoulders. It ought to have been simple enough- Dolly and Arjun are surrounded by friends - but going by Dolly's sullen expression and stony face it appears as if that were not quite the case. Shukla has been made to feel as if she has asked for a handful of the moon plucked straight out of the night sky. Dolly has, apparently, found herself too busy to even shop for the little girl's present. Shukla has done it all by herself. With Arjun working all hours of the week, she has taken the bus into the shopping district, she has wandered with purpose around the mall. She has made the discovery that the Indian store is not nearly as far away as Dolly claims. Shukla has been able to surmise that those multiple trips a day are simply a mark of laziness, a desire to get away from keeping house.

Shukla looks at the clock. Time marches on by, the girls remain at school, Dolly does not appear.

When the bell does ring, it is a woman she has never met before, standing on the front steps with a little girl in her arms. The girl in turn holds a weather beaten-looking toy kitten to her cheeks.

There is no sign of Dolly. There is no peace to be had. It is Shukla who must make the tea.

****

Dolly

"Hey guys, just thought I'd create a group for local mums who are expecting in 2015. Let's help each other out!"

Dolly can almost hear the Facebook post. It has anthropomorphised and now speaks with a cheery, Gaelic accent. Dolly doesn't know why it is Gaelic but it is. She has found it on the local mothering group. Towards autumn, posts such as these pick up in frequency. As the mother of pre-teens, Dolly has little use for the mothering groups themselves. Queues and queues of questions regarding sleep, feeds, endless to-ing and fro-ing regarding breast or bottle, raising readers, blogs about travel, blogs about toys, multi-level marketing and the like.

Once upon a time they had been useful. Dolly had once found the companions of her soul there. Kindred spirits bound together with the unexpected nature of motherhood.

Now, all she really needs is someone to commiserate with her because those babies she has raised have decided to talk back and there appears to be no remedy for that. But the post needles another part of her, one that sits on the wormhole of a sucking wound. She quickly leaves the group - something that she has been meaning to do for years now - presses down on the home button furiously, returns the phone to flight mode and throws it into the pit of her bag or the hell mouth as her girls have taken to calling it. The IKEA trolley stands next to her looking despondent. It is, predictably, unused.

Dolly looks around. It is evening now, and unexpectedly, autumn. The weather continues to be searingly hot in the afternoons but the temperatures plummet overnight. The moon has risen and it shines a pale, washed-out gold. The sky is descending into ink. The lake looks serene. But as with everything else in Bramblebury, nothing's quite what it seems; 'The Lake' is just a man-made reservoir. The awareness of its artificiality makes her love it less.

With sunset long gone and the girls' pick-up time long past, Dolly realizes that it is far too late to return home. This - what she is doing now - could not have been a mistake. It would defy logic to dress it up as so. And of course, Arjun is logical. There is no escape from his growing need for precision. She will have to talk, she will be made to explain herself. She cannot face it.

The girls know the way home, the school has their father's number. Knowing full well that they will receive something to eat at home, she feels dispassionate. Instead, her mind turns inwards. It's a pity that she has now started thinking of Arjun as their father and only that. He is no longer her lover, he has never really been a friend and now she has received full confirmation if that - after the events of the last few months - were needed that he is not, in fact, even on her side.

Dolly picks at the skin of her forefinger, a childhood habit. She knows that she has been missed. She also knows that they are concerned about her whereabouts rather than her well-being. She is absent without leave. Somewhere in the distance, the sky growls. It might rain, Dolly thinks, still unmoved. She has not brought an umbrella and in her light denim jacket and her *Janpath* scarf, she is now decidedly chilly. She has not planned this. She has not meant to stay away. She had just needed to get away, she had felt a visceral need to distance herself from her mother-in-law's need for pomp and ritual. Using the shopping trolley as camouflage is the only way that Dolly knows how to survive these everlasting, yearly visits. Twice a year this year. Once upon a time, not so very long ago, she would seek the company of friends but a recent misstep on her part has put an end to that.

Dolly hadn't meant it. It had slipped off the end of her tongue before she had even realized.

"Didn't they mind when Ahalya turned out to be, well, a girl? I can't believe the doctors got it so wrong!" Dolly had chuckled. "Didn't your in-laws say something?"

Ahalya's mother, Sayori, and Dolly's oldest friend in Bramblebury, had looked aghast. Adjusting her expression into one of muted horror, she shook her head.

" No", she had said tightly, "They were very pleased". Silence had settled and had pulled itself taut within them. It wasn't until that moment that Dolly realized that something had gone very, very wrong. She had unwittingly revealed a part of herself that was ugly. She had unveiled a part of her prejudices that she had never even known that she had had. She! The proud mother of twin daughters! Sayori had left soon after.

Nowadays, Facebook tells Dolly that while Sayori is meeting everyone else, she isn't meeting her. The latter has taken to leaving pointed messages of congratulations on recent births.

Congratulations on being a girl-mummy!

Happy hatch day chica! I'm so happy when anyone has a girl! #girlpride

In the meantime, within their circle of friends, Dolly has been recast as the crazy lady who has had a miscarriage and can now no longer bear anyone else's happiness. For Dolly, it runs deeper than *tha*t but now, without friends, she has no one to talk to. All the friends she had were mothers too. Like her, they too mothered without support. It wasn't quite the sisterhood of solidarity that she read about but they had all rubbed along together. Fundamentally different people, they had simply been thrown together thanks to their tenure in Bramblebury. And now, she had been edited out of that group too.

<u>The Past Lives In The Present</u>

The breeze picks up but Dolly feels like the air is being pulled from her lungs.

And boom, she is back.

Autumn has been whooshed away and she is back in the clinical seafoam green of a NHS bereavement suite.

The saddest Dolly has ever been is when she had fought her way through a mist of tears only to find herself, alone, in a room. Alone, with her born-too-early-daughter wrapped in a towel.

Since then, every waking moment she spends is a decision. Dolly walks a tightrope between her present and her recent past. The grief is a wormhole, it sucks her in and renders her body useless. Entire weeks, even months, have gone by while she has lain prone on the sofa while the girls have taken themselves to school and Arjun has gone to work, sulking because he has been unattended. She has stared blankly at daytime TV before forcing herself to watch 'One Born Every Minute' as an act of masochism, a punishment which she feels she deserves.

For awhile, the sympathy had been immediate. Bramblebury settled a blanket of the stuff on her. Bramblebury had furnished her with home cooked meals until her fridge heaved with it; Bramblebury had even told her that she need not bother returning the Tupperware which she interpreted, at the time, as true concern. Dolly was told she never need to worry, that they were there.

Until, of course, they were not.

At the time of her daughter's death - because in her eyes, this is how she sees the loss and cannot understand why she should settle for any other words - sympathy had sat uncomfortably with her. The thought that intruded upon her grief then and continues to rob her of her peace now is that she is to blame. She has got what she deserved. The tiny, hopeless little bundle that had lain in her arms for one, all-too-brief hour had never stood a chance.

Dolly thinks that she ought to have gone absent without leave before.

The past and present have blurred. Her tenses are in a jumble. As much as Dolly feels the chill of the present, her mind has retreated to the past. Every second is a palimpsest of time. Every moment has been lived twice.

Arjun's perfection was never something that Dolly had questioned. Tall and broad shouldered, he was conventionally handsome. That he would look at her, that he would seek her out, that he would hold her in his arms and find her beautiful...All of it was unprecedented. Arjun's mother had made no secret of the fact that she had found Dolly wanting. But...The magic mantle of Arjun had been enough for her. So, while Shukla raged and muttered that Dolly's parents should have taken better care of their daughter (her skin was an issue that Shukla had fixated upon), Dolly herself basked in Arjun's gaze, in love. Their sudden marriage, their arrival in England on a misty October day as fresh as this one, the swift arrival of their daughters, their youth - Dolly had been in love with all of that. Whatever Shukla's hesitations might have been, Dolly herself had no cause to worry. She lost herself in the family of her own making; she plunged headlong into the lifetime role of being a wife and mother.

Later, at the school gates, she would sometimes catch herself wondering if this was all there was and wondered if she should be doing more. Dolly had found her newborn twins to be all-consuming. Once they were older, she found herself chasing opportunities and play dates, for them and it had never seemed to be a good time to begin something of her own. It was only once the girls had started going to school full-time that she started to look around. Now that they were both in Year 7 and had after-school clubs to attend to alongside all of their other extra-curricular activities, Dolly had enrolled herself in a distance learning course to learn how to design websites.

Once upon a time, not too long ago, she had entertained hopes of one day, running her own business. Now, she isn't sure whether that future will come.

Dolly and Arjun had always had their future mapped out. One thing was for sure, they weren't prepared for another pregnancy. Dolly had felt settled. But, at 35, with eleven year old girls, she had read the two lines on the positive pregnancy test as a new beginning, as a new starting over from square one, from scratch. More hard work, late nights, mornings passing by in a blur, personal ambition buried somewhere. In the dark grey of the bathroom, Dolly had pictured the sniggers both within the community and her family. She had wondered how her girls would take it. They had each other, they had never hankered for more.

Yet, when they heard the news that there was to be a new baby, they appeared to be overwhelmed. Excited. It was to be their baby. Witn an eleven year age difference between her oldest and youngest children, Dolly had not thought that her thirties would be for childbearing. Her twenties had been for that. She had been a very young first-time mother. But, in the end, her daughters' excitement was infectious.

After the first couple of weeks, she started looking forward to being a mother to another child. It had never occurred to her that Arjun would not be able to come around to the idea. It had never occurred to her that while she worried about genetic tests and Googled 'geriatric pregnancy', Arjun would take his mother into his confidence. His growing distance had led to arguments breaking out all over the place. Cracks everywhere, walking on eggshells. All the idioms.

Before the pregnancy, Arjun and Dolly had always managed to keep their tensions secret from the girls. It had been possible to pass off the occasional raised voice as a disagreement. With the pregnancy and their polarized opinions, hiding and secrecy stopped being possibilities.

She was moody.
He was unfeeling.
She was too loud.
He had an allergic reaction to her voice. She was disorganized.
 He was controlling.
She had let herself go.

Hadn't she been the one who had raised his children while he chased his pipe dreams?

She lacked motivation.

He had succeeded while standing on the skeletons of her ambitions.

Oh, so she was ambitious?

Typical of him to twist her words. Why was ambition bad? Why had she, for all these years, been pretending to be someone she was not? She was hormonal.

He was a pig.

She was careless.

He was callous.

She was neglectful.

He was ambitious.

She was bossy.

He was suffocating.

She was cold.

He was volcanic.

However, in spite of all that, Dolly had read it all as a tale of another marriage temporarily not working, a belated onset of the seven-year itch. They had been married for thirteen. Parents for eleven. It was bound to happen sooner or later. The honeymoon period did not last forever. Their friends were always telling them how lucky they were, her friends specifically were always telling her how lucky she was, as if it wasn't common for a husband to actually love his wife or even care for her. Dolly now thought that they had tempted fate and therefore, the evil eye had now struck.

****

The rain drizzles down. It is late and Dolly knows if she turns off the flight mode, she will be flooded with notifications, voicemail messages and missed calls. The crevices of the trolley are pooling with water. The spray of the rain catches her in the face. But she can't move, she is transfixed and now that the floodgates have opened, the thoughts don't hold back.

****

Things finally came to a head at the gender scan. The baby was revealed to be a girl.

'Oh Dad', the radiographer had clucked, "Don't look so disappointed! What do you have at home?"

"Two girls", Arjun had said. He was polite, more or less. His tone was strained, terse even.

"Ah well, now you'll have three! Aren't you lucky?"

Three girls. Three girls. Three girls was one too many, two too many, three too many.

After the gender scan, Dolly found it hard to keep track of the direction her life was taking. Her mother-in-law, who had already been displeased by the notion that Dolly was adding to her precious son's burden with another mouth to feed, wanted - in no uncertain terms, to terminate the pregnancy. Arjun, man of science, took her side.

It was an abnegation, they said, three girls. An exaggeration. A laugh, a piss-take, it was everything but right. Three girls! Three girls? Shukla kept on saying it, as if the prospect was ridiculous. Wasn't she one of five, Dolly had asked.

How will she manage, Shukla had asked Arjun loudly over Skype. She had ignored Dolly who was sitting next to him. In that moment, a memory had burst like a thunderclap. Dolly had remembered right then how, upon holding the twins for the first time, poring over the smooth, perfect faces, Shukla had commented that this was why one needed to bring home fair mothers, so that the children would not be dark. The girls did not resemble Arjun, Shukla had insisted. They had inherited Dolly's coloring. Dolly had got up and left but not without hearing a comment that may or may not have been intended for her ears.

If this was India. Over there, what can you do? You have to think of money also. Now this one, another year later, another one. She wants a cricket team?

After Skyping with his mother, Arjun had begun to insist with further ferocity that Dolly was being ridiculous and that he had, for awhile now, made his opinion quite clear about the third child. It was she, he insisted, who had dawdled.

Ultimately, Dolly had screamed at him.

What do you want me to do?

Get rid of it.

No.

You were angry before but now you want to abort because she's a girl. You don't want a girl.

You are being ridiculous. I love our girls. I never said anything about an abortion.

Your mother did.

Keep my mother out of it.

You never do.

You are ungrateful. After everything she has done for us...

With July on the horizon and Arjun's perennial paranoia about ticket prices rising, he had booked tickets for India. With every passing week, Dolly had grown more and more fearful. She wrote long, passionate messages, begging Arjun to return to normal. He never replied. She begged for the baby's life. He did not reply. Arjun maintained that it was just not possible but the rest of it -her accusation that a termination had been planned and that it was driven by the baby's gender - was in her imagination.

What will happen once I'm in India? Nothing, he said, nothing.

Will you force me to have an operation? Say it, say it.

I will not force you to do anything. The decision is yours.

It's not my decision if you are backing me into a corner.

No one is backing you.

You are gaslighting.

What does this word even mean? It wasn't a word two years ago. You will believe anyone as long as they run a Facebook group.

Don't make me go to India. It's a geriatric pregnancy, what if something happens? Oh, so you won't get on a plane but you will raise a child? For the rest of your life?

****

By now, the rain has increased to a steady drumbeat. Dolly doesn't wear a watch. She has become so accustomed to looking at her phone for all her needs. She doesn't know what time it is. It must be night. The houses - posher, larger houses, in these parts - are slowly turning off their lights, one by one. The kitchen lights usually remain on. Dolly has walked past these houses before, wondering how lovely the lives inside must be. And now she knows.

Inside there is just a person, at night, after the lights have gone off, loading the dishwasher resentfully while the other people sleep.

Her face is wet now, not from the rain but from her tears. The sobs come from somewhere deep within, her whole body shakes, her shoulder blades sting with the force of it.

****

Dolly had rung her parents. They had never been happy about the new pregnancy. They had been happy with her marriage, they prided themselves on having accomplished the task of marrying their daughter off early. They were happy that she had proved herself fertile with twins, no less. They were unhappy that those twins were girls. The conversation had been brutal, their words were left etched onto the skin of her mind.

"You can't even raise two, how will you raise three? They will be heathens, urchins, waifs.Money? With what money? We are with Arjun."

The day after Arjun brought down the suitcases from the attic, and the sudden, hot temperatures of a summer (an Indian summer, the tabloids heralded) soared, Dolly woke up in a pool of sweat. Upon going to the bathroom, she saw that it was blood. On the phone, the midwife had been calm. She advised her to wait and see. In the morning, Arjun didn't go to work, for the first time in eleven years. The girls went to school as normal. As she bled slowly in the bedroom, Dolly found that she still had nothing to say to her husband and he, apparently, had nothing to say to her. He had sat in the front room, accompanied by the soothing murmur of daytime TV and his laptop. Eventually, Dolly decided that she could not wait any longer. The drive to the hospital had been silent. Arjun looked ahead, he parked responsibly. The young midwife who had first seen her in triage was practical, like her husband.

"You need to prepare yourself, love. Babies who come this early, they don't stay."

"In another week or…"

"Not this early sweetheart. Not so soon. Let's get you up here shall we? Let's have a look".

There was no heartbeat.

There is nothing, Dolly thinks now , as sad as a mother willing her lost child to live. Having had a Caesarian with the girls, it had been her first experience of giving birth naturally. Arjun had been there and in spite of him and all that he had come to represent during the worst of it, she had sought him out.

The hospital did everything that they knew to do. There was a memory box, there were photographs. Sometime later, there was even a memorial. Other fathers came but not Arjun. He stayed at work.

The girls had been devastated. It had been their first encounter with death. Dolly had been conscious that she had to keep a lid on her grief, the girls' SATS had been around the corner. Once the exams were over, Arjun saw it as enough time as having passed and high time for normalcy to be restored.

Dolly held Arjun and Shukla accountable. Your thoughts, she wrote to him while he sat in a funding meeting, did this. You willed this to happen, she called to tell him when he was sitting at lunch with his colleagues. *You killed her, she knew she was not loved, you killed her*, she emailed him as he sat in a seminar. *You and your mother killed her. Three girls, three girls, three girls…You will have no girls, you will see.*

Eventually, Arjun rang the GP only to hang up when he remembered that their GP too was a family friend and perhaps Dolly didn't need help, perhaps, he thought, she could make it through on her own. In the end, in the middle of the night, he called for his mother, he asked her to return. He was flailing, he said. Drowning.

****

The Now

The skies crackle with thunder and lightning, the storm is directly overhead. The day has long misted away into evening and now twilight draws near. A reckoning will have to be made, Dolly thinks, should she return home to face the music or should she stay put instead. Her mind is full of things unsaid.

The rudeness of grief has taken Dolly by surprise. She hunts, feeling rootless. She hunts for places in order to hook and place blame. In the recent months, she has lashed out at Arjun, launching volleys that he tiredly tries to duck. He has stayed at work later and later and left in the morning earlier and earlier. He has no answers. The very thought of him makes her seethe with rage.

As the rain falls, Dolly turns her mind to Shukla.

If it weren't for her, she is sure that Arjun would never have felt this way. He would never have been the way that he was. Shukla had been only too ready to dig up seedy doctors who would see a termination through; she had always mourned the fact that her only son had had twin daughters and that left only expenses to bear and no one to carry on the family name. Such irony, she had said, given that her daughter had only had sons. Her own parents' reaction had cut her deep. When she spoke or spoke too much, Arjun was always ready to throw this volley back at her.

Dolly thinks of Shukla as a forever denying presence in her life. Denying Dolly or herself or her daughter of food (in that way she was fair) because she believed that the men of the house, should always receive the largest portion, the greatest serving, the most generous helping. Shukla saw herself as a bit player in her own life and she had relegated her own daughter along with Dolly and her daughters, to walk-on roles, had condemned them to a lifetime of being bit-part players, extras in their own life. How else could one justify how Shukla and Arjun had forgotten everything? How could they have forgotten the recent past and insisted on hosting an Ashtami celebration at home *on the very day* that her youngest granddaughter would have been born? How could they celebrate a girl and worship the divine in her when they had rejected another girl in their own home?

Dolly's mind reels with questions and she remains rooted to her spot, the cold plastic seat of a bus shelter, in the rain.

****

Arjun

Arjun has returned home earlier than usual. Shukla has called him, all in a frenzy.

Dolly is nowhere to be found.

Before he had a chance to return the phone to its home - his back pocket - the phone rings again. This time it's the girls' tutor. No one has come to pick them up from their after-school chess club. Should they walk home alone?

At home, his mother is agitated. With *Ashtami* rituals concluded but not to her satisfaction, she is now angry. His father flaps about, apparently helpless. Shukla throws her empty suitcases on the bed and Arjun finds her pulling her things out of the cupboard and dumping them inside haphazardly and without ceremony.

"Enough, enough", she snarls, "You let her get away with too much. Are you a man or a mouse? She didn't come! I was left to look like such a fool in front of your friend's wife! She showed me up, she showed me how unwelcome I am in my own home! Oh sorry, sorry, her home!"

Arjun's head begins to pound and he looks on, alarmed. The girls look scared. Later, when the house is quiet and Shukla's anger is spent and she has collapsed in a heap in one of the armchairs, dates and months start tumbling into place. He pulls conversations out from the depths of his memory and starts to fit the puzzle pieces together.

But it is too late. He doesn't know who to call anymore. Whoever he did, would then know. He will be found out and he can't face the thought. His one hope - his mother - has failed him. And Dolly.

Arjun allows the girls to watch as much TV as they like. He hopes that it will stupify them and absolve him of questions.

By midnight, when Dolly still has not returned, he turns to Shukla who is warming dinner in the microwave - she is less fiery now that her bags are packed and she is ready to go, "Perhaps, Ma, all of this was not necessary. Not today".

They each understand exactly what they wish to and look down, never at each other.

Glossary

Navratri: a nine day Hindu festival. On each day a different goddess is honoured. The manner of celebrations vary greatly according to local custom.

Kanjak: *Kanjak* or *Kumari puja* takes place on the eighth day of *Navratri*. Young girls are worshipped as it is believed that they are in their holiest form and are therefore representatives of the spirit of the goddesses.

Filmy: anything that has been touched or inspired by Bollywood or Indian cinema. Another way of saying 'Melodramatic'.

Janpath: a place in Delhi which is known to be

popular with tourists. Lots of handicrafts are sold here.

One Born Every Minute: A British fly-on-the-wall documentary series set in a labour and delivery ward.

Radha and Govind

By Richa Chauhan

I open my eyes and find myself in a hospital!
Why am I here?

What happened?

It's so difficult for me to recall. And oh, my head hurts
...The last thing I remember is that, I was in a forest
in Kanatal, near Dehradun. I had gone there with a
group of friends, six of us. My close friend Chitra
had planned and arranged this trip to the forest. I
remember arriving at Dehradun airport, ah what was
the name … Jolly?… Grand? No, Grant airport. From
there, I remember taking a bus first to Mussoorie and
then to Kanatal. From Kanatal we hired a taxi to go to
that Koudia forest. I was having so much fun and then
something happened that changed my life forever.

How do I begin? Let's start from the time when I was
in school.

It was a Sunday morning and suddenly the alarm
rang. Startled out of my slumber, I saw the time was
7 am! Definitely early for a Sunday morning. The
alarm had woken me up from a dream. Why did I

have to wake up so early? I was so angry. It was such a nice dream.

I was in the middle of a garden with colorful flowers, with a swing in the center of it. I was swinging with my eyes closed, feeling the fresh fragrant breeze on my face. My hair too was swaying along. Far away was a single tree, deep and so dense that the shadow underneath would not let a single ray of the sun pass through it. It suddenly seemed like night in the middle of the day, and I opened my eyes to see the faint contour of a person standing under the tree. It was difficult to see where that person was exactly looking at. I was trying to see harder but a sudden sound snapped me out of the dream..

Yes, that was the alarm. I switched it off and again closed my eyes, trying to continue with my dream where I left it, but it was too late. Anyways, I did have to get up because my mother had told me that it was *Janmashtmi* today. I must shower early, dress up and help her in preparing a festive meal to eat after our fasting during the day. *Panjiri* made with condensed milk, shallow fried *makhane*, tapioca *khichdi, kuttu* flour cutlets, *makhane kheer,* boiled potatoes with rock salt – delicacies to be savoured especially after a fast.

I always waited for this one day of the year. Partly because of the delicacies we got to eat and partly because I felt connected to Krishna. My mother once told me, "Do you know you were born a day before Janmashtami? Everybody congratulated us that day saying Radha was born." I was so thrilled to hear that.

As per our mythological stories Radha is one day older to Krishna. That's how I got my name, Radha. I am Radha. Since then I felt connected with Krishna. I would fancy I was special and this soon made me a dreamer!

Janmashtami celebrations usually end with a specific tradition of *puja*, presenting all the food we are about to eat in small quantities to God, offering water to the moon and ending the fasting with food. My mother would wait till midnight to perform the rituals. I was allowed to dine when I felt hungry. So, I quickly ate without any delay. After all, I had been desperately waiting since the time my mother prepared them. After watching *Chitrahaar* on TV with special songs about Krishna, it was the time to go to bed. Sometimes, before falling asleep, I would even think about what dreams that night I would have.

Next morning the alarm rang at 5.30 and I had to get up because I had a tuition class from 6.30 to 7.30 My mother was not in favor of it but in my town, it was quite a trend and some of my school teachers were taking full advantage of it. After all who would not want one more source of income, that too without much effort? They just taught what they would or should in the school. Anyways, I did not think so much about the unethical issues prevalent in our education system at that time. I just went with the flow.

Like always, I would roll out with my eyes still closed, go straight to the bathroom, freshen up, and then get ready. I would quickly drink a glass of milk and have two slices of toast with butter. That had always been the quickest breakfast without much ado and on top of that, I always loved it. Now, we had two perpendicular streets outside our home connecting the center of the town. One was a clean but longer route to get to my tuition class - it took 15 minutes longer on a bike. The other one was uneven, messy and in the middle it had a barren field except few trees randomly planted on it on both sides, and it was a shorter route. As always, I ran short of time and preferred to take this short and secluded route. Sometimes, I had to get off my bike to walk across an open drain in front of the field with uneven stones. Today, as I was doing it with my eyes totally focused down on the drain to cross it without any slip, I suddenly heard someone cough. Normally, at this early hour, people preferred to go to the park nearby and would never want to come to this street with a stinking open drain. So, I was surprised. After landing safely on a flat stone, I looked up and around. The street light was still shining partly on the nearest tree in the field.

I almost fell off my bike when I spotted somebody standing right under that tree in such a way that only the body below the neck was visible. That person's face was under the shade. All I could see was a pair of jeans with white sports shoes and the hanging edge of a brown shawl wrapped on the upper body. I could figure out that the person – a man – was standing facing me.

Maybe he was looking at me or somewhere else? I tried to analyse but was a bit scared and as I was also in a rush, I quickly hopped on my bike and dashed off. I reached my tuition class on time. After it finished, I rode back home through the same street, wondering if the person would still be standing there. But there was no one and the field was like always, lonely and quiet. I rode back home thinking maybe it was some kind of illusion, maybe I was sleepy and didn't see clearly.

I arrived home by 8.00 am. By that time my mother had packed my lunch box for school. A half an hour break at home, and then I would leave for school. Our school was co-ed.

Last year, a boy named Govind had joined our class. I heard he had failed in one year senior class and therefore was sent to our's. He had a peculiar look that couldn't be ignored at first sight: brown eyes which were mysterious, deep and passionate; slightly long, dark brown hair with a flick falling on his forehead; and an honest smile from the heart. He was taller too than the other boys of our class. A carefree, satisfied look on his face, sleek body, wearing a loose shirt with top few buttons open. Quite honestly, I was attracted to him from the very first moment I spotted him in our class! Soon after he joined, my friends started gossiping about him, that he was not at all an academic. He was slow in his studies as well as in sports. I also came to know that he had a hole in his heart, so his parents never forced him to do what he did not want to. He apparently was weak physically and mentally. That explained his behavior. I nevertheless was attracted to him, I developed sympathy for him, and would observe him from the corner of my eyes, always. Where he went, where he ate at lunch time, how he talked to his friends, the things that made him happy. Over time, I didn't even realize that I had been observing him so profoundly that he could even catch my vibes, or was it just by chance, that I came to know from my friends that he too liked me? I felt flattered. But as he was not good in studies, and had a pretty 'low' profile in all school activities, none of my friends were fond of him, so I felt reluctant to express my fondness for Govind in front of them. There was a conflict between my brain and my heart. My heart said my attraction towards him was natural and justified, but my brain warned me to proceed any further!

As time passed by, as if he was able to grasp my feelings even if we never spoke, strange coincidences started happening. Whenever, I would think of him intently, he would appear from somewhere, not always, but most of the times. I was able to feel his presence whenever he was in the vicinity. Slowly, unlike me watching him from the corner of my eyes, he started gazing at me openly, which after a while started getting embarrassing. My days changed from feeling terrific, being the center of attention of somebody, to feeling terrible. While we were playing in the break, eating or sitting in the class, his eyes would pierce through me. Everyone at school at that point knew that he was after me. As I began encountering harassment rather than love, I started ignoring him. But once Cupid's arrow has left the bow, perhaps it cannot be retrieved. There was no turning back. My friends started avoiding me, because he would always make a scene of following me and staring at me. I had to run away, many a time or hide in a corner of the classroom, out of his view. My friends did not want to be part of my struggle trying to escape this embarrassment that seemed to be happening too frequently for me to handle in an amicable way. This discomfort and uneasiness was becoming part of my school life. I would often return home tired and emotionally spent.

Thankfully my mother used to arrive before me from her school where she used to teach social science. She would help me with my homework whenever possible. I always felt so proud of her.

I always had another meal at home, after school. That was like my second lunch while watching TV. After lunch, I would sleep for about half an hour or so, finish my homework, and then go to our neighbor's and play until it got dark. I so much enjoyed my time at home, more than at school, that should always be part of my fond childhood memories. For most others, school time was the best time, unlike me.

Again my day would start with the same route to tuition and there that stranger was as always, standing under the tree doing nothing, saying nothing, just conveying unspoken words with his presence. Uncomfortable with his incessant persistence, I decided to change my route and leave for my tuition classes 15 minutes early.

Minor adjustments here and there, and I somehow

survived school and got admission into an engineering course outside my town. From there I started a new life.

After four years of BTech, I got a job in Delhi. I now had a new circle of friends. The life in my school and my hometown became a matter of the past, a past I was too keen to leave. Rather, I ran away from it.

In the company where I started working, our colleagues annually planned a week-long trip to the hills for sightseeing and hiking. This year my friend Chitra, suggested a place called Kanatal near Dehradun. It turned out to be a long journey first by flight, then by bus and then finally we reached our resort with a taxi. We arrived at the resort booked for us in a forest, spent an hour settling down and freshening up, and then got ready to venture to the nearby grounds. Everyone was excited to explore the place at least a little bit on our very first day. But it soon got dark and since we too were worn out after our long journey we returned to our resort and decided to start early the next day.

The same childhood dream came to me again. I was swinging in the middle of a flower filled garden with a tree far away, with shadows underneath covering something or someone else. A voice from a distance woke me up, "It's getting late, wake up Radha". I opened my eyes and saw Chitra sitting next to me, nudging me to wake up. I got ready for our hike.

The weather was splendid, not too sunny and with a pleasant cool wind in a romantic hilly landscape. All six of us went out of the resort, ready to explore on this beautiful day. We carried a map, and planned to spend the first day in the forest of Koudia. The forest stretched around for 6 km with dense tall trees. The possibility of spotting few wild animals in the vast expanse of hills and valleys, excited us. We set out to keep walking for several hours, trying to capture every beautiful view with our cameras, but we agreed to stick together in a group and not venture out alone, that would be too risky.

The surroundings were mesmerizing, lush green everywhere interspersed with some trees loaded with colorful leaves, tall trees sometime random, sometimes growing in an aligned geometric pattern. Trees in a straight-line alternating with shrubs growing in between, and in some places giving way to a clear passage to walk along.

Suddenly, I spotted a very strange looking small animal with orange and black stripes right in front of us. Scared, it withdrew into the shrubs. I desperately wanted to take a photo of this animal, so I started following him slowly, so as not to scare him further. The animal sensed being chased, and sped ahead. I took it as a challenge and started running after it with my camera dangling from my neck in a strap. 10 minutes later, I felt tired of running, and paused to catch my breath. Sitting on a rock, I looked around and realized that I had come into a deeper part of the forest with more dense trees, so thick that one would think it was already night out here. I realised I was alone and had got separated from the group! Fear of the unknown was creeping in, but I tried to take it easy and forced my mind to stay calm.*The forest was quiet, if I would shout they would perhaps easily hear me*. Not to ruin the peacefulness, I decided to make a call instead with my cellphone. I tapped on Chitra's number and called her but there was a busy tone. I tried again. Still busy! That's when, I began to panic and attempted to call others in vain. My realisation that I was alone in this wild forest stepped up my heartbeat and I panicked.

A little later, I found out that there was actually no network in that zone. To make matters worse, I heard a clap of thunder, and dark clouds started covering the tiny blue patch of sky that was still visible above the trees. I had to find some shelter, but where? I started running in the direction from where I thought I had come. I was getting lost, there was no marked path and then all of a sudden, I spotted a person walking far away; I was so relieved, that I shouted and ran faster to reach him.

Luckily that person heard me, stopped in his tracks and turned around.

While dashing towards him, I saw the edges of his face and felt as if I had seen him before: *where, and why did he look so familiar*? As I got closer, the rain washed away all my doubts and his face became more clear. My pace slowed down, and as I reached him, I felt, shocked and aghast. Could I really believe my eyes? I had never imagined in my wildest dreams, I would ever meet Govind again. How was it possible? Govind too in the same state as me, appeared shocked and stunned.

"Is it really you?" We both said at the same time. That moment froze in time, the raindrops felt like flowers, the whole world around me was overflowing with a hypnotic fragrance. We smiled at each other, trying to hold our deepest laugh. We were still so awestruck that we simply didn't know how to start a conversation. After few moments, I broke the magical moment first and asked him, "How come you are here, Govind?"

"I moved nearby recently, wanted to explore the area around but got lost in these woods. And you?" He asked with a twinkle in his deep-brown mysterious eyes.

"I came here with my friends for hiking, and while following an animal, I got lost. I was so scared, thank God I found you!" I replied back, with a deep urge to hug him and hold him tight to feel if he was for real or not, appearing out of the blue to rescue me out of this situation!

He looked at me, deep into my eyes, also understanding my emotional need to hold him tight, to feel safe and secured. Now that I was older, without any fear of expressing my feelings, I matched his direct gaze and wanted to say so much. *Yes, I meant it, I really felt lucky to find you, and I have been wanting to tell you this all my life. You made me uncomfortable, but still, I was loving you unknowingly even then.*

Instead, we just smiled at each other, standing still, not knowing how to make up for the time we had missed since school, till another lightning struck and we returned to our senses. We both laughed again and started walking. We talked about our life in general, not mentioning anything about our time spent together at school.

"What have you been doing?"

"Where did you move?" I didn't even realise when we crossed the forest and all of a sudden spotted a bungalow in the middle of the forest. We were astonished but in the rain any shelter was more than welcome, and this looked grand!. We knocked at the door. We saw someone turning on the light inside and coming to open the door. As the door opened, an old couple stood there and ushered us inside. They too were surprised to see someone outdoors in this weather. We immediately explained our situation. First, they looked reluctant to let us stay, thinking we were probably some teenage boy and girl who had run away from their homes and were searching for a shelter. I anticipated their apprehension and out of desperation, mentioned that we were a married couple too!

Govind looked at me speechless. I had sensed it right, the old couple immediately let us spend the night in their home and return next day, back to our place. They offered us warm tea and some biscuits too. They suggested that we stay in their guest room. The rain outside was getting stronger, and the wind was howling and scaring me to bits. During dinner time, we all cooked together in the kitchen, and prepared *daal, bhindi,* some *roti* and *rice*. It was a very simple yet delicious meal. After dinner, we all again sat together for a while chatting, talking about our families, about our lives and how lucky we felt to have found this house. An hour later they retired to their bed and showed us the guest room.

Finally Govind and I had some time for ourselves. I wanted to ask him so many questions, and now that we were both grown-ups, I wanted to ask him what was the actual reason behind what he did to me during our school days? Did he really have feelings for me or was it just to harass me, some idle muse in his aimless life. I looked at him and realized that he was also looking at me back and trying to read my mind.

Before I could ask him, he suddenly said, "I love you Radha. Don't you see this?"

I looked deep into his hypnotizing eyes, trying to judge if he really meant it. Next thing I realised, was that I was hitting him with all my rage and tears flowing unhinged from my eyes, as I kept repeatedly asking him, "Why did you do this to me? Why didn't you say this before? Why did you have to ruin my school life, stalking me madly, if you loved me so much?"

I kept punching him and he tried to hold my hand and stop me. In this hustle, he got real close, and I too slowed down, as if we were guided by some unseen force. Our faces moved closer and before I knew it, we both started kissing each other. I could not remember how long or how short that moment was. After that everything that happened was out of my control. I also could not remember when I fell asleep. Next morning as I woke up, I saw Govind sitting next to me, smiling and looking at me lovingly. I smiled back at him. Sun rays were streaming into our room. We got ready, cleaned up the room and came out. The old couple was busy making breakfast.

"Good morning. So, all good?" They asked politely.

"Yes all perfect" I said a bit shyly.

I prepared a special ginger tea for everyone while they prepared toast and omelet. After finishing our breakfast, we bid them goodbye. I really liked them. They had almost become our guardians. Since they hardly got any visitors, they were happy to have us. Govind and I left the bungalow and started walking back towards the next village. This time the couple had given us direction, and how to get to Koudia resort, without entering the forest. On our way Govind asked me for my address and contact number saying that he too needed to contact his parents, they must have been worried. He said once we would settle back to our normal lives, he would call and introduce me to his parents. I felt so excited and shy at the same time, and it all felt like a happy and romantic dream, where Radha had met her Govind for the infinite time, destined to be lovers forever, through all ages.

Before departing, we kissed again, and he murmured into my ears, "*Never be afraid to take shortcuts.*"

I couldn't understand, but I just smiled. I took the bus and reached my resort. The battery on my cellphone had died so I recharged it and called my friends. They were really anxious and had even lodged a complaint at the police station. My friends were amazed to see me glowing with a mysterious contentment on my face. Chitra jumped when I arrived and said, "You look so happy and different, this is definitely not the same Radha!"

I wanted to tell her what happened, but just then I received a call from my parents, who had been informed by my silly friends that I was missing! Poor them, they must have been worried sick. I picked up the phone. I could hear from my mother's tone that she must have been crying for a long time. I started feeling guilty and tried to explain the situation, slowly she calmed down. I then told her the strangest incident of my life.

While I explained, I sensed that she was shocked, she didn't utter a single word for the next few minutes. I said, not really comprehending her silence, "I understand it was shocking for me too, may be God wanted us to meet…." and my voice trailed off.

I wanted to say more but before that she interrupted me and said something that turned me deaf until I blacked out.

I still do not understand anymore where I am, why I am standing or lying, and what I am doing swinging in the garden and talking to my 'invisible' friends….My mother keeps saying, 'Govind passed away few months ago!'

What a lie, don't they know that I am Radha, Govind's eternal beloved?

And we plan to spend a life together?

Epilogue

Radha and Govind (popularly called Krishna), as per Hindu mythology are eternal lovers, they spent time together in the forests of Vrindavan, as Govind would play his flute and Radha would sit near him enchanted and forgetting all her daily chores. Later, Krishna left Vrindavan and Radha, to follow his own course of life. But till date, Radha and Krishna are worshipped together in India. Several festivals are based on Radha and Krishna.

Glossary

Janmashtmi: An annual Hindu festival that celebrates the birth of Krishna, one of the Hindu Gods.
Panjiri: A staple from the Indian subcontinent. It is made from whole-wheat flour fried in sugar and ghee, heavily laced with dried fruits and herbal gums.
Makhane: Fox nuts grown in the wetlands of Asian countries. They are also known as phool makhana (because of their flowery appearance) and lotus seeds.
Khichdi: A dish from the Indian subcontinent made from rice and lentils.
Kuttu: Buckwheat or grass seed flour.
Puja: Worship.

Chitrahaar: A television program on Indian National channel featuring song clips from Bollywood films.
Daal: Lentil.
Bhindi: Okra or okro, known in many English-speaking countries as ladies' fingers or ochro, is a flowering plant in the mallow family. It is valued for its edible green seed pods.
Roti: Indian flat bread.

Durga's New Dawn

By Pallabi Roy-Chakraborty

Floating about in the ethereal mist, Durga was incessantly interrupted by a faint throbbing noise.

The noise was unrelenting, amplifying by the second and rapidly invading her senses.

"Someone please make the damned thing stop!" Durga groaned and drowned herself further in the warm welcoming embrace of the covers.

"It can't be 6 am already!" she screamed inwardly.

Even as she drifted through the haze, unwilling to let go, her mind screamed "Wake Up! Waaaaaaaaaaaake Up!"

The fog shifted abruptly, mercilessly jolting her back to reality.

"Damn! Another Monday!" Her hands went instinctively to the shrieking alarm clock, faintly annoyed at the sudden end to her hours of bliss.

Switching off the alarm, Durga turned to look at the peaceful form of her husband, Bhairav, still deep in slumber.

"Boy, the man could sleep! He would probably sleep through anything!"

She sighed and forced herself off the bed.

Walking out the door, she quickly peeked into the rooms of her children. Her daughters occupied the first room, while her sons took up the room adjacent to theirs. She couldn't help but smile as she looked at them, fast asleep, blissfully unaware of her daily morning hustle.

Still smiling to herself, Durga started heading to the kitchen, listing the things in her mind that needed to be done within the next hour.

This was one of those rare occasions when she was genuinely happy about her ten hands! More often than not, they were mostly hindrances to the outfits that she so admired and wanted to try on.

At least, with her daily chores, her multiple hands were still serving some purpose now that her demon slaying days were behind her.

Reaching the kitchen, Durga started readying herself to begin the preparations for the day.

Halfway through her chores, beads of sweat started forming on her forehead as she quickly glanced at the clock merrily ticking away. She sometimes wondered how the women down there managed, when she being the "Goddess" was rapidly running out of breath.

"May be, I should also offer them some extra hands!

Hmmm…. maybe, not to all, but to a select few as a pilot."

She took a mental note…. She would need to run it by the innovation department and also do a feasibility check before taking it across for implementation. She felt a tinge of excitement. It had really been a while since she had the opportunity to try something different.

Earlier she still had a number of cases where mortals were interested in super powers and performed rigorous and strict penance to obtain them. The supreme trio were forced to grant them whatever they wanted. She had been fortunate enough to be a part of several such cases, it had always been fun to design and implement them. But over the last few years, everybody seemed to be sufficiently happy with what had been handed down to them.

 Sure, the complaints department was still stacked up with grievances of all kinds…. Parents unable to find suitable partners for their children, married couples unable to have children, some with many children (all daughters) and still seeking that one elusive son and so on….

What continued to amaze her was the sheer number of requests that came in for a husband like hers. She almost had the mind to grant them all and then sit back and have fun watching them dealing with his fits. *"Bam Bholey!"*

The complaints were many and varied, but, unfort-unately, none amongst them were different, they were all run of the mill. Not that the supreme trio were unhappy about it…. With so many of such "different" cases gone bad and the big bosses themselves being called down to handle the situations, they wanted the mortals to stick to being normal as much as possible.

The beeping microwave curtly snapped her out of her reverie. She took a quick fearful look at the clock. Time waited for none, not even for her!

Taking a long deep breath, Durga went about waking Bhairav and getting the children ready for school as soon as breakfast was served and school bags and lunch boxes packed and ready to go.

She frowned, as she realized that the morning madness had just begun!

Durga was already exhausted by the time she pressed the elevator that would take her to her work station. She had a 9 am meeting that morning on the much needed modernization of the divine weaponry. With the new variant of the mutant demons and their state of the art artillery, it was high time that the divine weaponry be overhauled as well.

She hardly had the time to look into the details and was grossly underprepared to take any kind of calculated decisions.

She clucked impatiently, if the elevator did not arrive any time soon, she would not even have the time to grab a quick coffee before the meeting took off!

Scurrying between meetings, the next time Durga looked at her watch, it was already lunch time. She had promised to have lunch with Mary, an expat and a dear friend, who was here for a 2-year term.

"Phew! Finally, time for a break!" said Durga, feeling relieved.

She took the elevator to the office restaurant. Mary was already there, waiting for her.

"Hi dear! What's up?" asked Durga.

"Don't ask! Just because I am 'THE Mother', nobody seems to think of me as anything other than a mother! At least you still get to be a goddess; all that I get to be is a saint!"

"Ohhh…. Don't fret dear!" Durga tried to calm her down. "Tell me all about it…."

In an attempt to calm her down, Durga veered her towards the one topic that always gets all mothers gushing….Their children! She, herself, was no different.

Even as they spoke, Durga's mind swiftly moved back to her children. With Saraswati, her younger daughter, there was nothing to worry about. As far as academics were concerned, she was perfect. But the other three, Laxmi, Karthik and Ganu seemed to have minds of their own. She was perpetually dreading the parent calls that seemed to have lately become quite frequent for her children (of course, none for Saraswati, her darling Swati, as she fondly called her).

Their teacher had suggested some kind of sibling pressure, with Saraswati, always outperforming the entire school.

Durga had once tried to take this up with Bhairav so that he could have a heart to heart chat with the boys while she would subtly discuss the issue with Laxmi herself.

All Bhairav had done was close his eyes and nod his head while blowing out smoke rings from his mouth!

"Huh! So much for shared responsibilities!" thought Durga sourly.

Lunch done with, Durga bade farewell to Mary and took the elevator back to her work station. While in the elevator, she did a quick evaluation of the grocery stock in her house. Even as she tried to mix and shuffle all the probable combinations in her head, Durga sighed as she realized that none of the available combinations would make it possible to mete out any known dish of any cuisine.

She looked at her watch. If she could wrap up in time, she would probably be able to manage a quick trip to the local supermarket.

If not, then it would be another hitherto unknown-of food item that would be dished out of her kitchen.

Of course, she could always snap a finger and get whatever she desired. But there was no fun in that! She preferred the earthly ways.

She chuckled to herself. Bhairav called her kitchen 'Delectable Durga's'. Her children, on the other hand, were not so kind. For them it was mostly 'Disastrous Durga's'.

Reaching her work station, Durga glanced at the calendar adorning her desk, willing it to scoot on to her favorite part of the year, just a few months away.

How she loved these annual sojourns! The five days that she spent at home every year, were only hers, to be pampered, revered and loved.

She could almost hear the rhythmic beat of the *'dhak'* calling out to her. The alluring *'kash'*, swaying gently and in perfect harmony, seemed to be filling the air all around her.

"Now, now Durga!" she chided herself, "There's still a while to go. Back to work now!"

Durga forced herself to focus on her assignment. She had been entrusted to identify ways of establishing respect and equality in today's mortal-land.

For her bosses, this was key, since once identified, this would definitely help to keep the defence budgets to a minimum and increase the spend in the other areas that were desperately in need.

Her mortal correspondent, Narada, who had been conducting the field operations to gather the relevant data, had done his part well. Now it was up to her to decipher the rest.

As she shifted through the analytics, gloom and doom loomed all around her. Abuse and assaults were rampant everywhere she looked!

The only solace was that, amongst the many soulless kinds, there still remained a few worthy of being called human.

Maybe, now, it was time again, to select the good few and begin afresh.

But was that really the only way out? She had not yet found her answer!

Brows knitted together, Durga pressed herself to arrive at a solution. But the harder she tried, the more disheartened she felt.

Taking a break, Durga decided to switch to her wish list instead.

Her bosses had recently started "Mannat" (not to be confused with the house of a celebrated film star down under). Theirs was a strategic program to streamline the collation, review and approval of the wishes and demands of the mortals.

Each of them had their own wish lists, which was nothing but the prayers that were offered to them by their devotees.

But of course, there were no free lunches and each prayer was always accompanied by a wish that had to be granted. They had each been given monthly quotas and based on that they had to review and grant a certain number of requests.

As she ran through her list, the absurdity of some of the requests made her roll her eyes.

A certain Mrs. Das from Bagbazar had offered her 10,001 rasgullas in return for a favor.

"Seriously, man!", Durga muttered under her breath. With the rapid surge in the number of diabetics worldwide, diabetes was now a truly global epidemic, one that had made its presence felt here in Mt. Kailash as well. Who, in their right minds, would make such an offering?

She continued sifting through the requests, granting some and rolling her eyes more and more the further she progressed.

She floundered, dumbfounded, as she came across a request from one of her most loyal devotees. He had most magnanimously offered his new born daughter in return for a son that he had been lusting for.

"No!", she thundered, pained to the core.

Why could they never see it? This was her way of shielding them from what had happened on that fateful day, many many eons ago.

Tears welling up, Durga turned her face away from the screen to compose herself.

Memories, long repressed, came flooding back.

With her final blow, Mahish had disintegrated into a billion pieces scattering into the heart of the mortal realm, forcing himself upon the unsuspecting milieu.

His last laugh, loud and taunting, had streaked the air, leaving her with an unease that she could not shake off even now.

To her, it was only a matter of time. Mahish would rise again and she too wanted to be equipped for the combat.

Since then, she had been systematically sending off pieces of herself into the mortal world, into the homes of the select few, who she thought, had been most loyal and trusted.

Alas! She could not have been more wrong! Her devotees, it seemed, were more than generous in building her temples but extremely miserly when it came to offering her a place in their hearts and homes.

"This will not do!" Durga thought to herself, struggling to contain the rising wave of dejection within her. She needed to think about an alternate arrangement.

Closing her eyes, Durga tried to calm herself. It was quite a while, before she could regain her composure again.

Glancing briefly at her watch, she continued moving through the items on her list.

By the time Durga finished running through her list, dusk had just begun to set in. She could see the queue of the homeward bound traffic getting longer by the minute.

Now came her favorite part of the day. She felt herself relaxing as she looked forward to what awaited her back home.... Smiles and snuggles galore. Gathering her things, Durga started moving towards the elevator.

Back home, after a grand welcome by Bhairav and the kids, Durga immersed herself in the remnants of the household chores that needed to be completed for the day, smiling to herself every now and then, as a few fragments of the conversation between Bhairav and her children caught her ear.

Each of them had a different story to tell, each eager to go first.

Humming to herself as she rigorously scrubbed the kitchen counter, a sudden thought flashed across Durga's mind. Even as she had been trying so hard to think of ways to establish respect and equality, she herself, had been endorsing just the reverse all along!

She was taken aback, as she realized that there was nothing equal about the sharing of her responsibilities, familial or otherwise.

There was nothing respectful in how she was always essential, but never principal. This was exactly what she had seen mirrored all across.

"No more!" Durga promised herself.

"It is now time to bring in the change! And where best to start but right here and right now!", were her last thoughts, as she lay in bed, retiring for the day.

Hours later, as she wafted, once again, through the familiar mist, Durga could hear the faint throbbing noise, over and over again, growing louder by the minute. A determined Durga, undaunted and resolute, firmly buried herself into the warm welcoming embrace of the covers!

Today was a new dawn, and a new beginning....

Epilogue

Durga, is a much worshiped Goddess in India, and she lives with her husband Shiva in Kailash (Himalayas) with her four children, Laxmi, Saraswati, Kartik and Ganesha— each blessed with special powers. As per Hindu mythology, Goddess Durga came into being to destroy Asura, who was the invincible demon, whom none of the powerful Gods could defeat. Durga who had ten hands, and possessed powers of several Gods was in the end the slayer of Asura, the one who rescued the world. In West Bengal, India, 'Durga Puja' is a popular festival celebrated each year. This story is based on these mythological characters.

Glossary

Dhaak: Drum like instrument from South Asia which is played during 'Durga Puja'.
Kaash: A form of grass native to the Indian subcontinent. The appearance of the Kaas indicates the beginning of the festive season.

Sita's Vacation

By Brindarica Bose

R am would return any minute now from his football practice. Sita kept turning her gaze towards the window, whenever a car whizzed past. The total absence of shouting, jumping, conversation, allowed every extraneous sound to be heard. She loved these prolonged moments of silence. It enabled her to think, to relax and to plan.

Lying on her beige leather sofa with both her feet up, she tossed the olive green cushion on top of her tummy and tried to flatten it. Her tummy grew back to the same size after the cushion was removed.

Sita shifted her attention back to the movie 'La La Land' which she was watching for the second time. She had first seen it at a cinema hall in Zurich. She had watched it alone on her way back from work on a Friday evening. She had loved it enough to watch it twice.

Sita sighed when the movie ended. She felt Mia's tears in her own eyes.

She thought about a life full of dreams, like Mia's and of lost love. Love, that was the creation of poets and authors—love that was born out of romantic proses, prized with thorny red roses, and mourned over twisted divorces. Sita's mind wandered and she felt distraught. Tomorrow would be a big day for her.

It was too dark outside. And even if it was drizzling, Sita couldn't hear it from her living room. Her windows were closed almost twenty-four hours a day—now that autumn had set in and the temperature had to be regulated inside their two storied house in Switzerland.

Sita sprawled across her sofa in her living room and looked out of her window into the muted night. She turned down the volume of her TV.

Her 11 year old twins—Luv and Kush were fast asleep.

Sita had discussed with her boys several times '*their gameplan*' for the coming month—when Mamma would not be at home. Both boys unconditionally accepted the fact that their Mamma was keen to play 'hide-and-seek' in real life with their father. 'Where' mamma was going to hide—would be a top secret—that they would have to safeguard like two dragons protecting a treasure.

Luv and Kush were the reason, that Sita doubted her plans again and again. What if one of them developed a sore throat and flu? Who would take care of them? As such both boys were independent in their daily routines, but they were still quite young. They were also unaware of any emotional impact this vacation of hers might have.

Luv and Kush had each other's companionship—which was a big advantage. Their entire world spun around all the tangible elements that typically made up a young boy's life—football matches, Pokémon cards, UNO, Asterix Comics, Lego and their most recent acquisition—a mobile phone, which they had to share between themselves.

Unlike her boys, Sita lacked true companionship in her life. Blame it on her taciturn nature—she also had a limited number of friends. All her friendships remained on the surface—brief conversations at birthday parties and limited comments on Facebook posts. None with whom she could enjoy a heart-to-heart talk. Lately, Sita often complained to her husband Ram that she was suffering from an odd sensation in her stomach—as if there was a fist sized knot and someone had cinched a band tightly on top of it. Sleep would not take that feeling away. Ram advised her to go for walks in nature. But where was the time?

She felt as if the mist, which permanently hung over the river Limmat outside her house, had permeated through her windproof windows and barged into her body and was slowly engulfing her brain, her heart and all her visceral organs. It was grey outside and grey inside too. Indeed, inside, there was chaos. There were wishes that had turned into echoing whispers and screaming voices which had turned into pathetic whimpers.

Sita had plunged into a misery which transcended her role as a mother and a wife; she was undergoing a silent struggle to retain her psychological existence.

Afraid of turning too hermetic—her instinct of self-preservation was getting stronger day by day.

She needed a break. Yes, a vacation!

A 'vacation' that was longer than a weekend—always intercepted by umpteen number of duties and chores. She was now aware consciously, of her strong desire to be alone—to give herself some time and not lose her existence entirely.

Her husband remained unaware of her condition or desire as always.

Sita's packing was done. Documents, laptop, adaptors, clothes, all that she would need for a month—were neatly packed in two medium-sized Easy-Pack suitcases. She had also arranged the next month's routine with the nanny. She had spoken to everyone except Ram, who still knew nothing about her plans.

Sita was afraid that Ram would convince her to scrap her plans for a vacation, and make her feel guilty. She was afraid like every time, he would make her believe that 'she' and her needs were less significant. That Sita needed to have only one priority in her life, and that was her children and her family. Without whom, her existence would have no meaning, which often made her wonder, *'Who am I?' 'Why was I born as Sita?'*

Ram was always busy and never noticed any of the silent preparations that had been going on over the last few weeks—the list of emergency numbers hanging near the telephone, the nanny who seemed to be helping with groceries on weekdays, the house key which had a thick red band around it and the extra stock of washed socks.

In the last fourteen years of her marriage, apart from moving to seven new houses around Europe and the birth of her twins, Sita's life had remained the same. Ram was travelling for work most of the time. Sita, was packing, unpacking, and moving all the time. It was only in the past year that she had started working in a publishing firm in Zurich, i.e. after they decided to settle down in Switzerland.

Earlier, who would pay for a nanny, full time? It would be more than the salary she would earn! So Ram had decided that Sita didn't have to search for a job until both boys were independent enough to look after themselves. Sita also felt that was the best choice, since they were living abroad. But with every passing year, she felt that she was losing touch with herself, her own dreams, her wish to live her own life as an individual, and not just as a caretaker.

As a couple, Ram and Sita barely got any 'we' time. The only way Ram could express his love for her was to take out the trash every alternate day without fail and remind her constantly that she needed some exercise to stay fit. They barely managed to go out together. One parent always had to stay back for the kids. By default that parent had been Sita. But things were slowly changing. The boys were more independent and didn't mind staying alone for a while.

Sita had turned 40 last year. Call it mid-life crisis or a self-preservation 'wake-up call' she discovered that she still could not be weaned away from all her childhood dreams. Her *biggest dream* had been to write a book. The way her health was deteriorating (or was it just her grey cells?) she felt time was slipping away fast, and she had to at least give it a try.

She needed a vacation soon, to sort out her life and to search for an answer to, 'Who is Sita? What does SHE want?'

****

Sita's mind jolted back from her thoughts to present, as the door knob turned and Ram entered the house. Ram dropped his Adidas bag on the floor, removed his shoes and went upstairs to take a shower without even a 'hi' or a 'hello'. Sita sighed at his chronic lack of interest in her.

Sita didn't want to sleep before seeing him tonight.

Ram was unaware and hence had no rush to see his wife.

For the readers, Ram' and Sita's background needs a bit of description here.

To start with, Ram and Sita were quite different in their mannerisms and lived in different worlds. Sita walked with a slight stoop, always in a hurry to hide her existence from the world. She had striking features but preferred not to highlight them. Her thick black hair was wrapped in a no-fuss ponytail, her big eyes bore no hint of eyeliner or mascara and she barely wore any lipstick or make-up.

Ram on the other hand was tall and walked with his head held high, a natural posture which Sita often envied. He was handsome, and aware of the effect he had on others. Ram's endearing nature made him very popular amongst his colleagues and friends. His world revolved around his football pals, matches, work and his twins. Sita existed too, but like the dark matter in the universe—invisible and all-consuming, relevant but mostly unknown. Ram came from an illustrious family of business entrepreneurs, but Ram himself preferred not to join the family business, but instead chose to wander around the world. He chose an IT job which would enable him exactly that. He didn't mind moving houses and countries, until last two-three years when his family started complaining that they missed friends and their old home. Ram loved sports and travelling, and wherever he went he had a group of people following him, on football grounds or in Instagram. His profile photo always showed him placed with his football pals in the ground, whereas Sita always posted a flower's photo as her display image in Whatsapp or Facebook, and she had no Instagram account.

Sita had been adopted. Her adoptive parents (were both Professors of Anthropology) and Ram's father—were college friends, and that is how their marriage had been arranged. Sita's parents were well-known academics and Sita spent most of her time with her paternal grandmother, whom she lovingly called *'Thammu'*. Thammu must have been around 55, when she started learning how to read and write in English.

She would often ask Sita to write down five new English words for her and then she would memorise them day and night. She would chant those words just like *Krishna's* name with her fingers running over the beads, which she carried in her jute purse.

When Thammu would finish memorizing all the new words, she would stitch them together and write a poem for Sita. There would always be several rounds of corrections, but Sita loved doing that. Thammu would patiently revise her poems and when they would have around 20 corrected poems, both Sita and Thammu would neatly copy them in a notebook and store these notebooks under lock and key in an aluminum suitcase below their bed. It was their secret plan to publish them one day. They never showed the notebooks to anyone, neither to Sita's father, nor to her mother—both were always at work anyway.

Sita didn't realise what Thammu was doing to her subconscious mind at that time. She was seeding a dream in her granddaughter's mind—*a dream to be a 'writer'*. Irrespective of age, gender or education.

Sita completed her BA in English and unlike her erudite parents, she didn't want to study further. Instead she worked for an advertising firm for few years and then she got married. Her parents were completely charmed by Ram—whom they knew from childhood actually. Thammu passed away in the same year. Till then Sita had been a woman who was offbeat, eccentric, irreverent and not conventionally pretty. She had loved literature, writing, and one day planned to publish her own book, i.e. till she got married and started a family. The latter had always seemed like an inevitability.

After marriage, Sita couldn't work on her plans, due to her husband's constant travelling and the birth of both her boys. After a complicated pregnancy, her life changed for good and bad. Luckily after arriving in Switzerland, Ram announced that they had moved enough and he would push for a long-term residence permit. Sita and both boys had always complained that they wanted to live in a place longer and the boys also couldn't keep changing schools at this crucial stage. After they settled down, Sita started looking for a job and she found one too—as an Account Manager in a publishing firm. But after 14 years, her blood was not as warm as before. She felt being a mother exposed her to constant scrutiny by others, and her worst critic was her husband. Her married life had somehow restructured her DNA, she lacked the energy to start anything new. She remembered Thammu and their joint plans, but that seemed like a fairytale now. The idea of writing a book stirred up different emotions—pity and a deep sigh, more than enthusiasm and joy these days. But those stale emotions were shifting gears, whether she wanted to acknowledge them or not…

****

Sita lay on the sofa, mulling over the prospect of writing her own book and about *Balmiki's proposal.*

So alluring was her vision about the proposal, that it dominated her entire existence. At first she had felt only the pleasurable thrill, she once had shared with Thammu, then came in the 'not my cup of tea, let it pass' phase, and then it changed to 'why not give it a try?' Balmiki was in Sita's mind all the time now. And their plan for a vacation.

The entire episode had started about a month ago.

One evening, while preparing dinner, Sita had suddenly collapsed on the floor and had lain there senseless for a minute or two. The knots in her stomach had intensified and she felt pain right below her navel. When she came back to her senses, she realised what had happened, and was a tad disappointed to find that neither her boys, nor her husband had come downstairs to check on her. She moved heavily towards the dining table and sat on a chair, staring anxiously at her reflection on the dark glass window. She continued to stare unseeingly in the glass window, until she felt another wave of discomfort and got up quickly to drink some water from the sink.

'They are probably not even aware', Sita thought to herself.

Her boys were indeed glued to the television watching *Pokémon* episodes and her husband was still in the bathroom—zapping through world news on his mobile.

There was not much space between the kitchen cabinet and the dining table where Sita had been standing, so even though she had collapsed on the floor, she did so in a 'sitting' position, and was therefore not hurt. As always even her falls left no visible scars.

Sita wiped her hands on her apron and reached out for her mobile and Whatsapped her husband,

"I fell down. Come downstairs."

Five minutes passed. No one came.

A little piqued by their indifference, Sita switched off the stove.

Her pasta was no more *aldente*. The tomato sauce too had splashed all over the kitchen counter like proxy spots of blood—instead of her own.

The stress of daily work and now this sudden fall was proving to be tough for her. She was losing her patience. Sita didn't wait any longer. She quickly cleaned up the red sauce stains from the kitchen platform, served pasta in four plates, placed them on the table with forks, entered the living room, switched off the TV, seated herself on the table and started eating, all within ninety seconds.

The fantastic three—Luv, Kush and Ram arrived in the next three hundred seconds. The boys came in grumbling about TV, but were happy to start eating immediately, hungry always. Ram took more time to arrive. He arrived, unhurried, with his wet hair neatly brushed back and his skin glowing in the late autumn evening, wearing a T-shirt that proclaimed that he was the 'Best Dad in the World'. Once seated, he threw a quick sideways glance towards Sita and asked, with an inconspicuous chuckle, "So, you fell off your chair?" Sita twitched and sensed the hidden sarcasm and didn't reply.

Ram didn't prod her further, instead he poked at the soggy pasta, sniffed at it, and finally started eating. No verbal complaints. Just twitches and sighs everywhere and Sita's dogged silence.

By the time Sita had finished all her chores that evening, it was already 10 pm, and even if she wanted to pick up her diary and write, she had no energy left. The next morning she had an appointment with the famous writer, who went by the alias of *'Balmiki'*. She was slightly apprehensive, since this would be her first meeting with him. His account had been passed on to her this year. Her boss, Mrs. Pfister, spoke highly of him and had encouraged Sita to work with him.

****

Sita's meeting with Balmiki the next day was quite out of the ordinary.

Instead of meeting in the office as they usually did with major clients, Balmiki had asked her to come down to Zurich HB, to the new Hiltl outlet next to the Hauptbahnhof, for lunch.

Sita agreed since this was their first meeting and she didn't want to sound too complicated or rigid.

Balmiki was a man with poise and style, in his fifties, with salt and pepper hair.

He wore a pesto-green linen shirt, and sat outside the entrance under an umbrella, waiting for her. Sita had seen his photo before, so she could spot him easily. She fixed a stray strand of hair behind her ear and walked up to him.

Balmiki looked up with an effortless smile, pushed back his chair and stood up extending his hand for a handshake.

It was self-service at Hiltl, so they went and ordered a light lunch and after the initial pleasantries were over, they began to discuss Balmiki's book project—a historic tome he was writing for Sita's publishing house.

They had to discuss the characters, timelines, contract signing and the book release details. Their discussion took almost an hour and a half. The table was tiny, and Sita was having trouble placing her papers on it. Balmiki helped her neatly pile them on an extra chair and helped her organise herself. Once they finished discussing the main points and agreed on the timelines, Balmiki picked up the folder with the printed papers and shoved it inside his dossier. Sita told him that she would also send him a soft copy, and Balmiki nodded with a smile. He then wiped off some salad sauce from his chin, put down his reading glasses on the table, leaned back and asked Sita with a faint smile, "So, tell me something about yourself!"

"Mrs Pfister was saying that you have been working with her for almost a year now? What were you doing before joining this publishing house, if I may ask?"

Sita gulped down her last morsel of risotto with a sip of white wine and then cleared her voice, taking few extra seconds to carefully summarise what she would say.

"Well, my husband and I were travelling for fourteen years all around Europe, so I really couldn't take on a permanent job. I followed him around, and also had to take care of my two young boys, Luv and Kush, who are eleven now."

Then she added immediately, so that Balmiki wouldn't find her professionally lacking any experience, "I was freelancing as a copyeditor, in between..." And in the same breathe added, "I also did a Bachelors in literature and worked for an advertising agency before I got married."

"You have been busy Sita, and you do have sufficient experience," Balmiki said, slightly disappointed with her apparent lack of self-worth. "And I must admit, you were a tough negotiator when it came to deadlines and royalty today."

"As you know, my plot is still developing, and I will need *you* to help me finish my story, I am in search of a character, who will be the companion of my protagonist", he said. "And you can help me find one," Balmiki added with a wink.

Sita checked her watch. It was getting late. She would have to take the next train to reach home on time. Her nanny had sent her a SMS, she would be leaving earlier today.

Balmiki was observing Sita closely, still waiting for her reply.

He leaned in and said, "I guess you need to leave now? Well, it was a pleasure meeting you Sita!"

And then, Balmiki dropped the bombshell, which made Sita sit up all of a sudden.

"I won't take much of your time Sita, but I wanted to invite you to a writing retreat that I am organizing in London next month."

Balmiki gave her a colourful brochure with the title, *'Writing my first novel at Balmiki and Ravana's Writers Den'*.

A kind of joyous madness seized Sita.

As if a total stranger had invaded her mind and had discovered her secret dream. Sita being in a swither about the proposal didn't know how to react.

Balmiki added, "Who knows Sita, with all these writers around and ongoing workshops, you too may start working on your own book—whether you want it or not!"

Sita blushed, her voice choked, almost.

Balmiki was offering her an *'official vacation'*—everything was coming together, and even if it made no sense, her heart was leaping wildly already!

Balmiki was observing the cascade of emotions on Sita's face keenly. He gave her a lopsided grin as though her bewilderment amused him. It was a brief moment, when his eyes sparked and then he lapsed into a sobre gravity again.

Balmiki was a writer who was constantly in search of stories and he had found his plot around this interesting character already, and if she really had the writing skills Mrs. Pfister had proudly exclaimed, then she could become his next protégé. He had helped launch many aspiring authors' career. Sita was much older than his earlier candidates, but then why not help someone.

Sita kept quiet. Her emotions were still too high and she didn't trust herself to utter a single word. She stammered after a while and asked, "That's an amazing offer thank you so much, Balmiki. Just in case I do come to this Writers' workshop, how long would I have to stay and how much would it cost?"

"The Writers workshop which I am organizing is for a month. Course fees and all costs will be covered by your company, they have always sent one representative and this time Mrs. Pfister recommended you. She wanted me to announce this to you."

Sita's eyes lit up. Then she replied with a hesitant smile, "On second thoughts this is perhaps not suitable for me. I have two kids and my husband will never agree to something this long."

"Then, don't tell him Sita. I shall ask your boss or my partner Ravana to kidnap you," Balmiki added with a twinkle in his eyes and got up to leave.

And just like that, the *'vacation'* came into being!

In the train, she had read and re-read the brochure, checked the website and the archive photos online. She was convinced that her Thammu had somehow conspired with the universe to get this offer for her. She had been her literary agent up in the stars!

Sita continued worrying, "What if Ram doesn't let me go? He has always said that I, shouldn't wander out of my limitations (exactly how his brother had described it at a family gathering—*every woman's Lakshman Rekha*). What if I step out of it? Will Ram be happy with my boldness or feel disappointed?"

The *Lakshman Rekha* had burned an imprint in her skin, in her mind, and she forbid herself to step out of it. But now that invisible line was forming an uncomfortable knot around her, and she was desperate to get out of it. Her life could not be limited anymore by that line.

The more she thought about Balmiki's *bona fide* offer the more she lost control over her good wife and good mother's genes and all *Lakshman Rekhas*.

A vacation away from all her mundane duties with the prospect of starting on something she had always wanted to—how could she not consider such a proposal?

She thought aloud, would she be an utterly neglectful mother?

Yes she would be.

But, was one month too much to ask for, in a lifetime?

All these thoughts made knots in her mind. Something about Ram always made her inordinately timid. She almost always gave up her case the moment he frowned and made eye-contact with her, and if he hesitated she would always leave the conversation with a 'Forget it' and walk away without complain. 'What had changed? Was it because she had turned 40 and didn't feel the need to conform with all rules, expectations and prejudices anymore?'

"It's your life lady, you decide," Balmiki had said, his parting words to Sita.

That is what had happened a month ago.

****

Sita had almost dozed off on her beige sofa, when Ram entered the room, after his shower. Immediately she switched off the TV. She smiled at him with guilt and sadness. Ram looked so innocent, so guilt-free, did he deserve this secrecy? Would he blame her if she told him that she had planned this vacation with Balmiki and that she would be living in a writers' resort run by a Sri Lankan for four weeks across the sea? Would that bother him more than the inconvenience at home? Would he blame Balmiki and Ravana for kidnapping her or would he feel ashamed to know that she had eloped with an older man, who had promised to fulfil her secret dream? A dream he, her husband, was not even aware of. Ram would perhaps turn to his kingdom, his football pals for advice. Their opinion would be his opinion and his decision.

****

Next morning arrived. It was a Saturday.

When Ram woke up, it was already broad daylight but there was no sound in the kitchen downstairs. The house appeared oddly calm. Ram looked at his watch. It was twenty past nine.

The other side of the bed was empty.

Sita must be practising yoga downstairs, *finally*, he thought. His intention was to always initiate good habits in her, and not to provoke. She had never understood that.

He checked on the boys, they were both asleep, with their covers pushed to the rim of the bed, sleeping like two babies.

Ram came downstairs.

The living room was empty. The kitchen was empty.

No one was outside as well.

He went near the sink for a glass of water, and that is when he saw a handwritten note stuck below a bowl, with freshly cut fruits.

"Ram, fruits for today's breakfast. The fridge is stocked for the week. I am leaving. Please don't start a search party. I am well and leaving with my own 'free will' (yes it still exists). Mother earth shall crack and take me back into her

womb, and I shall emerge again with the hope to live a life I have always wanted to. Take care of my boys till then, thank you! Sita."

Ram, read the note two-three times, still it made no sense.

He called Sita, first through whatsapp, then through normal paid call.

The voicemail spoke in Sita's voice.

"Hi, I am on Vacation. Please call Ram for urgent matters."

Sita's train entered the long tunnel beneath the English Channel. The earth cracked, the train moved in high speed below the sea, into mother earth's womb enroute to Balmiki and Ravana's writer's den in London.

Sita updated her Whatsapp status, 'Do not disturb. On Vacation.'

Glossary:

Thammu: Short form for thakuma, which means grandmother in Bengali.
Krishna: Hindu God.
Lakshman Rekha: The imaginary line 'Lakshman' (Ram's brother) marked on the ground to protect Ram's wife 'Sita' in the epic 'Ramayana', and asked her not to step beyond it for self-preservation. The area within that circle was protected by special powers. But Sita had stepped out of it and got abducted by Ravana.

Epilogue:

Sita and Ram are Hindu mythological characters from the famous epic Ramayana, written by Balmiki thousands of years ago. As per Ramayana, Ram and Sita were banished to a life in the forest for 14 years, during which Sita was kidnapped by Ravana and taken to Lanka from where Ram had to rescue her after a difficult battle. After their return to their Kingdom Ayodhya, Sita had to pass through a 'fire-test' to prove her chastity. When she got pregnant, residents of their kingdom questioned her once again, and then to retain peace in his kingdom Ram banished his wife Sita to the hermitage of Balmiki in a forest, where his twin sons Luv and Kush were born. Years later when Ram went to the hermitage to bring them all back to their palace, after yet another fire test, Sita refused to return and asked mother Earth (she was the daughter of 'Janaki'/Mother Earth) to take her back forever. Sita's loyalty for her husband, her endurance, her sacrifice, her strength to bring up her twin sons alone, and finally her decision to retain her self-esteem has always been a mystery and a source of inspiration for many.

Author Profiles

KAMALIKA RAY, India
kamalikaray333@gmail.com

Writing, photography, art, and filmmaking sends Kamalika Ray to cloud nine. Her work experience and continuing education in the financial services sector brings her back, to Mumbai. Her writings have found a place in an anthology published by Penguin Random House (Tell me a Story), awards in the Wordweavers India contests and special mentions in other digital platforms. Her photography has been featured in the Times of India newspaper, and has also won multiple awards. She is currently working on a collection of her poetries.
You can follow her work on Instagram: @kreative_kamalika

ASHWATHY MENON, India
menonashwathy26@gmail.com

A Post Graduate in Marketing and HR, Ashwathy spent her Corporate Career in the Service Industry affiliated in Sales and Marketing functions besides being involved in Training interventions. An unexpected entry into high school teaching post a sabbatical led her to discovering her love for teaching and evolved her as a person. Besides donning the mantle of a super mom for her super busy daughter, she is driven by her passion for singing and painting, deriving a great meaning from them. Based out of Mumbai, this is her first work at fiction writing.

SHWETA DASGUPTA, India
shwetaghosh699@gmail.com

Shweta Dasgupta, a teacher by profession, has freelanced for many years in leading newspapers like the Hindustan Times, Times of India and The Indian Nation. She writes in English, Hindi and Bangla. Her short stories have been published earlier. Nowadays she juggles her time between being a mom, daughter and wife. Shweta is passionate about writing, pens poems, short stories and *shayeries*. "I like to express myself this way. Every Writer has this deep down desire to be read, appreciated and be accepted by his/her reader and I am no exception to this." Shweta adds. She lives in the City of Joy, Kolkata, with her teenage daughter, a son (four legged Joe) and her mother.

SINDHUJA MANOHAR,
New Zealand
sindhuja.manohar83@gmail.com

Sindhuja is a finance professional by day and an aspiring writer by night, currently living in New Zealand. She was born Indian, nurtured Indonesian, adopted Singaporean, and educated American. She is a complex product of multicultural upbringing, globetrotting homes, and blurred geographical borders. She considers herself the luckiest mother to her boys who mean the world to her. A devoted daughter, loving sister, and loyal friend, Sindhuja has seen many ups and downs, but she continues to have hopes and desires, ideas and visions. She has faith in the inherent goodness of people. She believes in the wisdom of children and the beauty of nature. She trusts in the honor of honesty and the magic of forgiveness. She believes in the necessity to survive, and more importantly, the craving to thrive.

TANIA BASU, Australia
tania_basuin@yahoo.co.in

Tania Basu was born in Kolkata and has spent her early childhood in Hyderabad, India. After finishing school, she did her graduation and Post Graduation in English from Calcutta University before exploring the field of Special Education in Intellectual Disability. Currently she lives in Melbourne, Australia with her husband and three and a half year old daughter and is enjoying every moment of the experience of bringing her up. Having been part of a big and close extended family with a number of powerful female role models has had a strong impact in Tania's identity formation and understanding of the role of women in the modern world. The experience of migrating to a new country and raising a girl child in a bilingual and bicultural environment has given her an opportunity to reflect on certain fundamental aspects of what India represents. She has written journal articles and newspaper columns in the past but this is her first attempt to write a short story.

EKTA SHARMA, Australia.
ekta.sh@gmail.com

Born and raised in India, Ekta Sharma Khandelwal now lives in Australia with her tribe, consisting of her husband, a son and a daughter. Ekta is an avid reader drawn to stories which embodies themes of inspiration, adventure and insight. She is a polyglot and speaks six languages fluently. Her weekday is consumed in researching the challenging aspects within the quirky world of artificial intelligence alongside her comrades in the advanced data analytics group. Ekta believes all problems can be fixed by a well-made hot cup of ginger cardamom tea. There are no words to fully capture the depths of her love and passion for Fridays. When she is not twisting her brains you can find her seeking out opportunities for sleep, sanity and The Shire.

POPPY CHOUDHURY, Indonesia
choudhurypoppy@gmail.com

Poppy Choudhury is a social chronicler who accidentally got on to the life train living, working and experiencing varied cultures in ASEAN and Europe. She loves 'people watching' and enjoys listening to, reading and writing life stories. She holds a Masters degree in Mass Communication (Pune University, India) and Corporation Social Responsibility (Nottingham Business School, UK) and a doctorate in Social Responsibility and Workplace Disability from Monash Business School. She currently lives in Indonesia with her family and teaches at the Undergraduate and Masters program at BINUS Business School.

MUNMUN GUPTA, Indonesia
munmun_gupta@hotmail.com

Munmun Gupta is presently working as an English language lecturer at Binus International University in Indonesia. In the past, she has worked as a kindergarten teacher in India and Indonesia. She holds a Master's Degree in English Literature and has always been fascinated by the world of literature. Munmun loves to write and deliberately tries to encourage young readers with the written word. Her books *More Carrots for Me* and *The Mighty Banana*, which describe the benefits of eating healthy foods, are loved by mothers and children alike. Her book *The Boy Who Loved his Caterpillar* is also an excellent read. When not writing, she spends a lot of time running after her boys, Dev and Neil, who inspire her work. She continues to create imaginative picture books, uplifting her readers and bringing smiles to their faces through her joyful tales. Her story provides insight into what it means to be alive in this time of rapid change

SUMONA GHOSH DAS, USA.
sumona29@gmail.com

Sumona Das resides in Washington DC, with her entrepreneur husband and two daughters. Sumona is a science grad and has a Masters in Business Administration. She is the co-owner of her husband's management consulting firm. Simultaneously she pursues her childhood love for art, music, and literature. Her stories and poems have been published in several books and journals. She writes in her blog www.sumonasworld.blogspot.com. Her principle of giving back keeps her involved with nonprofits that support orphan children around the world. Sumona's experience and exposure to different cultures inspired her to write, 'A Journey to Remember'.

SUPARNA BASU, USA

Suparna.ubrb@gmail.com

Suparna is a mother of two boys and a public school educator in Ohio, USA. Between a game designer 7th grader and midnight academic discussion calls about Japanese language, planets and life, with her aspiring planetary physicist, college going son, Suparna's life is busy as a mom, as a teacher and as a mentor to her students. She ran a handmade (book binding) publishing shop for almost 10 years to encourage young writers to write more. She currently is in the committee of her local high school's academic scholarship program. She passionately reads history books but also loves to quilt and crochet in her free time. Suparna is a courageous, indomitable 'burn' survivor, who appreciates life's blessings, everyday.

SUJATHA RAMANATHAN,
USA
indivas@gmail.com

Sujatha Ramanathan is a Medical Writer by profession. She has always been captivated by nature and enjoys photography and reading. She is a positive and outgoing person who believes in encouraging, lifting and strengthening one another with thoughts, words and actions. Suja's personal life experiences have made her value and trust in the power of the present, take life and all its experiences as they come. She lives in New Jersey and is truly convinced that gratitude, appreciation and smiles have the ability to change the world. This is her first attempt at short story writing although she has been penning poems in her spare time as a hobby.

AGOMONI GANGULI MITRA,
Scotland
agomoni.ganguli@gmail.com

Agomoni Ganguli-Mitra was born in Geneva, Switzerland and loves raclette and rosogolla in equal measure. A global citizen at heart and an unrepentant feminist, her current anchor is Scotland, where she works and lives with her family. She loves music, dance and stories.

ABHILASHA KUMAR,
Switzerland
abhilasha.kumar@gmail.com

Dr. Abhilasha kumar is an out-of-lab researcher interested in a myriad spectrum of subjects, from neuropsychology to evolutionary biology, wildlife, traveling, astronomy, the occult, the esoteric and the metaphysical. Occasionally, she delves in wildlife poetry as an experimental and educational art form. Abhilasha currently lives in Basel, Switzerland, with her husband and two sons, where she can be seen walking her dog around the countryside. Her only confessed sin remains Swiss chocolate and bicycling in the countryside.

IPSITA BARUA, Switzerland
barua.ipsita@gmail.com

Copywriter by profession, writer by interest, photographer by passion and wanderer at heart, that's what defines Ipsita who's been in the advertising chaos for more than a decade in various countries. After living in Dubai for several years, she now lives in Zurich, and is always on the lookout for compelling stories to share and inspire. An imagination that collides with her own experiences. While the world today is skewed towards visual communications, she believes it's never a complete picture without words woven well and a story scripted to engage. That is where she holds her power of the pen... or keyboard!

JYOTI KAPOOR, Switzerland
Jyoti.kapoor.ch@gmail.com

Jyoti Kapoor is a software engineer by education and holds a masters in business administration, works with a leading stock exchange as an manager in IT. She loves to travel, cook and listen to music. Writing has been an all time ambition and love. A five-year old son, caring husband, inspiring parents and loving friends complete her life. She is empathetic and expressive, therefore storytelling comes as part of this package full of words for every moment. By participation in this book she has molten the reflections from her emotional as well as professional worlds into one quick shot of an anecdote from a time travel experience into the future.

REJINA SADHU, Switzerland
rejina.ramachandran@gmail.com

Dr. Rejina Sadhu is a neurobiologist turned regulatory medical writer who finds the world of written words absolutely thrilling, adventurous and fascinating. A Malayali born in Mumbai, she moved to Switzerland for her PhD, got married to a Bengali and continued to explore the world through books, travel, music and food. She speaks five languages fluently and started writing poems and stories at a young age for her school magazine and moved on to publish in university publications. The organizers of the Bombay Hindi Sahitya

Parishad published her Hindi poems, which she read at their annual event. Her scientific essays earned critical acclaim from the Nobel Laureate Harold Kroto. A mother of two school-going children, she hopes to encourage them to read and use the written medium to generate a positive wave of hope, fun and faith that may lead to better solutions and a healthier world. In her free time, she loves to bake cakes and Indian delicacies.

NAYANA CHAKRABARTI,
Switzerland
nayanachakrabarti@gmail.com

Born in Kolkata and brought up in Cambridge, Nayana's writing seeks to try and make sense of the immigrant experience. She currently lives in Zurich with her husband and two children.

RICHA CHAUHAN, Switzerland
chauhan.richa@gmail.com

Richa Chauhan is a laser scientist in a Zurich based company. She has done PhD in spectroscopy in University of Basel, Switzerland. Her masters was in laser physics from IIT, Roorkee and IIT, Delhi. She loves to paint, travel, read about science, and dance like no one is watching, in addition to taking care of her 8 year old son Tanish. She is currently involved in a monthly kids workshop "Wonder kids" and teaches kids science with fun experiments.

PALLABI ROY-CHAKRABORTY,
Switzerland
pallabi.roy82@gmail.com

Pallabi currently lives in Zurich with her husband and son. A Software Engineer by profession, she is also a dancer and writer in her free time. Whilst her profession keeps her firmly rooted in logic, she is a strong believer in the power of imagination. Her son Reyan is her greatest inspiration and she strictly adheres to his way of living….miracle and magic in even the most mundane, happiness without a reason, forgiveness with a smile and most importantly rising after every fall.

BRINDARICA BOSE, Switzerland
brindarica@gmail.com

Brindarica Bose lives in Wohlen, with her husband and two sons Adhrit and Jeet. Her first published book was 'Swiss Masala' (2018) and this is her second attempt. Born in Mumbai, she lived in Kolkata, Ranchi and Coimbatore before coming to Switzerland in 2002. After completing her B.Sc. and MBA in India, she worked for the newspaper 'Times of India', in Mumbai and later joined an international association in Zurich, as Publications Manager. She started teaching fine arts professionally to adults and children since last three years and frequently exhibits her paintings worldwide. www.brindarica.com

Made in the USA
Middletown, DE
08 September 2019